Record of
Miraculous Events
in Japan

TRANSLATIONS
FROM THE ASIAN CLASSICS

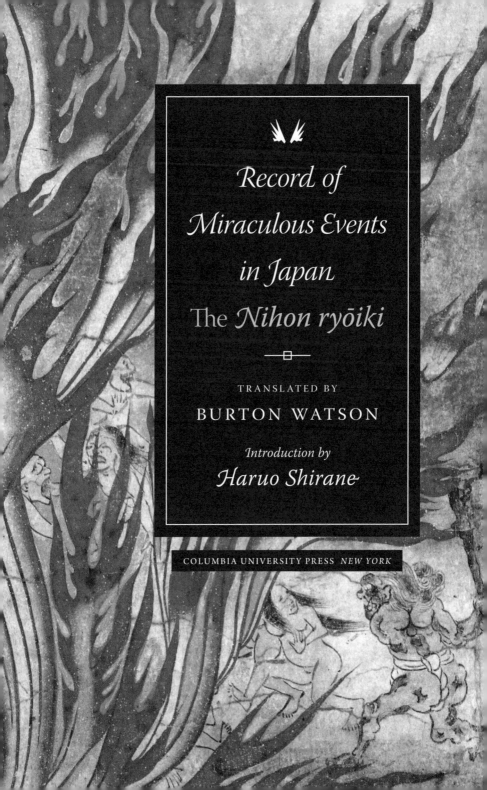

Record of Miraculous Events in Japan

The *Nihon ryōiki*

TRANSLATED BY

BURTON WATSON

Introduction by
Haruo Shirane

COLUMBIA UNIVERSITY PRESS *NEW YORK*

Columbia University Press wishes to express its
appreciation for assistance given by the Pushkin Fund
toward the cost of publishing this book.

Columbia University Press
Publishers Since 1893
New York   Chichester, West Sussex
cup.columbia.edu
Copyright © 2013 Columbia University Press

Library of Congress Cataloging-in-Publication Data
Keikai, 8th/9th cent.
  [Nihon ryoiki. English]
  Record of miraculous events in Japan : the Nihon ryoiki /
translated by Burton Watson ; introduction by Haruo Shirane.
       pages cm. — (Translations from the Asian classics)
  Includes bibliographical references.
  ISBN 978-0-231-16420-7 (cloth : alk. paper)
  ISBN 978-0-231-16421-4 (pbk. : alk. paper)
  ISBN 978-0-231-53516-8 (e-book)
  1. Buddhist legends—Japan.   2. Tales—Japan.
3. Buddhism—Japan—Folklore.   I. Watson, Burton, 1925–
translator.   II. Shirane, Haruo, 1951– writer of added
commentary.   III. Title.
  BQ5775.J3K4413 2013
  294.3'8—dc23

                                        2012048487

Columbia University Press books are printed on permanent and
durable acid-free paper.

This book is printed on paper with recycled content.
Printed in the United States of America
c 10 9 8 7 6 5 4 3 2 1
p 10 9 8 7 6 5 4 3 2 1

COVER IMAGE: *Jigoku zoshi* (*Scroll of the Hells*, twelfth to
thirteenth century), detail. (TNM Image Archives)
COVER DESIGN: Lisa Hamm

CONTENTS

Volume II

Volume III

*Record of
Miraculous Events
in Japan*

Haruo Shirane

The *Record of Miraculous Events in Japan* (*Nihon ryōiki*, ca. 822), compiled in the early Heian period (794–1192), is Japan's first major collection of anecdotal (*setsuwa*) literature and, as such, had a huge impact on the formation of Japanese literature. It is also the first collection of Buddhist anecdotal literature, establishing a major precedent for this genre, which would come to be popular throughout the medieval period. *Setsuwa* (anecdotes), a modern term that literally means "spoken story," are stories that were orally narrated and then written down. These recorded stories were often used for oral storytelling, resulting in new variations, which were again recorded or rewritten. The result is that *setsuwa* frequently exist in multiple variants, with a story usually evolving over time or serving different purposes. In being told, written down, retold, and rewritten, *setsuwa* presume a narrator and a listener, but not necessarily a specific author. The author of the *Nihon ryōiki*, Keikai or Kyōkai (either reading is acceptable, but for the sake of consistency I follow the latter, which is the variant used in the translation that follows), was in fact more of an editor and a collector than an author in the modern sense.

Premodern *setsuwa* survive only in written form, sometimes (as in the *Nihon ryōiki*) in Chinese-style (*kanbun*) prose, providing a glimpse of the storytelling process but never reproducing it. The following example is titled "On Mercilessly Skinning a Live Rabbit and Receiving an Immediate Penalty" (1.16):

In Yamato province, there lived a man whose name and native village are unknown. He was by nature merciless and loved to kill living creatures. He once caught a rabbit, skinned it alive, and then turned it loose in the fields. But not long afterward, pestilent sores broke out all over his body, his whole body was covered with scabs, and they caused him unspeakable torment. In the end, he never gained any relief, but died groaning and lamenting.

Ah, how soon do such deeds receive an immediate penalty! We should consider others as we do ourselves, exercise benevolence, and never be without pity and compassion!

In a manner typical of the genre, the *setsuwa* is compactly written (usually no more than one or two pages), is plot and action driven, turns on an element of surprise or wonder, and is didactic (teaching karmic retribution, for the sin of killing animals, and urging compassion). In contrast to the later vernacular tales (*monogatari*), which admit to being fiction, the *Nihon ryōiki*, like subsequent *setsuwa* collections, insists on the truth of the stories it includes—however miraculous they may be.

The *setsuwa-shū*, or collection of *setsuwa*, which can be very long, was inspired in part by Chinese encyclopedias (*leishu*). In contrast to the *setsuwa*, which had its roots in oral storytelling, the *setsuwa-shū* was a literary form that provided a structured worldview (in this case, centered on karmic retribution). Often the same *setsuwa* appear in a number of collections. Indeed, many of the *setsuwa* in the *Nihon ryōiki* reappear in later collections, including *Notes on the Three Treasures* (*Sanbōe kotoba*, 984), *Biographies of Japanese Reborn in the Land of Bliss* (*Nihon ōjō gokurakuki*, 985–987), and *Tales of Times Now Past* (*Konjaku monogatari shū*, ca. 1120). The *setsuwa* in the *Nihon ryōiki* were probably collected and edited as a supplementary sourcebook for sermons by Buddhist priests who preached to commoner audiences that could not read *kanbun*. They also reflect Kyōkai's desire to demonstrate the different ways in which the law of karmic causality is manifested.

Little is known about the author of the *Nihon ryōiki*, except that he was a *shidosō* (self-ordained priest), as opposed to a certified priest affiliated with a major temple and ordained by the state. At some point (probably between 787 and 795), he became affiliated as a low-ranking cleric with the Yakushi-ji temple in Nara (one of the great centers of Buddhism at the time). At the time, the central (*ritsuryō*) state attempted to keep a tight control on the priesthood and cracked down on private priests, who took vows without official permission. A recurrent figure in the *Nihon ryōiki* is Gyōgi (Gyōki, 668–749), a self-ordained priest from the early Nara period, who gained a wide and popular following and was consequently prosecuted by the government before he accepted an invitation from Emperor Shōmu (r. 724–749) to build the large statue of the Buddha at the Tōdai-ji temple in 741. The prominent position of Gyōgi in the *Nihon ryōiki* indicates that he represents an ideal for Kyōkai, who was likewise an active private priest before eventually joining the Yakushi-ji temple. One of Kyōkai's own accounts of himself in the *Nihon ryōiki* states that in 787, he realized that his current poverty and secular life were the result of evil deeds he had done in a previous life, and so he decided to become an ordained priest.

Kyōkai edited the *Nihon ryōiki* sometime in the early Heian period (around 822 or earlier), but the stories themselves are set in the Nara period (710–784) and earlier. In Kyōkai's time, during the reigns of Emperor Kanmu (r. 781–796) and his son Emperor Saga (r. 809–823), the country was rocked by considerable social disorder, famine, and plagues. It was a particularly hard time for farmers, many of whom fled from their home villages. Some of these refugees were absorbed into local temples and private estates, and others became private priests like Kyōkai. Unlike the officially ordained clergy in the major temples in the capital, who were of aristocratic origins, these self-ordained priests attracted a more plebian following, and many of the stories in the *Nihon ryōiki* are about poor commoners and farmers. The *Nihon ryōiki* deals at times with high-ranking aristocrats such as Prince Shōtoku, but most of the stories concern commoners on a much lower level of society. Kyōkai sought to teach Buddhist principles to society as a whole. In this regard, the *Nihon ryōiki* differs significantly from the elite literature being produced at this time, such as *Nostalgic Recollections of Literature* (*Kaifūsō*,

751) and *Collection of Literary Masterpieces* (*Bunka shūreishū*, 818), two noted collections of Chinese poetry and refined Chinese prose written by aristocrats. Instead, the *Nihon ryōiki* is written in a rough, unorthodox style of Chinese-style prose that gives us a glimpse of the underside of society and the reality of everyday commoner life.

Eighty percent of the stories in the *Nihon ryōiki* take place in the Yamato region (in and around the capital of Nara), but the place-names come from almost every part of the country—from Michinoku (in northeastern Honshū) to Higo (in Kyushu)—strongly suggesting that the private priest may have preached at a certain village, gathered stories, and then told them at another village. In contrast to the compilers of the *Chronicles of Japan* (*Nihon shoki*, 720), who combined local and provincial myths and legends into a larger state mythology, itinerant Buddhist priests absorbed and transformed local folk stories into Buddhist anecdotes; they included folk tales about animals and serpents, which often take on allegorical or symbolic functions.

Kyōkai arranged these stories, which were drawn from a variety of sources, in such a way as to demonstrate the Buddhist principle of karmic causality, as reflected in the full title of the compilation, *Miraculous Stories of the Reward of Good and Evil from the Country of Japan* (*Nihonkoku genpō zen'aku ryōiki*). Kyōkai seems to have been inspired by a Chinese work, the *Mingbaoji* (Jp. *Myōhōki; Record of Invisible Works of Karmic Retribution*). Deeds in the course of a lifetime, whether good or evil, have a direct consequence in this life or in the next existence (in which one can be reborn, depending on one's deeds, in paradise or as a nonhuman animal, such as a cow, which represents a lower rung of existence). The compiler sought to gather stories that illustrate this concept, particularly those that show an immediate retribution for good or evil conduct. Other stories demonstrate the miraculous powers of Buddha, the bodhisattvas, sutras (particularly the Lotus Sutra), and Buddhist paintings or sculptures.

The *Nihon ryōiki* is also notable for its portrayal of a Buddhist Hell presided over by King Yama, who metes out just punishment (see 2:5). (The Western Paradise is assumed to exist, but there is no description here.) In the early chronicles, such as the *Nihon shoki*, the underworld (called Yomi) is a place marked by pollution where bodies decompose. By contrast, the *Nihon ryōiki* depicts a terrifying Buddhist Hell where past actions are met with extreme physical punishment. In the ancient period, sin was the result of transgressing the communal order, usually agricultural violations or pollutions, but in the *Nihon ryōiki*, sin takes on new meaning as a moral and social violation, with the individual responsible for his or her own actions. In the early chronicles, disease was cured by communal means, by purification and cleansing. But here, disease, which figures prominently, is the punishment for sin, the result of previous karma.

The *Nihon ryōiki* contains 116 stories and is divided into three volumes, which are arranged in a roughly chronological order, beginning, in volume 1, with the description of the introduction of Buddhism to Japan from the Korean state of Paekche. The first four stories are from the pre-Nara period: from the reigns of Emperors Yūryaku (r. 456–479), Kinmei (r. 539–571), Bidatsu (r. 572–585), and Suiko (r. 592–628), respectively. This rough narrative of Buddhism in Japan reaches its height in volume 2, which focuses on the Tenpyō era (729–749) and on the reign of Emperor Shōmu, who built the great temple of Tōdai-ji, with its colossal image of the Buddha, and, after abdicating from the throne in 749, declared himself to be the "slave of the Three (Buddhist) Treasures." Priest Gyōgi—who represents an ideal for the editor and who was active in the Tenpyō era—figures prominently in this volume (see, for example, 2:7, 2:12, and 2:30). Volume 3 focuses on stories from the post-Tenpyō era, primarily from the reign of Empress Kōken (r. 749–758). As he notes in the preface to this volume, Kyōkai regards this time (which includes the period in which he lived) as an age of Buddhist decline (*mappō*), the last of the three ages of the Buddhist Law, in which Buddhist teachings are gradually abandoned. In Kyōkai's view, the principles espoused by *Nihon ryōiki* are all the more necessary in such a degenerate age, in order to save people from their many sins.

Volume

I

If we inquire into the matter, we find that the inner, or Buddhist, writings and the outer, or non-Buddhist, writings were first transmitted to Japan in two groups. Both of them came from the country of Paekche,[1] the latter in the reign of Emperor Homuda [Ōjin, r. 270–312], who resided at the Toyoakira Palace in Karushima, and the former in the reign of Emperor Kinmei [r. 539–571], who resided at the Kanazashi Palace in Shikishima. However, it was customary for those who studied the non-Buddhist writings to denigrate the Buddhist Law, while those who read the Buddhist writings made light of the other works. But they are ignorant and foolish, embracing fatuous beliefs and disbelieving in the consequences of evil or good action. People of true wisdom regard both types of writing with seriousness and have faith in and are fearful of karmic causation.[2]

Among the successive emperors, there was one who, ascending a high hill, was moved to compassion and, content to live in a palace where the rain leaked in, brought succor to his people.[3] Or another who was born with great ability and knew the direction things were taking. He could

1. Paekche (18 B.C.E.–660 C.E.), located in southwestern present-day Korea, was one of the three kingdoms of Korea, along with Koguryŏ (37 B.C.E.–668 C.E.) and Silla (57 B.C.E.–935 C.E.).
2. According to karmic causation, evil acts or karma beget evil, and good acts or karma beget good, although they may take considerable time to do so.
3. Emperor Nintoku (r. 313–399).

listen to ten men expounding without missing a word. When he was twenty-five, at the request of the emperor, he lectured on a Mahayana sutra, and his commentaries on the scriptures have long been handed down to later ages.[4] Or there was an emperor who, making great vows, reverently created a Buddhist image. Heaven assisted his vows, and the earth opened up its treasure.[5]

And among the great monks, there were those whose virtue led them to the ten stages of bodhisattvahood and whose Way transcended that of the two lower levels of voice-hearer and *pratyekabuddha*.[6] Grasping the torch of wisdom, they lit the dark corners; riding in the boat of compassion, they rescued the drowning. Because of their pursuit of difficult actions and bitter practices, their fame spread to foreign lands. As to the truly wise men of our time, we cannot as yet tell how great is their accomplishment.

Now I, Kyōkai, a monk of Yakushi-ji in Nara, observe the people of the world carefully. There are those who, though possessing ability, are petty in their actions. Greedy for treasures, they outdo a magnet that attracts an iron-rich mountain and pulls out its iron; eager for others' goods, stingy with their own, they are harsher than a grinder that splits each millet seed and sucks out its core. Some covet temple property and are reborn as calves to repay their debt; others speak evil of the doctrine or of monks and meet with calamity in their present lives. But some seek the Way, pile up practice, and gain recognition in their present existence, or are deeply faithful, practicing good in their lives, and are showered with blessings.

The rewards of good and evil are like a shadow following a form; the recompense of suffering and bliss is comparable to a valley echo following a sound. Those who observe such occurrences shrink in alarm, but forget them in a moment's time. Those who are shamed by them with-

---

4. Prince Shōtoku, who lectured on the Lotus Sutra.
5. Emperor Shōmu (r. 724–749), who had difficulty completing his huge statue of Rushana Buddha until, in 749, gold was discovered in Japan.
6. In the Mahayana teachings, both the voice-hearers, or Hinayana believers, and the *pratyekabuddhas*, or "private buddhas" or self-enlightened beings, were regarded as being inferior to believers.

draw in perturbation, but soon lose all memory of them. If the disposition of good and evil were not known, how could we straighten these tangles and make clear the right and wrong of them? And how, without evoking karmic causation, could we mend evil hearts and advance the path of goodness?

Long ago in the land of China, the *Myōhōki* [Ch. *Mingbaoji; Record of Invisible Works of Karmic Retribution*] was compiled; and during the great Tang dynasty, the *Hannyagenki* [Ch. *Bore yanji; A Collection of Stories on the Kongō-hannya-kyō (Diamond Sutra)*] was written.[7] But why should we respect only these records of foreign countries and not credit the miraculous stories that occur in our own land? Since these events occurred here and I saw them with my own eyes, I cannot let them go unrecorded. After pondering them for a long time, I can no longer remain silent. Therefore, I have written down what I have chanced to hear, entitling it *Nihonkoku genpō zen'aku ryōiki* [*Miraculous Stories of the Reward of Good and Evil from the Country of Japan*], compiling it in these three volumes and handing it down to future times.

I, Kyōkai, however, am not blessed with a wise nature, but one muddied in content and hardly clear. Like a frog in a deep well, my understanding goes astray when sent on distant wanderings. I'm like a clumsy craftsman working on a piece carved by a master, only afraid that I will suffer long-standing injury to my hand. My work is no more than one pebble from Mount Kunlun.[8] But my sources in the oral tradition are so vague that I fear there is much I have left out. In my zeal to attain the finest product, I fear that I have let even inept flute players play.[9] May the wise men of later times not laugh at my efforts. My prayer is that those who read these strange accounts will shun what is wrong, enter the right, refrain from various evil practices, and carry out all that is good.[10]

---

7. Tang Lin, comp., *Myōhōki*, in *Taishō shinshū daizōkyō* 51:no. 2082; Meng Xianzhong, comp., *Kongō-hannya-kyō jikkeiki* (718), 3 chaps., in *Dainihon zokuzō-kyō*, part 2, *otsu*, case 23:1.
8. Mount Kunlun was the source of fine jade.
9. A reference to King Xuan of Qi, a state in ancient China, who was so fond of playing the flute that he allowed even inept players to take part in his orchestra.
10. The last two clauses are a popular Buddhist maxim.

※

On Catching the Thunder (1:1)

Chiisakobe no Sugaru was a favorite attendant of Emperor Yūryaku (called Ōhatsuse-wakatakeru no sumeramikoto, who reigned for twenty-three years at the Asakura Palace in Hatsuse).[1]

Once, when the emperor was living at the Iware Palace, he and the empress were sleeping together in the Ōandono and were intimately engaged. Unaware of this, Sugaru walked in, whereupon the emperor, embarrassed, stopped what he was doing. At that moment, there was a clap of thunder in the sky.

The emperor then ordered Sugaru, saying, "You—invite that clap of thunder to come here!"

"I shall do so," replied Sugaru.

The emperor said, "Yes—invite it here."

Sugaru, leaving the palace, wore a red headband on his forehead and carried a halberd with a red banner.[2] Mounting his horse, he galloped past the heights of Abe and past the road to Toyura-dera until he reached the crossroads of Karu no Morokoshi. There he called out in invitation, "You god of the echoing thunder of heaven, the emperor invites you!" Then, as he turned his horse around and headed back, he asked himself, "Even though it's the god of thunder, why wouldn't it accept the emperor's invitation?"

On the way back, between Toyura-dera and Iioka, lightning struck. When he saw this, Sugaru called for priests to place the lightning in a portable shrine and take it to the royal palace, where he announced to the emperor, "The god of thunder accepts your invitation!"

---

1. Throughout the stories, the text in parentheses is Kyōkai's explanations, comments, or interpretations.
2. The color red indicated an imperial messenger.

At that moment, the god gave off a brilliant blast of light that dazzled and frightened the emperor. He made many offerings to it and then had it sent back to the place where it had struck, which is now called Thunder Hill. (It is situated north of the Oharida Palace in the old capital.)[3]

Later, Sugaru died. The emperor issued a command that his corpse remain in its coffin for seven days and seven nights, in recognition of his loyalty and good faith. Then he had a grave built where the lightning had struck, with a memorial pillar that said, "The grave of Sugaru, who brought the thunder." But this enraged the thunder, which struck the pillar and stomped on it. In destroying the pillar, however, its feet became caught in the splinters. When the emperor heard of this, he freed the thunder so it did not die. The thunder remained in a confused state for seven days and seven nights. When the emperor's envoy erected a new pillar, he inscribed it, "This is the grave of Sugaru, who in both life and death ensnared the thunder."

This is said to be the origin of the name Thunder Hill in the time of the old capital.

ON TAKING A FOX AS A WIFE AND PRODUCING A CHILD (1:2)

This took place long ago in the reign of Emperor Kinmei (Emperor Amekuni-oshiharaki-hironiwa no mikoto, who resided at the Kanazashi Palace in Shikishima). A man of the Ōno district of Mino province set out on his horse in search of a good wife. At that time in a broad field, he came on an attractive woman, who responded to him. He winked at her and asked, "Where are you going, pretty miss?" She answered, "I am looking for a good husband." "Will you be my wife?" he then asked.

3. The "old capital" refers to the site of the pre-Nara capital.

She replied, "I will." So he took her home, and they married and lived together.

After a time, she became pregnant and gave birth to a boy. At the same time, on the fifteenth day of the Twelfth Month, their dog gave birth to a puppy. The puppy constantly barked at the wife and threatened to bite her. She became so frightened that she asked her husband to kill the puppy, but in spite of her request, he would not do so.

Around the Second or Third Month, when the annual quota of rice was being hulled, the wife went to where the female servants were pounding rice to give them some refreshment. The puppy ran after her, trying to bite her. Startled and frightened, she changed into a fox and jumped on top of a hedge.

The husband, seeing this, said, "You and I have together produced a child. Therefore, I can never forget you. Whenever I call, come and sleep with me." Thus, following the husband's word, she came and slept with him. (Hence she is called a *kitsune* [meaning both "fox" and "come and sleep"].)

At that time, his wife, wearing a red dyed skirt (what now would be called peach-flower color), would move slowly and gracefully, trailing her skirt as she went. The husband, gazing at her figure, sang a love song that went

> Love fills me
> completely.
> But after one moment,
> a fleeting gem,
> that one—she's gone!

Therefore, they named the child who they had produced Kitsune, which became his surname: Kitsune no atai. The child was famous for his great strength and could run as fast as a bird flies. He is the ancestor of the Kitsune-no-atai family of Mino province.

On a Boy of Great Strength Who Was Born
of the Thunder's Rejoicing (1:3)

Long ago in the time of Emperor Bidatsu [r. 572–584] (who was named Nunakura-futotama-shiki no mikoto and resided at the Osada Palace in Iware), there was a farmer living in the village of Katawa in the Ayuchi district of Owari province. He was preparing his rice fields and flooding them with water when a light rain began to fall. Accordingly, he took shelter under a tree and stood there holding a metal rod.[4] Presently, it began to thunder. Frightened, the man held the rod over his head, whereupon the thunder dropped down in front of him, taking the form of a young boy who bowed politely.

The man was about to strike him with the rod, but the thunder said, "Please don't harm me! I will repay you for your kindness!"

"How will you repay me?" the man asked.

"I will repay you by seeing that a son is born to you," the thunder replied. "So you must make me a boat out of camphor wood, fill it with water, and float bamboo leaves in it."

When the man had done as the thunder asked, the thunder said, "Don't come any closer!" and withdrew to a great distance, rising into the sky in a cloud of mist. Later, a child was born who had a snake twined twice around his neck, born with the head and tail of a snake hanging down behind.

When the boy had grown to be ten years and more, reports spread of a man at the imperial court who was very strong. Thinking that he would like to try challenging him, the boy made his way to the emperor's palace.

At this time, there was a prince of the royal family who excelled in strength and was living in separate quarters by the northeastern corner of the imperial palace. At the northeastern corner of his quarters was a stone that measured eight feet around. The strong-man prince came out

---

4. The metal rod presumably was some kind of farm implement.

of his quarters, picked up the stone, and threw it some distance. Then he returned to his quarters, shut the gate, and did not admit anyone.

The boy, observing this, thought to himself, "This must be the strong man I've heard about!" That night, when no one was looking, he picked up the stone and threw it one foot farther than the prince had done. The prince, seeing this, rubbed his hands together, picked up the stone and threw it, but was unable to throw it any farther. The boy then threw the stone two feet farther than before. The prince, seeing this and hoping for greater success, threw it again, but did no better than before. When the boy picked up the stone and threw it again, his heels dug three inches into the ground and the stone went three feet farther. The prince, seeing the marks where the boy had stood, thought, "This must be where the boy is!" and ran after him, but the boy ducked through the hedge and fled. The prince leaped over the hedge in pursuit, but the boy turned and fled back to the other side of the hedge. The prince, mighty as he was, was never able to catch him, and realizing that the boy surpassed him in strength, he gave up the chase.

Later the boy became an apprentice at Gangō-ji temple.[5] At this time, the boys who rang the bell in the bell tower were being killed night after night. The boy, learning of this, said to the monks, "I will catch the ogre, kill him, and put a stop to this plague of death."

When the monks agreed to this, he had four men stationed with lamps at the four corners of the bell tower, and told them, "When I seize the ogre, remove the shades from your lamps!" Then he took his stand by the door of the bell tower.

In the middle of the night, a huge ogre appeared but, spying the boy, withdrew. Later in the night, it came again. The boy seized hold of the ogre's hair and began to pull; the ogre pulled to get away, the boy pulled toward the inside of the bell tower. The four men who had been stationed in the tower were so terrified that they could not lift the shades from the lamps. The boy then pulled the ogre to each of the four corners of the

5. Located at this time in Asuka, Gangō-ji later moved to Nara and became one of the seven great temples of Nara.

tower and was thus able to uncover the lamps. When dawn came, it was found that the boy had pulled out the ogre's hair by the roots and the ogre had fled. The next day, they followed the trail of the ogre's blood to see where it would lead. It led to a crossroads where a wicked servant of the temple had been buried. Thus they knew that the ogre was the ghost of the wicked servant.[6] The hair from the ogre's head is preserved to this day in Gangō-ji and is looked on as a treasure of the temple.

The boy later became an *upāsaka* [lay brother] and continued to live at Gangō-ji. The temple was preparing its rice fields and getting ready to flood them with water. But some princes of the royal family cut off the water supply to the fields, so they became parched. The boy said, "I'll see that the water gets into these fields," and so the monks agreed to leave things to him.

The boy had a plow handle made so large that it required more than ten men to carry it. Then he picked it up like a staff, carried it to the sluice gate, and stuck it there. But the princes pulled out the plow handle and threw it away, so the sluice gate was once more blocked and no water flowed into the temple fields. The boy then brought a stone that was so big it would take more than a hundred men to carry it and propped open the sluice gate, allowing the water to flow into the temple fields. The princes, awed by his strength, no longer attempted to stop him, and as a result the temple fields did not dry up but produced an excellent crop.

Because of this, the monks agreed to let the boy become an ordained monk with the name Dharma Master Dōjō. When people of later times tell of Dharma Master Dōjō of Gangō-ji and his feats of strength, this is who they mean, and it is right that they should speak so. No doubt he performed many good and powerful acts of karma in his previous lives and thus was able to acquire this kind of strength. This was a wonderful event that occurred in the land of Japan.

---

6. Persons who had died unfortunate deaths were buried in a roadway, that the feet of people traveling the road could prevent their spirits from moving around and causing harm.

✳

On Imperial Prince Shōtoku's Showing Unusual Signs (1:4)

Imperial Prince Shōtoku was the son of Emperor Tachibana-no-toyohi, who resided at the Ikenobe-no-namitsuki Palace in Iware. He became prince regent for Empress Suiko,[7] who resided at the Owarida Palace.

He had three names: Umayado no toyotomimi, Shōtoku, and Kamitsu-miya. Umayado, or "stable door," because he was born in front of the stables. Toyotomimi, or "intelligent ears," because he was born by nature so wise that he could attend to ten men arguing legal claims at the same time without missing a single word. And because he not only was scrupulous in his conduct like a monk, but also wrote commentaries on the Shōman-gyō [Śrīmālā Sutra] and the Hoke-kyō [Lotus Sutra], spread the Way, brought profit to the nation, and was so well versed in the Chinese classics that he instituted the system of court ranks and honors, he was called Shōtoku, or "Sacred Virtue." And because his residence was above that of the palace of the empress, he was called Kamitsu-miya, or "Prince of the Upper Palace."

When the prince was living at the Okamoto Palace in Ikaruga, he had occasion to leave the palace and go for a pleasure ride. When he reached the village of Kataoka, he came on a beggar lying sick beside the road. Seeing this, the prince got down from his palanquin, questioned the beggar, and, taking off his cloak, placed it over the man. Then, his visit concluded, he returned to his palanquin and went on his way.

On his way back, he saw his cloak hanging on the limb of a tree, but the beggar was gone. When the prince put on the cloak again, one of his ministers said, "Are you so poor that you have to wear a dirty cloak worn by a beggar?" The prince replied, "It's all right—you wouldn't understand."

7. Empress Suiko (r. 592–628) was Prince Shōtoku's aunt.

The beggar, meanwhile, went someplace else and died. When the prince heard of this, he held a temporary burial for him, and then had a grave made in the village of Okamoto, in a corner of Mount Moribe, northeast of Hōrin-ji, and placed the body in it. It was called the Hitoki Grave. Later, a messenger he sent to the grave found that the door could not be opened and no one could go inside. Only beside the grave door was a poem that read:

> The little stream of Tomi
>   in Ikaruga—
> should it dry up,
> only then would the name of My Lord
> be forgotten!

On his return, the messenger reported this. The prince, hearing it, remained silent and said nothing. Thus we know that a sage recognizes sagely worth, but an ordinary individual does not. The eyes of an ordinary man saw only a humble person, but to the keen eyes of a sage, his hidden identity was apparent. This was a miraculous event.[8]

≈

Also, Master Ensei, a disciple of Dharma Master Ai, was a national preceptor of Paekche. He lived in the Takamiya Temple at Kazuraki in Yamato province. At that time, there was a monk living in the northern lodge of that temple whose name was Gangaku. This monk would always leave at dawn, go to the village, and come back in the evening—always in the same manner. When an *upāsaka* [lay brother], a disciple of Ensei, reported this to his teacher, Ensei said, "Don't say anything about this— just keep quiet!"

---

8. For a slightly different version of this story, see *Nihon shoki* (*Chronicles of Japan*), chap. 22; and *Nihongi: Chronicles of Japan from the Earliest Times to A.D. 697*, trans. W. G. Aston, Transactions and Proceedings of the Japan Society of London, suppl. 1, 2 vols. (London: K. Paul, Trench, Trübner, 1896), 2:144–145.

The lay brother secretly bored a hole in the wall of Gangaku's room to spy on him and found the room filled with a dazzling light. Again, he reported this to his master, who replied, "That's why I warned you to keep quiet about him!"

Not long after, Gangaku suddenly died. At that time, Ensei told his disciple to cremate him and bury the ashes, and this was done. Later the lay brother came to live in Ōmi. At that time, he heard someone say, "The monk Gangaku lives here." When he went to see, he found that it really was the monk Gangaku. Gangaku said to him, "It's been a long time since I saw you, but I've been thinking of you all along. How have you been?"

Thus we know that he was incarnated as a sage. Eating the five kinds of strong herbs is forbidden in the Buddhist precepts,[9] but if a sage eats them, it does not count as an offense.

On Having Faith in the Three Treasures and Gaining an Immediate Reward (1:5)

Lord Ōtomo no Yasunoko no muraji of the Great Flower Rank was an ancestor of the Ōtomo no muraji in Uji, in the Nagusa district of Kii province.[10] He was endowed by Heaven with a clear mind, and he revered the Three Treasures.[11]

According to the annals, in the reign of Emperor Bidatsu, sounds of musical instruments were heard off the coast of Izumi province. There were sounds of flutes, *shō* [panpipes], and various types of stringed instruments, or others that sounded like rolls of thunder. They were heard in the daytime, and at night a bright light spread to the east.

Lord Ōtomo reported this to the emperor, but he was silent and disbelieving. When it was reported to the empress, however, she said,

9. The strong herbs are garlic, scallion, onion, ginger, and leek.
10. Muraji was a hereditary title for high-ranking administrators.
11. The Three Treasures of Buddhism are the Buddha; the Dharma, or doctrine; and the Order, or community of believers.

"You—go and find out!" He accordingly went to see and found that it was just as reported. While there, he came on a camphor-tree log that had been struck by lightning. On his return, he reported to the empress, "While I was at the beach at Takashi-no-hama, I found this log. I humbly request permission to make Buddhist images out of it." The empress replied, "Your request is granted."

Yasunoko, delighted at this, announced the imperial decree to Shima no Ōomi [Soga no Umako, sixth century], who, in great joy, commissioned Ikebe no atai Hita to carve three bodhisattvas. They were placed in the Toyura Hall to inspire awe and reverence. However, Lord Mononobe no Yuge no Moriya no Ōmuraji addressed the empress, saying, "These Buddhist images should not be displayed in our country. Put them away somewhere far away!" Hearing this, the empress said to Lord Yasunoko no muraji, "Quickly hide these images!" Thereupon, he had Hita no atai hide them among the rice sheaves. Lord Yuge no Ōmuraji eventually set fire to the hall and had the images thrown into the canal at Naniwa. He upbraided Yasunoko, saying, "The cause of our present trouble lies in keeping unauthorized images sent from a nearby country to our own land. Throw them away at once and let them flow back to the land to the west!" ("Unauthorized images" means "Buddhist images.") But Yasunoko firmly refused. Yuge no Ōmuraji, his mind deranged, began to plot rebellion, looking for a chance to carry out evil. But Heaven disliked him, and Earth too hated him. In the reign of Emperor Yōmei, he was at last overthrown, and the Buddhist images were brought into the open and handed down to later ages. At present, the image of Amida enshrined at the Hiso Temple in Yoshino and casting out its light is one of them.

In the first month of spring in the year with the cyclical sign *mizu-noto-ushi* [593],[12] the empress was enthroned at the Owarida Palace

12. From very early times, the Chinese have used a combination of two sets of signs, the so-called Ten Stems and Twelve Branches, to form a sixty-term chronological sequence that, when it ends, begins again. This may be used to designate years, months, or days. When the Japanese adopted the use of the sixty-term cycle, they read the terms in the Japanese equivalents of the Chinese names.

and reigned for thirty-six years. In the first year of her reign, in the summer, the Fourth Month, the month *kanoe-uma*, on the day *tsuchinoto-u*, Prince Umayamado was appointed prince regent, and Yasunoko no muraji was made his personal attendant. In the thirteenth year of her reign, the year *kinoto-ushi* [605], in the summer, the Fifth Month, the month *kinoe-tora*, on the day *tsuchinoe-uma*, the empress gave him the Great Faith Rank, saying, "Your distinguished services shall long be remembered." In the seventeenth year, the year *tsuchinoto-mi* [609], in the spring, the Second Month, the prince regent bestowed on him 273 acres of rice fields in the Iibo district of Harima province. When the prince regent died at the Ikaruga Palace in the twenty-ninth year, the year *kanoto-mi* [621], Yasunoko no muraji expressed a desire to leave lay life and become a monk, but the empress would not permit this.

In the thirty-second year, the year *kinoe-saru* [624], in the summer, the Fourth Month, a high monk took an ax and struck his father. Seeing this, Yasunoko no muraji immediately petitioned the throne, saying, "Monks and nuns should be examined and a presiding officer appointed to regulate them. If there are any found guilty of evil, they should by all means be discharged." The empress gave her assent to this proposal. Yasunoko no muraji's proposal revealed a total of 837 monks and 579 nuns. The monk Kanroku was appointed Daisōjō, and Yasunoko no muraji and Kurabe no Tokosaka were appointed Sōzu.[13]

In the thirty-third year, the year *kinoto-tori* [625], in the winter, on the eighth day of the Twelfth Month, Yasunoko no muraji died suddenly at his home in Naniwa. His corpse gave out an unusually fragrant odor. The empress decreed that it be retained for seven days in honor of his loyalty. But on the third day, he came back to life and spoke to his wife and children. "There was a five-colored cloud," he said, "like a rainbow stretching to the north. I was walking along it, and that cloud was fragrant, as though fine incense were there. At the end of the road, I could see a golden mountain, which, when I reached it, dazzled my eyes. There

---

13. Both Daisōjō and Sōzu are high officers charged with the regulation of the clergy.

the Imperial Prince Shōtoku, who has departed this life, was waiting for me and together we climbed the golden mountain. On top of the golden mountain was a *bhikshu* [monk], who bowed to the prince and said, 'I am a servant in the Eastern Palace. In eight days you will encounter a sharp sword. Please drink this elixir of immortality!' The monk then handed the prince a goblet in which a jewel had been dissolved, which he drank. Then the monk said, 'Recite three times the words "Homage to the Bodhisattva of Miraculous Power,"' after which he withdrew. The prince then said, 'Go home at once and prepare for the making of a Buddhist image! When I have finished the rite of repentance, I will come to your place to make it!' So I came back here along the road I've mentioned. And so, to my surprise, I've returned to life!"

Accordingly, people called him the "Returned-to-Life Muraji." In the sixth year of the reign of Emperor Kōtoku, the year *kanoe-inu*, in the autumn, the Ninth Month, he was granted the rank of the Great Flower, Upper Grade, and died at over the age of ninety.

In appraisal we say: "How praiseworthy, this member of the Ōtomo family! He revered the Buddha, honored the doctrine, was pure in nature, and valued loyalty. He was blessed by both heredity and good fortune, living a long life without fault. His military might was boundless, and his filial piety has passed to his descendants. Truly, in his devotion to the Three Treasures of Buddhism, he was aided by the protection of the good deities."[14]

Looking back, it is apparent that the sentence "In eight days, you will encounter a sharp sword" refers to the rebellion raised by Soga no Iruka. "Eight days" means "eight years." By "Bodhisattva of Miraculous Power" is meant Bodhisattva Mañjuśrī. The "jewel" that he drank refers to the medicine that allowed him to avoid danger. The "golden mountain" is Mount Wutai in China,[15] and the "Eastern Palace" is Japan. When he

---

14. This appraisal section, in four-character phrases with occasional rhyme, is in imitation of similar sections in Chinese histories such as Ban Gu's *History of the Han*. It was also used in Chinese Buddhist works, which is probably from where Kyōkai took it.
15. Mount Wutai, one of the four sacred mountains in Chinese Buddhism, is devoted to the worship of Bodhisattva Mañjuśrī.

was told "go home at once and prepare for the making of a Buddhist image," this was made manifest by the birth of Emperor Shōhō-ōjin-shōmu [Shōmu, r. 724–749], who was from Japan, built a temple, and fashioned a statue of the Buddha. The Most Venerable Gyōki, a contemporary of Emperor Shomu, is an incarnation of Bodhisattva Manjuśrī. This was a miraculous event.

On Gaining an Immediate Reward for Faith in Bodhisattva Kannon (1:6)

The Venerable Monk Gyōzen, when he was in lay life, was a member of the Tatebe family. In the reign of the sovereign who resided in the Owarida Palace, he was sent to Koguryŏ for study.[16] When that country was overthrown, he was forced to wander.[17] Suddenly he came to a river, but the bridge had been destroyed and there was no boat, so he had no way to get across. Standing on the broken bridge, he began to meditate on Kannon. As he did so, an old man in a boat came along, greeted him, and ferried him to the other side of the river. But after he got over and was on the road ready to set out, both the man and the boat disappeared. Then he began to wonder if the man had been an incarnation of Kannon. Immediately, he made a vow to fashion an image of Kannon and worship it.

Eventually, he made his way to Tang China, where he fashioned an image, to which he paid devotion day and night. He was known as Dharma Master Riverside. He excelled by nature in the practice of the virtue of forbearance and was revered by the Chinese emperor. In the second year of the era Yōrō [718], he returned home to Japan with the party of the Japanese envoy to China. He lived in Kōfuku-ji temple and continued to

---

16. Probably in the reign of Empress Suiko. Koguryŏ (37 B.C.E.–668 C.E.), located in northern and central present-day Korea, was one of the three kingdoms of Korea, along with Paekche (18 B.C.E.–660 C.E.) and Silla (57 B.C.E.–935 C.E.).
17. Koguryŏ was invaded and overthrown in 668 by Tang China.

venerate the image of Kannon until his death. Indeed, we know that Kannon possesses powers that are difficult to fathom.

In appraisal we say: The Venerable Monk went far away to study, met with trouble, and could not return. Having no way to escape, he rested on the bridge, meditating on the Sage or Bodhisattva. He depended on the power of the heart, and this caused the appearance of the old man, who disappeared suddenly once they had parted. In time, he made an image and always paid it honor, never ceasing his devotions.

On Paying For and Freeing Turtles and Being Rewarded Immediately and Saved by Them (1:7)

Meditation Master Gusai [Universal Salvation] was a native of the country of Paekche. When that country encountered a period of troubles, an ancestor of the governor of the Mitani district of Bingo province was put in charge of reinforcements and sent to Paekche.[18] At that time, the present governor's ancestor vowed to build a temple to the deities of Heaven and Earth if he returned home safely. Eventually, he escaped harm and thereupon invited Meditation Master Universal Salvation to return to Japan with him. Mitani Temple, as well as other temples, were founded by him, and he was looked on with reverence by monks and lay folk alike.

Once, in order to create a Buddhist image, he went to the capital to purchase supplies. Having bought gold and paints and other supplies and paid for them, he returned to the port of Naniwa. At that time by the sea, he saw people on the beach offering four large turtles for sale. He ordered them to be bought and set free.[19] Then he rented a boat belonging to some men, and he and his two acolyte companions set out to sea.

18. Paekche was attacked in 660 by forces from both Tang China and neighboring Silla. It was invaded and overthrown in 663.
19. The practice of buying captive fish, birds, or other animals and setting them free was highly recommended in Buddhism.

When it grew late and the dark of night had fallen, the sailors manning the boat began to plot. And when they reached the area of Kabane Island in Bizen, they threw the two acolytes into the sea. Then they said to the meditation master, "You, too, quick—into the sea!" He tried to reason with them, but they refused to listen. Then, after making a vow, he jumped into the water.

When the water came up to his waist, he felt something like a rock under his feet, and when dawn came, he saw that he was being carried by the turtles. They left him on the beach of Bitchū, after nodding to him three times. The turtles that had been ransomed and set free, it appeared, had come to repay their debt to him.

Eventually, the guilty sailors, six men in all, came to his temple to sell the gold and paints they had stolen. The patron of the temple first came out to make an estimate, followed by the meditation master himself. Seeing him, the sailors were completely dumbfounded, not knowing what to do. But he forgave them for their crime and exacted no penalty. Instead, he fashioned a Buddhist image, placed it in the pagoda of the temple, and performed rites before it. Later he lived by the seaside, where he preached to those who passed by. He died at the age of over eighty.

Even beasts do not forget an act of kindness, but are careful to repay it. How, then, can human beings fail to have a sense of gratitude?

ON A DEAF MAN WHOSE HEARING WAS RESTORED IMMEDIATELY, OWING TO HIS FAITH IN A MAHAYANA SUTRA (1:8)

In the reign of the sovereign who resided at the Owarida Palace, there was a man named Kinunui no tomonomiyatsuko Norimichi, who suddenly became seriously ill. He lost the hearing in both ears and suffered from skin disease all over his body. And these ailments never healed. He said to himself, "These are the result of past karma, and there is no hope they will end soon. Rather than living a long life and being hated by others, it is better to do good now and quickly die!" Therefore, he swept the ground, decorated the hall, and summoned a monk who was well read in scriptures. Then, after purifying himself with holy water, he devoted himself to listening to a reading of a Mahayana sutra.[20]

Then he had a strange feeling. He said to the monk, "I am hearing the name of a bodhisattva in one of my ears. So I beg you, Most Venerable Master, to continue the reading!" The monk continued the reading, whereupon the hearing in one ear was completely restored. Norimichi was overjoyed and pleaded with the monk to go on. When he did so, the hearing in both of Norimichi's ears was restored.

All those both near and far who heard of this were filled with wonder and amazement. So we know that tales of a mysterious correspondence are not false.[21]

On a Baby Carried Away by an Eagle and Reunited with Her Father in Another Province (1:9)

In the reign of the sovereign who resided at the Itabuki Palace in Asuka Kawara, in the year *mizunoto-u* [643],[22] in the spring, around the Third Month, there was a man in a mountain village who had a baby girl. She was crawling in the courtyard when an eagle seized her, flew into the sky, and headed toward the east. Her father and mother, startled and shocked, grieved and tried to run after her, but it was impossible. Therefore, they held a Buddhist memorial service for better luck in her next existence.

---

20. Hōkō-kyō, or the sutras of the Correct and Equal period, is a term designating the third of Zhiyi's classification of the sutras, the introductory Mahayana sutras. But here it may mean the Lotus Sutra.
21. The "mysterious correspondence" is between Buddhas and sentient beings.
22. The second year of the reign of Empress Kyōgoku (r. 642–645).

Eight years later, in the reign of the sovereign who resided at the Nagara-no-Toyosaki Palace in Naniwa, the year *kanoe-inu* [650],[23] in the autumn, the Eighth Month, the latter part of the month, the father whose child had been seized by an eagle, having business in the area, happened to put up for the night in the Kasa district of Tamba province. When the little daughter of the family went to the village well to draw water, the man, wishing to wash his feet, went with her.

Around the well were gathered some girls of the village, who snatched away the pail from the daughter of the family and would not allow her to draw water. The other girls joined together in speaking insultingly to her, saying, "You—you're something that the eagle wouldn't eat! Why don't you have any manners?" They abused her and hit her, so she went home crying.

When the head of the family with whom the man was staying asked her why she was crying, the man described to him in detail what had happened at the well, including the fact that the other girls had abused and hit her and called her "something that the eagle wouldn't eat!" He asked why they said that.

The head of the family replied, "Some years ago, on such-and-such day of such-and-such month, I had climbed into a tree to catch some doves when an eagle with a baby girl in its talons came flying from the west and dropped the baby into its nest for the young eagles to eat. The baby was terrified and crying. The eaglets looked at her but were too surprised and frightened to peck at her. When I heard the baby crying, I took her from the nest, climbed down the tree, and raised her as a daughter."

When the two men compared the dates of the events, they found that they agreed, and that this was clearly the daughter of the traveler.

For his part, crying bitterly, he told in detail how the eagle had made off with his child. The other man, recognizing the truth of his words, relinquished all claim to the girl.

Ah, this father—he stayed by chance with a family that had a daughter, and in the end it came to this! Thus we know that, through the help

23. The first year of the Hakuchi era of the reign of Emperor Kōtoku (r. 645–654).

of Heaven and its pitying, the bond between a father and his child is deepened. It was a miraculous event!

On a Man's Stealing from His Son, Being Reborn as an Ox, and Showing an Unusual Sign (1:10)

In the central village of Yamamura in the Sou district of Yamato province, there was once a man called Lord Kura no Iegimi. In the Twelfth Month, he decided to atone for his past sins by having a Mahayana sutra recited. Therefore, he said to his servant, "Go and call a monk!"

The servant asked, "What temple should I go to in order to find a monk?"

The master replied, "You don't have to go to a temple. You can invite any monk you happen to meet." The servant, following these instructions, brought home a monk he happened to meet on the way. The master, satisfied with the arrangement, made offerings to the monk.

That night, after the monk had performed his service and it was time to go to bed, the host spread quilts for him to sleep under. The monk thought to himself, "Rather than waiting to see what kind of offerings I get in the morning, it would be better to make off with these quilts!" Then he heard a voice saying, "Don't steal those quilts!"

The monk, greatly startled, looked around the house for someone who had spoken. But all he could find was an ox that was standing in a shed beside the house. When the monk approached the ox, it began to speak. "I am the father of the master of this house. Some years ago, I stole ten sheaves of rice belonging to my son without telling him what I was doing, in order to give them to someone else. Because of that, I was reborn as an ox in payment for that deed. You have become a monk—how dare you even think of stealing these quilts? If you doubt the truth of my words, make a place for me to sit down. I will sit in it, so you will know I am really his father!" The monk was filled with shame and went back to bed.

The next morning, after he had completed his religious service, he said to his host, "Please have the other people withdraw." Then, summoning the members of the immediate family, he told them what he had heard. The host, his heart full of grief, got up and went to where the ox was. Spreading a seat of rice straw, he said, "If you are really my father, come sit down here!" The ox knelt down and lay on the seat. All the family members began weeping bitterly and saying, "He really is our father!" Then the host stood up, bowed politely, and said to the ox, "I will cancel all the accounts in your former life!" The ox, hearing this, wept great tears and heaved a sigh; the same day, around four in the afternoon, its life came to an end. Afterward, the host presented the quilts and other goods to the monk as an offering and did many good works for the sake of his father.

How can we fail to believe in the law of karmic causality?

On a Lifetime of Catching Fish in a Net and the Immediate Penalty Gained (1:11)

The Most Venerable Jiō, a monk of Gangō-ji in the capital, at the invitation of a patron of the temple, went on a summer retreat to lecture on the Lotus Sutra at No-no-o Temple in the Shikama district of Harima province. In the neighborhood, there was a fisherman who had been netting fish for a long time, from childhood to the present. Then one day, he suddenly crawled in among the mulberry bushes, crying in a loud voice, "The flames are about to devour me!" When his family tried to help him, he called out to them, "Don't come near me! They're about to burn me up!"

Meanwhile, his father rushed to the temple and begged the Most Venerable Jiō to help them. When Jiō recited spells, the man was eventually rescued from the flames, though the breeches he was wearing had been scorched. Thoroughly frightened, he went to the temple and, before the congregation, confessed his crime and promised to reform his ways. He made an offering of clothing and other articles to the temple and had sutras recited. Thereafter, he never did any evil deeds.

It is just as the *Yanshi jiaxun* [*Family Instructions for the Yan Clan*] says: "Once there was a man who belonged to the Liu family of Jiang-ling, who made his living by selling stewed eel. Later, he had a child born to him who had the head of an eel but from the neck on down had a human body."[24] This demonstrates the same principle.

On a Skull That Was Saved from Being Stepped On by Men and Beasts, Showing an Extraordinary Sign and Repaying the Benefactor Immediately (1:12)

Dōtō, a Buddhist scholar of Koguryŏ, was a monk of Gangō-ji. He came from the Eman family of Yamashina province. In the second year of the Taika era, the year *hinoe-uma* [646], he built the bridge at Uji. Once, when he was passing through the valley in the Nara hills, he saw a skull that had been trampled on by men and beasts. Sorrowing at the sight, he had his attendant Maro hang it on a tree.

On New Year's Eve of the same year, a man came to the gate of the temple, saying, "I would like to see the Venerable Dōtō's attendant Maro." When Maro came out, he said, "Thanks to the pity of your master, I have gained the blessing of a peaceful existence. And only on this one evening am I able to repay your kindness." Then he took Maro to his home.

Passing through the closed gate, they entered the back part of the house, where they found plentiful food and drink prepared. The man divided up the fare with Maro, and they ate together.

Later, when night had fallen, they heard voices, and the man said to Maro, "Go quickly! Here comes my elder brother, the man who killed me!" When Maro, wondering at this, asked what it meant, he replied,

---

24. Written by Yan Zhitui (531–590), this Chinese work, which presents a synthesis of Bud-dhist and Confucian teachings, was popular in Japan in the Nara period (710–784).

"Long ago, when my elder brother and I were traveling on business, I came into possession of forty catties of silver.[25] My brother, out of envy and hatred, killed me and took the silver. For many years now, my skull has been trampled on by men and beasts passing by. But now, thanks to your master, I've been freed of that wrong. Therefore, in remembrance of that debt, I have repaid you tonight."

At that time, the man's mother and elder brother entered the room to pay their respects to the various deities. Seeing Maro, they were surprised and alarmed and asked how he happened to be there. When he told them what he had just heard, the mother said accusingly to her elder son, "Ah—it was you who killed my beloved boy! It was not someone else's doing!" Then she expressed her thanks to Maro and insisted that he eat and drink more. On his return, Maro reported all this to his master.

Even a spirit of the dead or a skeleton repays an act of kindness. How, then, can a living person forget such a debt?

On a Woman Who Loved Pure Ways, Ate Sacred Herbs, and Flew to Heaven Alive (1:13)

In the village of Nuribe in the Uda district of Yamato province, there lived a very unusual woman. She was a concubine of Nuribe no miyatsuko Maro. She practiced Heaven-approved ways, had gained enlightenment, and possessed a pure heart.[26] She gave birth to seven children, but being extremely poor, she had nothing to feed them. Having no means to raise them, she wove vines to clothe them. Every day, she would bathe her body, clean it, and put on ragged clothing. And when she went

---

25. A catty is a unit of weight that equals 1.5 pounds, so this would be 60 pounds of silver.
26. Although not a Buddhist, she followed practices that allied her to Buddhist modes of conduct. There is a strongly Daoist flavor to this tale.

abroad, she always gathered herbs, and at home was careful to keep her house clean. When she had gathered a mess of herbs, she would call her children, have them sit up straight, and remind them, "Eat this food reverently!" This was how she always conducted herself, so that in her manner she resembled a dweller in Heaven.

In the reign of the emperor who resided at the Nagara no Toyosaki Palace in Naniwa,[27] in the year *kinoe-tora* [654], her extraordinary ways prompted a response from the gods and spirits. When she went to the spring fields to gather herbs, she flew up to Heaven.

Truly we know that, although one does not practice the Buddhist Law, those who love such ways can communicate with those who drink the elixir of immortality. As the Shōjin nyomon-kyō says: "Even though you live the life of a layperson, if you sweep the garden with a pure heart, you will gain five kinds of merit."[28]

ON A MONK WHO RECITED THE SHIN-GYŌ AND, RECEIVING AN IMMEDIATE REWARD, SHOWED AN EXTRAORDINARY SIGN (1:14)

Shaku Gigaku was originally from Paekche,[29] but when that country was overthrown, in the reign of the sovereign who resided in the later Okamoto Palace,[30] he came to our country and lived at the Kutara Temple in Naniwa. He was seven feet tall, well read in the Buddhist scriptures, and particularly skilled in reciting the Hannya Shin-gyō.[31]

Egi, a fellow monk at the same temple, happened to go out alone one night around midnight. He found a bright light coming out of the room

27. Emperor Kōtoku (r. 645–654).
28. The identity of this work is highly obscure.
29. Shaku, short for Śākyamuni, indicates a follower of Buddhist teachings—that is, a monk.
30. In 660, in the reign of Empress Saimei (r. 655–661).
31. The Shin-gyō, or Hannya Shin-gyō, known in English as the Heart Sutra, is a very short work. See *Taishō* 8:nos. 250–255, 257.

where Gigaku lived. Thinking this strange, he secretly poked a hole in the paper panel and peered in. He saw Gigaku sitting up straight and reciting the sutra, and light was pouring out of his mouth. Being very startled and frightened by this, the next day he confessed what he had done to the congregation of monks.

Once Gigaku was talking with his disciples, and he said, "One evening, when I had recited the Shin-gyō a hundred times, I found that, when I opened my eyes and looked at the walls of the room, I could see right through all four walls and could see into the garden. Thinking this very strange, I then went out of the room and walked around outside, but when I looked, all the walls were closed up. When I stayed outside and recited the Shin-gyō, however, they once more became transparent. This shows you the extraordinary power of the sutra!"

In appraisal we say: How great is this child of Śākyamuni! He has heard much and expounds the teachings. When he recites the sutra in a closed room, his mind expands and moves abroad. It manifests itself in extreme quietude: What motion could it know? Yet when it passes through the walls of the room, it shines everywhere around!

On a Wicked Man Who Persecuted a Begging Monk and Gained an Immediate Penalty (1:15)

Long ago, in the time of the old capital, there was a foolish man who did not believe in the law of karmic causality. Once, seeing a monk begging for food, he grew angry and tried to stop him. The monk fled into the water in a rice field, but the man chased after him and caught him. The monk, not knowing what else to do, put a spell on him. The man went completely wild, running about in every direction. The monk, meanwhile, ran far away and could not be found.

This man had two sons. In order to free their father from the spell, they went to the temple and asked the meditation master to come and see their father. When the meditation master learned what had happened, he at first refused to go. But the two sons begged and pleaded, asking him to save their father, until at last he agreed. He had barely finished reciting the first passage of the chapter of the Lotus Sutra on Kannon when the man was released from the spell. Thereafter, he had a great awakening of faith, turned from wickedness, and did only good.

On Mercilessly Skinning a Live Rabbit and Receiving an Immediate Penalty (1:16)

In Yamato province, there lived a man whose name and native village are unknown. He was by nature merciless and loved to kill living creatures. He once caught a rabbit, skinned it alive, and then turned it loose in the fields. But not long afterward, pestilent sores broke out all over his body, his whole body was covered with scabs, and they caused him unspeakable torment. In the end, he never gained any relief, but died groaning and lamenting.

Ah, how soon do such deeds receive an immediate penalty! We should consider others as we do ourselves, exercise benevolence, and never be without pity and compassion!

On Suffering Damage in War, Showing Faith in an Image of Bodhisattva Kannon, and Gaining an Immediate Reward (1:17)

Ochi no atai, ancestor of the governor of the Ochi district of Iyo province, was sent to Paekche with the Japanese expeditionary forces.[32]

---

32. There are two possible dates for this: 660 and 663.

He was taken prisoner by Tang Chinese soldiers and brought to China. There, with other Japanese, eight men in all, he lived on an island. They acquired an image of Bodhisattva Kannon and worshipped it with deep devotion. Secretly, they worked together to cut down a pine tree and fashion a boat. Placing the Kannon image reverently in the boat, they made their vows to it and set off, their thoughts fixed on Kannon. They caught a wind from the west and proceeded directly to Tsukushi.[33]

When word of this reached the court, they were summoned to report on the affair. The emperor, deeply moved, agreed to grant their wishes. Ochi no atai said, "I wish to serve by establishing an estate." The emperor granted his wish. Thereafter, he established the district of Ochi and built a temple in which to place the image of Kannon. From that time until the present, his descendants have followed his example in worshipping and honoring it.

It was surely Kannon's power that brought about this remarkable display of faith. Even a wooden image of Ding Lan's mother appeared to be alive, and the woman in a picture loved by a monk responded with sympathy.[34] How, then, is it possible for the Bodhisattva not to respond?

ON REMEMBERING AND RECITING THE LOTUS SUTRA AND GAINING AN IMMEDIATE AND WONDERFUL REWARD (1:18)

In the Kazuraki upper district of Yamato province, there was once a devotee of the Lotus Sutra. He was a member of the Tajihi family. Even before he was eight years old, he could recite the Lotus Sutra, but with the exception of one character that always escaped his memory.

---

33. Tsukushi refers to the island of Kyushu in Japan.
34. According to the *Xiaozizhuan* (*Biographies of Filial Sons*) by Liu Xiang, when Ding Lan was fifteen years old, he lost his mother. He made a wooden image of her and cared for it as if it were alive. The story behind the second part of the sentence is unknown.

Even when he was in his twenties, it continued to escape him.

He prayed to Kannon, confessing his offense, and had a dream. In it, a man said to him, "In a previous existence, you were a child of Kusakabe no Saru of the Wake district of Iyo province. At that time, while reciting the sutra, you burned one character with a lamp so that you could not read it. Now, go and see!"

When he awoke, he was filled with wonder. He said to his parents, "I have urgent business—I want to go to Iyo!" His parents gave their consent.

Setting out, in time he reached Kusakabe no Saru's house and knocked on the door. A woman answered, and then reported to the lady of the house, "There's a visitor here who looks exactly like your deceased son!" On hearing this, she came to the door and found that the man was indeed the image of her dead son. Then the head of the house, Kusakabe no Saru, appeared and, wondering, asked, "Who are you?" The man replied, giving the name of his district and province. Then he asked the same question, and Kusakabe no Saru gave his full name. It thus became apparent to the man that these had been his father and mother in a previous existence. He knelt down in a gesture of respect, but Kusakabe no Saru greeted him warmly, invited him in, and, seating him in the parlor, asked respectfully, "Are you the spirit of our deceased son?" The man then described in detail the dream that he had had, exclaiming, "You elderly couple are my former parents!"

Kusakabe no Saru then began reminiscing, saying, "My former son was named such-and-such. He lived in the room over there, recited sutras, and used that water pitcher." The man, hearing him, entered the room, picked up the copy of the Lotus Sutra, and examined it. He found that the character he could never remember had been burned by a lamp and was missing. Once he had repented of this accident and had repaired the text, he was thereafter able to recite it without fault. Both the parents and the son looked on this with wonder and rejoicing, and the man never failed to honor this parent–child relationship.

In appraisal we say: How happy, the members of the Kusakabe family! He read the sutra and sought the Way in two lives, past and present, reciting the Lotus Sutra! He was filial to two fathers, his fine reputation handed down to posterity. This was extraordinary, surely not commonplace. Truly we know the authority of the Lotus Sutra and the wonderful workings of Kannon! As the Zen'aku-inga-kyō [Sutra on the Effects of Good and Evil] says: "If you want to know past causes, look at present effects. If you want to know future effects, look at present causes."[35] This is what it means!

ON RIDICULING A RECITER OF THE LOTUS SUTRA AND GETTING A TWISTED MOUTH AS AN IMMEDIATE PENALTY (1:19)

Long ago in Yamato province, there was a self-ordained monk. His family and given name are unknown. He used to play *go* incessantly. One day when he was playing *go* with a white-robed layman, a beggar came along, reciting the Lotus Sutra and asking for alms. The monk laughed scornfully at him, and then purposely twisted his mouth around in imitation of that of the man. The layman was shocked, saying with each play of the game, "How disrespectful!" He won every time at the game, while the monk lost. But while this was going on, the monk's mouth became twisted. No medicine could cure it, and in the end it never mended.

The Lotus Sutra says: "If anyone disparages or laughs at that person,[36] then in existence after existence he will have teeth that are missing or spaced far apart, ugly lips, a flat nose, hands and feet that are gnarled or deformed, and eyes that are squinty."[37] This is what it means. It is better to be possessed by evil devils and talk nonsense than to abuse the devotees of the Lotus Sutra. Remember that the mouth is often the source of evil.

35. The quotation is not from this sutra, but is in another text, the *Shokyō yōshū* (*Essential Passages from Various Sutras*). See *Taishō* 59:53c.
36. "That person" refers to one who accepts and upholds the sutra.
37. *The Lotus Sutra*, trans. Burton Watson (New York: Columbia University Press, 1993), chap. 28, "Encouragements of the Bodhisattva Universal Worthy," 324.

ON A MONK WHO GAVE AWAY THE WOOD USED TO HEAT THE BATH, WAS REBORN AS AN OX, AND LABORED UNTIL AN EXTRAORDINARY SIGN APPEARED (1:20)

Shaku Eshō was a monk of Engō-ji. Once, in the course of his daily life, he gave a bundle of wood to be used to heat the bath to someone else and then died. At that temple, there was a cow that gave birth to a male calf. When the calf grew up into an ox, it was tied to a cart and put to work, endlessly pulling a load of firewood.

One day, as it pulled the cart into the temple grounds, there was a strange monk at the temple gate who said, "Monk Eshō was good at reciting the Nirvana Sutra, but he's no good at pulling a cart!" The ox, hearing this, burst into tears, gave a long sigh, and abruptly died. The driver of the ox berated the monk, saying, "You put a curse on it!" and reported him to the officials. When in the course of investigation they called in the monk, they were surprised at his unusually noble appearance and radiant body. They took him to a better room and invited painters to paint him, saying, "This monk is to be painted exactly as he is, without any mistake!" The painters agreed to do so. And when they brought their efforts to the official lodge and the officials examined them, all of them were depictions of Bodhisattva Kannon. The monk, meanwhile, had suddenly disappeared.

Surely there can be no doubt—that monk was none other than an incarnation of Kannon. It is better to starve and eat dirt than to steal food meant for the daily needs of the monks! When the Daihōdō Sutra says, "I can save those who commit the four offenses or the five crimes, but I will not save those who steal from the monks!"[38] this is what it means.

---

38. Daihōdō is a shortened form of Daihōdō-darani-kyō. See *Taishō* 13:no. 397. The four offenses are killing, stealing, licentiousness, and lying. The five crimes are killing one's father, one's mother, or an arhat; injuring the body of a Buddha; and causing dissension in the Order.

On Mercilessly Driving Horses with a Heavy Load and Getting an Immediate Penalty (1:21)

Long ago in Kawachi province, there was a man named Ishiwake who sold melons. He would saddle a horse with a far greater load than the horse was capable of pulling, and then, when the horse failed to move, would whip it angrily and drive it forward. The horse would strain at the heavy load, tears pouring from its eyes. Once he had sold all his melons, he would kill the horse. After Ishiwake had killed a number of horses this way, he happened to peer into a cauldron of boiling water, whereupon both his eyes fell into the water and were boiled.

How swift is the penalty for evil deeds! We must believe in the law of karmic causality. Even looking at beasts, we see that they may have been our father and mother in past times. The six paths and the four forms of birth—they are the house we live in.[39] Therefore, we cannot be without pity and compassion.

On Working Diligently to Study the Buddhist Law, Spreading the Teachings for the Benefit of All, and, at the Time of Death, Receiving an Extraordinary Sign (1:22)

The late monk Dōshō belonged to the Fune family of Kawachi province. Under imperial auspices, he went abroad to study Buddhism, journeying

---

39. The six paths are the realms of Hell, hungry spirits, animals, *asuras* (demons), human beings, and heavenly beings. The four forms of birth are birth from the womb, from eggs, from dampness or moisture (as worms), and by transformation.

to Tang China.[40] There he met and became a disciple of Tripitaka Master Xuanzang.[41] The master said to his other disciples, "This man, when he returns home, will convert many people to Buddhism. You should not look down on him but treat him well."

Once his studies were completed, he returned home and founded a temple called Zen'in-ji, where he resided. He excelled in the keeping of the precepts, and his wisdom shone like a mirror. He traveled widely, spreading the teachings and converting others. In his later days, he lived in the temple and lectured to his disciples, summing up for them the essential doctrines of many sacred texts.

When he felt that his end was near, he bathed, put on a clean robe, and sat upright facing west. A brilliance filled the entire room. He opened his eyes and asked his disciple Chijō, "Do you see the light?"

Chijō replied, "Yes, I see it." The master warned him, saying, "Do not speak incautiously about this!" In the latter part of the night, the light emerged from the room, moved to the area around the pine trees in the garden, and then, after a long time, went away to the west. All his disciples were struck with wonder, and at that moment the master, sitting straight up and facing west, died.[42] We may be certain that he went to the Pure Land for rebirth!

In appraisal we say: This distinguished member of the Fune family journeyed far in search of the Buddhist scriptures. He was a saint, not an ordinary person. In the end, he died in a burst of light.

40. Dōshō went to China in 653, returned to Japan in 661, and founded the Hossō (Consciousness Only) school of Buddhism.
41. A famous Chinese monk and translator of Buddhist scriptures, Tripitaka Master Xuanzang (602–664) traveled to Central Asia and India and brought back numerous images and texts. He is the author of *The Record of the Western Region*, an account of his seventeen-year journey.
42. West is the direction in which the Gokuraku jōdo (Pure Land), the realm of Amida Buddha, is located.

On a Bad Man Who Neglected to Pay Filial Duty to His Mother and Got the Immediate Penalty of an Evil Death (1:23)

In the Sou upper district of Yamato province, there once lived a man whose family name is unknown; his personal name was Miyasu. In the reign of the emperor residing at the Naniwa Palace,[43] he became a student of the classics. He spent all his time with books and neglected to take care of his mother.

His mother had borrowed some rice from him and was unable to return it. Miyasu grew angry and pressed her for repayment. At that time, the mother was kneeling on the floor, while Miyasu sat on a sleeping mat. When his visitors saw this, they could not remain silent but said, "Good man, why do you go against the rules of filial duty? Other people establish temples, build pagodas, make Buddhist images, or copy sutras for the benefit of their father and mother, or invite monks to a retreat for their sake. You are rich and are fortunate to have much rice to lend. Why do you go against what you have learned and fail to treat your dear mother in a filial manner?" But Miyasu dismissed their complaints, saying, "That's none of your business!" The visitors paid the mother's debt out of their own money, and all hurried away.

The mother then bared her breasts and, weeping, sadly said, "When I was bringing you up, I never rested day or night. I have seen how other children repay their parents for the care they received, but when I thought I could rely on you, I got nothing but opposition and disgrace. I was wrong to count on you. If you demand repayment of the rice I borrowed, I will now demand repayment for the milk I gave you. Our mother–child relationship is severed from this day on. May Heaven and Earth take cognizance of this. How sad, how pitiful!"

---

43. Emperor Kōtoku (r. 645–654).

Without saying a word, Miyasu stood up, went into the back room, and, returning with the pledges his mother had signed for the rice, burned them all in the yard. Then he went off into the mountains, to who knows where, his hair disheveled, his body bleeding, wandering wildly this way and that. He returned to his home but was unable to stay there. Three days later, a fire broke out suddenly, and all his houses and storerooms were burned. In the end, his wife and children were left with no means of support, while he himself, with nowhere to turn, died of hunger and cold.

An immediate penalty is not far off—how can we fail to believe this? Therefore, the sutra says: "The unfilial are destined to fall into Hell; those who take care of father and mother go to the Pure Land."[44]

This is what the Thus Come One preaches,[45] the true teaching of the Mahayana.

On an Evil Daughter Who Lacked Filial Respect for Her Mother and Got the Immediate Penalty of a Violent Death (1:24)

In the old capital there lived a wicked woman whose name is unknown. She had no feelings of filial respect and did not love her mother.

Once, it being a day for fasting,[46] the mother cooked no rice at home but went to her daughter's place, thinking to eat there. But the daughter said, "Today my husband and I are fasting. So there's just enough for the two of us—nothing left over for you!"

At that time, the mother had a little child. As she and the child returned home, she happened to notice a packet of boiled rice that someone had left by the roadside. She picked it up, ate it hungrily, and then fell asleep exhausted. Late at night, someone came to the door, reporting, "Your daugh-

---

44. The quotation has not been located, but it represents typical Mahayana doctrine.
45. Thus Come One is Śākyamuni Buddha.
46. Days for fasting are set aside in Buddhism for the laity to eat vegetarian fare and observe various practices.

ter says that she has a nail in her chest and is about to die! Come at once and look at her!" But the mother was so tired that they could not wake her or get her help, and, in the end, the daughter died without seeing her.

It is better to give our portion to our mother and starve than to die without showing her filial respect!

ON A LOYAL MINISTER, SATISFIED AND WITH FEW WANTS, WHO WON HEAVEN'S SYMPATHY AND WAS REWARDED BY A MIRACULOUS EVENT (1:25)

The late Middle Councillor Lord Ōmiwa no Takechimaro, of the Junior Third Rank awarded posthumously, was a loyal minister of Empress Jitō.[47] According to the records, in the seventh year of the Akamidori era, the year *mizunoe-tatsu* [692], an imperial order was given to the officials telling them to prepare for the empress's visit to Ise on the third day of the month. The Middle Councillor, fearing that the visit would interfere with agricultural work, presented a memorial attempting to dissuade the empress. She dismissed this, however, saying that she would go anyway. He then took off his official cap and in court repeated his remonstrance. "Now, when people are busy with farm work, you should not go!" he said.

Another time, in a period of drought, he closed off the water to his own fields and directed it to the fields of others, leaving his own fields to dry up. But the gods of Heaven responded with sympathy and ordered the dragons to send down rain. It rained on only his own fields, however, and not on those of others. Yao's clouds gathered for him, and Shun's rains fell.[48] Truly he was a model of loyalty, a man of great humaneness and virtue.

In appraisal we say: This praiseworthy man of the Ōmiya family from childhood loved to study, was loyal and benevolent, his actions pure,

---

47. Empress Jitō (r. 686–697) was Emperor Tenmu's consort.
48. The clouds and rain fell in response to the ancient Chinese sage-rulers Yao and Shun.

never unclean. He looked kindly on the people, bestowing blessings on them, directing water to their fields, shutting off his own, until the sweet rain fell—his fame will last for long!

On a Monk Who Observed the Precepts, Was Pure in His Activities, and Won an Immediate Miraculous Reward (1:26)

In the reign of Empress Jitō, there was a meditation master of Paekche named Tara. He always lived in Hokiyama Temple in the Takechi district, following a life of strict discipline. He specialized in caring for the sick and the dying, who were restored to life through his art. When he recited a spell for a sick person, there was a miraculous result.

Once, when he was climbing a slope with the use of a staff, he stuck a second staff onto the first one, so that the two supported each other without falling, but acted like a chisel.[49]

The empress respected him greatly and constantly made offerings to him, and the people put faith in him and paid him constant reverence. This was because his virtuous way of life caused his fame to be known far and wide. The power of his pity and compassion will long be praised.

On an Evil Novice, Name Unknown, Who Tore Down the Pillar of a Pagoda and Gained a Penalty (1:27)

The *shami* [novice] of Ishikawa was a self-ordained monk who had no clerical name; his secular name, too, is unknown. He was called the

---

49. Some kind of stunt? The meaning escapes me.

Ishikawa novice because his wife came from the Ishikawa district of Kawachi province. Although he had the appearance of a novice, his heart was set on thieving. Once he falsely told people that he was collecting funds to build a pagoda, but then he and his wife privately spent the money on personal items. Again, when he was living in the Tsuki-yone Temple in the Shima-no-shimo district of Settsu province, he tore down a pillar of the pagoda and burned it—he was extremely wicked in this way, having no respect for the teachings of Buddhism.

In the end, when he had reached the village of Ajiki in the Shima-no-shimo district, he was suddenly taken ill. He cried out in a loud voice, "I'm burning up, burning up!" and jumped one or two feet off the ground. People gathered around to look, asking, "Why are you doing that?" He replied, "The fires of Hell are burning up my body! When I'm suffering like this, why do you ask such questions?" On that day, his life came to an end.

Ah, how sad! We know that punishment for wrongdoing is no fiction: Why, then, do we not reflect on this? The Nirvana Sutra says: "If a person does good works, his name will be noted among heavenly beings; if he does evil, his name will be noted in Hell. Why? Because retribution is sure to come."[50] This is what the sutra means.

On Learning the Chant of the Peacock King and Thereby Gaining Extraordinary Power to Become a Saint and Fly to Heaven in This Life (1:28)

E no ubasoku, or E the Layman, was of the Kamo-no-enokimi family, presently the Takakamo-no-asomi family. He came from the village of Chihara in the Kazuraki upper district of Yamato province. He was wise

---

50. Nirvana Sutra, Northern Version, vol. 12. See *Taishō* 12:524b.

by nature, had studied widely, and had attained the One.[51] He put his faith in the Three Treasures of Buddhism and made this his life work. His constant desire was to ascend a five-colored cloud, fly off to the vast blue, visit as a guest in the palace of the immortals, sport in the gardens of eternity, and lie among their blossoms and suck their nectar to nourish his vital force.

Therefore, when he was in his forties and growing old, he went to live in a cave, wore vines, ate pinecones, bathed in the fresh spring water, and thus washed away the dirt of the world of desire. He practiced the chants of the Peacock King Sutra and, in this way, gained extraordinary arts and powers. So he was able to command devils and gods and make them do his will.

Once he summoned all the devils and gods and said, "Build me a bridge between the peaks of Kane-no-mitake and Kazuraki-no-mitake in the land of Yamato!" They were perplexed by this. In the reign of the emperor who resided at the Fujiwara Palace,[52] Hitokotonushi no Ōkami of Kazuraki-no-mitake was possessed and slandered him, saying, "E no ubasoku plans to overthrow the emperor!" The emperor gave orders that he be seized, but because of his magical powers, this was not easy to do. Therefore, they seized his mother instead. To save his mother, he gave himself up.

He was exiled to the islands of Izu. At times, his body floated on the sea or seemed to climb the tall mountains. His form was at times ten thousand feet tall or flew like a soaring phoenix. In the daytime, he obeyed the emperor's orders and remained on the islands, but at night he went to the heights of Mount Fuji in Suruga to practice his art. His desire, however, was to be pardoned from the punishment of the executioner's ax and to be allowed to return to the vicinity of the ruler. Therefore, he lay down on the blades of a deadly sword and flew to Mount Fuji. Three years passed while he was suffering in exile on the islands, but in the first year of the Taihō era, in the First Month of the year *kanoto-ushi*

---

51. That is, he had gained enlightenment, but the expression is Daoist in nature, as is much of this account.
52. Emperor Monmu (r. 697–700).

[701], he was allowed to return to the capital. In the end, he became an immortal and flew up to Heaven.

The Dharma Master Dōshō, a saint of our country of Japan, received an imperial order to go to Tang China to seek for knowledge of Buddhist Law. There he was requested by five hundred tigers to go to the kingdom of Silla in Korea, where, in the mountains, he lectured on the Lotus Sutra. There was a man among the throng of tigers who spoke to him in the Japanese language. "Who are you?" he asked, and received the reply "E no ubasoku!" The monk, supposing him to be a Japanese sage, came down from his seat, looking for him, but he was gone.

Hitokotonushi no Ōkami was bound by the spell put on him by E the Practitioner, and to this day he has not escaped. Many other miraculous deeds are attributed to him, but they are too numerous to mention. Truly we know that the workings of the Buddhist Law are great and far-reaching. Those who put faith in them will surely gain proof of this.

On Being an Unbeliever, Breaking the Bowl of a Begging Monk, and Incurring the Immediate Penalty of a Violent Death (1:29)

Shirakabe no Imaro was a man from the Oda district of Bitchū province. He was evil by nature and did not believe in the Three Treasures of Buddhism.

One day a monk came to him, begging for food. Imaro offered him nothing, but on the contrary abused him, broke his begging bowl, and drove him away. Later, Imaro went on a trip to another province. On the way, he ran into wind and rain. He sought shelter in a storehouse and was killed when it was blown over.

Truly we know that retribution is close at hand in the present life. Why, then, are we not more careful? As the Nirvana Sutra says: "All evil deeds are caused by wicked minds."[53] This is what it means. The *Daijōbu-ron* says: "If you offer alms with a heart of compassion, your merit will be as great as the Earth. But if you do so for your own sake, your return in all cases will be as tiny as a mustard seed. To aid one person in trouble or danger is better than all the other kinds of offerings!"[54]

On Taking Goods from Others Unjustly and Causing Evil, Gaining a Penalty, and Showing a Miraculous Event (1:30)

Kashiwade no omi Hirokuni was an assistant governor of the Miyako district of Buzen province. In the reign of the emperor at the Fujiwara Palace,[55] in the second year of the Kyōun era, the year *kinoto-mi* [705], on the fifteenth day of the Ninth Month, the day *kanoe-saru*, he suddenly died. Three days passed, and on the fourth day, the Day of the Boar, around four in the afternoon, he came back to life and told the following tale:

"There were two messengers, one with the hairstyle of an adult, and the other with that of a child. They accompanied me, and we went about two stages.[56] There was a big river along the way, with a bridge that was painted in gold. When we crossed the bridge, we found ourselves in a very wonderful land. I asked the messengers, 'What land is this?'

"'This is the southern land,' they said.

"When we reached the capital, we found that there were eight officers carrying arms and following us. Before us was a golden palace, and when we went in the gate, we saw the king sitting on a golden throne. He said to me, 'I have summoned you because of a complaint brought by your wife.' Then he called in a woman. When I looked, it was my wife, who had died long ago. Iron nails pierced her from top to bottom and ran

---

53. Nirvana Sutra, vol. 35. See *Taishō* 12:573c.
54. The *Daijōbu-ron* is one of the texts in the compilation *Shokyō yōshū*. See *Taishō* 59:53c.
55. Emperor Monmu (r. 697–707).
56. One *umaya* (stage) was about twelve miles.

from her forehead to the nape of her neck, while her four limbs were wrapped with an iron chain. Eight men carried her in.

"The king asked me, 'Do you know this woman?' I replied, 'Indeed— she is my wife.' Then he asked, 'Do you know what offense you are accused of?' I replied, 'No, I do not.' Then he asked the woman the same question. She answered, 'I do indeed! He drove me out of the house, and therefore I hate him, loathe him, and still bear him a grudge.' The king then said, 'You are guilty of no real crime. You may go home. But take care that you do not speak rashly of the affairs of the land of the dead! If you want to see your father, go to the south.'

"When I went in the direction I had been told, I found my father. He stood, embracing an extremely hot copper pillar. His body was pierced by thirty-seven iron nails, and he was beaten every day with an iron rod, three hundred strokes in the morning, three hundred strokes at noon, and three hundred strokes in the evening—nine hundred strokes in all! I looked at him in sorrow and said, 'Ah, how could I have known that you suffered such pain?' As father and son talked together, the father said, 'I brought on these sufferings. I don't know if you know or not. In order to support my wife and family, I killed many living creatures, lent eight *ryō* of cloth and demanded payment of ten *ryō* in return, or lent a little measure of rice and demanded a big measure in repayment. Or I took by force the goods of others or committed adultery with their wives. I did not take proper care of my father and mother or show respect for my elders, and, even when they were not slaves, abused them as though they were. Because of these offenses, I have thirty-nine iron nails driven into my body, little though it is, and daily receive nine hundred beatings with an iron whip. How painful, how unbearable! When will I escape from these penalties? When will my body ever find rest? Please, as quickly as you can, for my sake make Buddhist images and copy sutras to pay for the burden of my offenses. Never forget this! When I was starving, on the seventh day of the Seventh Month, I turned into a large snake, went to your house, and was about to enter the kitchen, but you used a stick to drive me away. Again, on the fifth day of the Fifth Month, I turned into a red dog and went to your house. But you called a big dog to chase me away, and I came back hungry and exhausted. When, on the first day of the New Year, I turned into a cat and went to your house, I was able to eat my fill of the offerings of rice and meat and other things and was thus able to make up for three years' lack of food. It was because I and my younger brothers got all mixed up and lost our proper relationship that all this happened. Therefore, I became a dog, eating foul things and fouling myself as well. And I suppose I will end up a red dog. But if you make an offering of one quart of rice, you will gain a reward of thirty days of food; and if you make an offering of one set of clothes, you will gain a reward of one year of clothing. Those who have sutras recited will live in the golden palace of the east and afterward will, in accordance with their wishes, be reborn in Heaven; and those who make images of Buddhas and bodhisattvas will be reborn in the Land of Eternal Life in the western direction; those who free living creatures will be reborn in the Land of Everlasting Life in the northern direction; and those who fast for a day will gain the reward of ten years of food.'

"Having heard all this talk of retribution for good or evil, I became frightened and decided to go. When I got to the bridge, the guards watching the gate stopped me, saying, 'You can't go out the gate after having once been inside!' I wandered around there for a while, when a child appeared. The gatekeepers, seeing him, knelt in greeting. The child called to me, led me to a side gate, opened the door there, and, pointing, said, 'Hurry out!' I asked him, 'Whose child are you?' He answered, 'If you want to know who I am, I'm the Kannon Sutra that you first copied when you were little.'[57] Then he went back inside the gate, and when I looked around, I had come back to life."

As Kashiwade Hirokuni had visited the land of the dead and observed the penalties meted out for good or evil behavior, the results are recorded here for general circulation. The causes and conditions that

---

57. The Kannon Sutra, which is chapter 25 of the Chinese version of the Lotus Sutra, describes the salvational power of Bodhisattva Kannon, or Kanzeon. It is often treated as a separate sutra.

bring about retribution for sins are just as they are generally expounded in the Mahayana sutras. Who could fail to believe them? Therefore, the sutra says: "The sweet dew of the present life is the iron ball of the future life." This is what it means.

Hirokuni, for the sake of his father, fashioned Buddhist images, copied sutras, and paid honor to the Three Treasures of Buddhism, thereby repaying his debt to his father and atoning for the offenses he had committed. Therefore, he turned from aberrant ways and followed what is right.

✳

ON EARNESTLY BELIEVING IN KANNON,
PRAYING FOR HIS SHARE OF GOOD FORTUNE,
AND IMMEDIATELY RECEIVING GREAT
GOOD FORTUNE (1:31)

In the reign of Retired Emperor Shōhō-ōjin-shōmu, residing at the Nara Palace,[58] Miteshiro no Azumahito went to Mount Yoshino to practice the Buddhist doctrine and pray for good fortune. Three years passed, during which he praised Kannon's name, reciting, "Hail to Kannon. Please favor me with ten thousand strings of copper coins, ten thousand bushels of white rice, and lots of pretty girls!"

At that time Awata no asomi of the Junior Third Rank had a daughter who was unmarried and a virgin. She suddenly fell ill at her home in Hirose. Her suffering was so great that there appeared to be no possibility of a cure. Her father sent messengers in all directions, seeking meditation masters and lay believers. Azumahito was among those called and asked to heal her by chanting spells. Through the power of his spells, she was cured of her illness. She fell in love with Azumahito and, in the end, gave herself to him. Her family seized him and shut him up in a room. This was more than the daughter could bear, and she cried out pleadingly

58. That is, in the reign of his daughter and successor, Empress Kōken (r. 749–758).

and would not leave his side. On consulting together, the relatives decided to recognize the marriage, freed Azumahito, and established him and his wife in a house and put him in charge of her wealth. When this was reported to the throne, he was given the Fifth Rank.

After some years had gone by, she found that she was dying. She called her older sister and said, "I am going to die, but I have one wish. I wonder if you will heed it?" Her sister replied, "I will comply." She said, "I have long shared the love of Azumahito, a debt to be long remembered. I would like to have your daughter as a wife for him, so that she may carry on the household." Faithful to her wish, her older sister gave her daughter to Azumahito to be in charge of the family fortune.

Azumahito received a rich reward in his present life. This was due to the power of his devotional practice and the generosity of Kannon. How can you not believe this?

On Having Faith in the Three Treasures, Revering Monks, Having Sutras Recited, and Gaining an Immediate Reward (1:32)

In the fourth year of the Jinki era, the year *hinoto-u* [727], in the Ninth Month, Emperor Shōmu went hunting with his officers in the mountains in Yamamura in the Sou upper district. A deer ran into a farmer's house in the village of Hosomi, and the people in the house, unaware of where it had come from, killed it and ate it. Later, when the emperor received word of this, he sent officers to arrest the people involved. There were more than ten men and women implicated in the affair, and they shook with fear, having no one to depend on. Their only thought was that nothing but the divine power of the Three Treasures could save them from their sorry plight.

They had heard that the Sixteen-Foot Buddha of Daian-ji would respond to peoples' prayers. They sent a man to the temple with a request that sutras be recited. They also sent a request, saying, "When we are taken to the court, please open the southern gate of the temple so that we may pay homage to the Buddha. Also, we ask that you ring the temple bell incessantly, so that its sound will follow us when we are in court."

The monks, heeding their request, recited sutras and opened the gate as they had asked. Meanwhile, the people had been escorted to the court and confined in a guardroom. It happened, however, that an imperial prince was born, and, accordingly, the emperor granted a general amnesty and did not punish them. On the contrary, he bestowed alms on the people, and their joy knew no bounds.

Truly we know that this was due to the mercy of the Sixteen-Foot Buddha and the merit of reciting sutras.

On a Wife Who Had a Buddhist Picture Painted for Her Deceased Husband That, as an Immediate Reward, Miraculously Survived the Flames (1:33)

In Hata Temple in the Ishikawa district of Kawachi province, there is a painted image of Amida. The villagers say that a virtuous wife once lived in the neighborhood of the temple, though her name is not known. On the day her husband was dying, she vowed to have a Buddhist image created. But because of her poverty, many years went by with the vow unfulfilled.

Each autumn she gleaned the fields, and then she asked a painter to help her make an offering to the dead, weeping tears of sorrow. The painter, moved to join in her devotion, completed a beautiful painting. A ceremonial feast was held, after which the painting was consecrated in the golden hall of the temple, where it was constantly treated with honor.

Later, a thief set fire to the temple and the hall was completely burned, but this painting of a Buddha alone survived undamaged. Was this not an act of mercy designed to comfort the widow and the others?

In appraisal we say: What a good wife she was, holding a memorial ritual for her husband! She held it at the end of autumn. Truly we know the measure of her devotion. Even burning flames could not destroy her sacred image. The help of Heaven above is beyond our comprehension!

ON GETTING BACK SILK ROBES THAT HAD BEEN STOLEN THROUGH A PETITION TO BODHISATTVA MYŌKEN (1:34)

In front of the temple called Shinobu-dera in the Ate district of Kii province, there was once a house. When ten silk robes were stolen from the owners of the house, they prayed earnestly for their recovery to Bodhisattva Myōken at the temple. However, the robes were sold to a merchant in the town of Kii.

Before seven days had passed, a violent wind suddenly arose. The robes wrapped themselves around the body of a deer, which carried them south and left them in the garden of the owners, who exclaimed, "A gift from Heaven!" When the man who had bought them learned that they had been stolen, he did not ask for them back, but let the matter rest. This was a miraculous event!

*

ON A NUN WHO, IN GRATITUDE FOR THE FOUR KINDS OF BLESSINGS, GAINED THE POWER TO SHOW AN EXTRAORDINARY SIGN (1:35)

In the village of Yuge in the Wakae district of Kawachi province, there lived a well-disciplined novice nun. Her name is unknown, but she lived in a mountain temple at Heguri. She organized an association of devotees and painted a Buddha image with a picture of the six realms of existence in order to give thanks for the four kinds of blessings.[59] After the dedication ceremony, it was enshrined in the temple, where it helped to show to all the various circumstances of birth. But the Buddha image was stolen, and though she wept and searched for it, she could not find it.

Meanwhile, leading the members of her association, she thought to free living creatures,[60] and they traveled as far as the marketplace of the city of Naniwa. There they saw a basket hanging in a tree, and they heard the voices of various living creatures crying in the basket. They waited for the owner to return, because they thought there must be creatures in the basket and wanted to set them free.

After a while, the owner returned. The nun and her group said, "We heard the sound of living creatures in your basket. We would like to buy them—that's why we were waiting for you." The owner said, "No— there are no living creatures!" But the nun and the others begged him and would not stop. The merchants in the marketplace said, "You should open the basket!" The owner, growing fearful, abandoned the basket and ran away. When they opened the basket, they found that it contained the Buddha image.

They were overjoyed. Their tears streaming down, they exclaimed in delight, "We lost the image and have spent days and nights longing for it. Now, by chance, we have found it again. Ah—what happiness is ours!" When the people of the marketplace heard this, they gathered around in congratulation.

The nun and the others of her group set living creatures free and thus attained good fortune. The image was restored to the temple, where clergy and lay members alike paid it reverence. This was indeed a miraculous event.

59. The six paths are the realms of Hell, hungry spirits, animals, *asuras* (demons), human beings, and heavenly beings. The four kinds of blessings are those bestowed by parents, lords, all sentient beings, and the Three Treasures of Buddhism.
60. The practice of buying captured fish, birds, or other animals and setting them free was highly recommended in Buddhism.

Volume

II

PREFACE

If we survey the history of the early period, we see that in the time before
Emperor Senka, people followed non-Buddhist methods in inquiring
about the gods. But from the reign of Emperor Kinmei on, people honored the Three Treasures of Buddhism and believed in the correct doctrine. To be sure, there were some ministers to the throne who burned
temples and cast away Buddhist images.[1] But there were other ministers
to the throne who built temples and worked to spread the Buddhist
teachings. Among the latter was Retired Emperor Shōhō-ōjin-shōmu,
who built a colossal statue of the Buddha and established the long-last-
ing propagation of the Law. He shaved his head, put on the surplice, received the precepts, and dedicated himself to the good, governing the
people according to what is right. His mercy extended to animals and
plants, and his virtue excelled that of all past ages. He attained the One,
governing accordingly; he communicated with the Three,[2] bringing rest
to the spirits. Through his fortune and virtue, even insects flying in the
sky gathered sacred grass to thatch the temple roofs, while ants crawling
over the Earth brought grains of gold to build a pagoda. Banners of the
Law were raised on high, fluttering in eight directions. The bark of enlightenment floated lightly on the water, its sails reaching to the ninth

1. This refers to those at court who opposed the introduction of Buddhism to Japan.
2. The One is enlightenment; the Three are Heaven, Earth, and humankind.

level of the sky. Flowers of good fortune opened in rivalry, filling cities and towns. Good and evil appeared as immediate karmic retribution, signaling fortune or misfortune. Therefore, he was called Retired Emperor Shōhō-ōjin-shōmu, which means "Superb-treasure-corresponding-sacred-might." But the records of good and evil and of their results are very many for the reign of this emperor, which are due to his holy virtue. They are, in fact, so numerous that to record them . . .[3] I have put down here only those that I have heard of. Were we to examine the record thoroughly, the mind would . . .

. . . provide us with a suit of iron, while those who love the good are clothed in pearl-studded robes of gold. For example, although you push them away, they come all the closer; although you try to drag them toward you, they move farther off. Grasp, and they retreat; cease, and they crowd around. Some there are who eat the seeds of millet or cast away treasures like Zhu Ming; who wash their ears like Xu You and lead their oxen like Chao Fu.[4] Are they any different? Some there are who, when they die, return, like cartwheels revolving, to the threefold world; who, once born, pass through the six realms like a floating water plant.[5] Then, having died, they are born again, and they suffer all the ten thousand pains of life. Weighed down, as with a yoke, by evil causes, they meet with suffering; helped on by the power of good deeds, they are led into favorable circumstances. With nurture and love, they lie down at the foot of tigers; due to loving kindness, they soar on high with the birds. Meng Chang's seven good things, Duke Gong of Lu's three transformations—these are all within their power.[6]

3. The ellipses represent words that were lost or are unintelligible in the text.
4. Zhu Ming was famous for giving away his wealth to his younger brothers; Xu You, a sage of antiquity, for washing out his ears to cleanse them from the stain when he was offered the rulership of the empire; and Chao Fu, for leading his oxen.
5. The threefold world is the world of desire, the world of form, and the formless world. The six realms are those of Hell, hungry spirits, animals, *asuras* (demons), human beings, and heavenly beings
6. Meng Chang's seven good things have not been indentified. Duke Gong of Lu's three transformations are conditions brought about by his good governance: insects do not profane the Earth, his influence reaches to the birds and beasts, and perverse children develop kindly hearts.

But I, Kyōkai, was not blessed with a keen nature, and my mouth is not skilled in speaking. My spirit is dull, like a blade made of lead; I string out my lines of characters, but alas, they do not flower. I'm one with the man who notched the boat;[7] I write, yet cannot get my phrases into order. But such is my desire to do good that I cannot cease from wasting good paper. Reflecting on my errors, I can only feel ashamed, my face red, my ears burning. Those of you who peruse the results, please forget how they may offend Heaven and insult the reader, and bear with me. Make a master of your mind, never the mind your master.

May the virtue in my work on the right fly on the wings of good fortune, ascending to the heights, and on the left burn with the torch of wisdom, climbing the peak of the Buddha nature, dispensing alms to all living beings, until we all attain the Buddha Way.[8]

7. When someone accidentally dropped a sword over the side of a moving boat, a man put a notch in the gunwale of the boat where it fell so it could be found.
8. The last paragraph is in the form of a Buddhist prayer.

✳

On Depending on One's Exalted Virtue, Committing the Offense of Hitting a Humble Novice, and Receiving the Immediate Penalty of a Violent Death (2:1)

Retired Emperor Shōbō-ōjin-shōmu [Shōmu, r. 724–749], who resided at the Nara Palace and reigned over the Eight Great Islands, in the first year of the Tenpyō era, the year *tsuchinoto-mi* [729], in the spring, on the eighth day of the Second Month, held a great Dharma meeting at Gangō-ji in the eastern sector of the capital and paid honor to the Three Treasures of Buddhism. Prince Nagaya,[1] Chancellor of the Senior Second Rank, was directed by edict to take charge of serving food to the monks. At that time, there was a novice who brazenly went to the place where the food was being served and held up his bowl for some. The prince, observing this, to punish him struck the novice on the head with his ivory writing tablet, hard enough to draw blood. The novice, wiping the blood from his head and wailing pitifully, immediately disappeared. No one knew where he had gone, but both the clergy and the lay members of the gathering whispered in secret, "An ill omen—not good!"

Two days later, a man, acting out of envy, went to the emperor with false accusations, saying, "Prince Nagaya is plotting to overthrow the state and usurp the throne!" The emperor, angered, called up the troops and sent them against the prince.

The prince thought to himself, "I am falsely charged and about to be taken into custody. That means I will surely be put to death. Rather than being killed by another, better to kill myself!" After administering poison to his children and grandchildren and seeing them strangled, he

---

1. Prince Nagaya (684–729) was a grandson of Emperor Tenmu and a distinguished literary figure.

took poison himself. The emperor ordered their bodies to be thrown out of the capital, burned to ashes, and cast into the river that flows to the sea. Only the prince's bones were exiled to Toba province, where many people were sent to die. The people, fearful, petitioned the officials, saying, "All of us in this province will die because of the prince's angry spirit!" Hearing this, the emperor, so that the bones might be nearer the capital, moved them to an island off the coast of Hajikami in the Ama district of Kii province.

Ah, how pitiful! However widely known in the capital and beyond for his wealth and good fortune, when misfortune fell on him, he had nowhere to turn, but perished in a day. Truly we learn that taking pride in his high virtue, he struck a novice in punishment, and because of this, defenders of the Law frowned on him and the good deities hated him. We should respect those who wear the surplice, humble though they may seem, for there are sages hidden among them. The Kyōman-gyō says: "Even among the high ranking, those who accidentally stepped on Śākyamuni's head with their boots on were guilty of offense."[2] Needless to say, then, that those who strike one who wears the surplice are guilty of error!

ON OBSERVING LICENTIOUS BIRDS, RENOUNCING THE WORLD, AND PRACTICING GOOD (2:2)

Meditation Master Shingon was originally Chinu no agatanushi Yamatomaro, governor of the Izumi district of Izumi province in the reign of Emperor Shōmu. By the gate of his house, there stood a big tree in which crows roosted, gave birth to their young, and raised them. Once, the male bird flew off to search for food, leaving his mate to shelter the chicks. While he was away looking for food, other crows constantly came around, seeking companionship. The wife took up with one of them, soaring high

---

2. The source of this quotation has not been identified.

into the sky with her new friend, heading north, and flying off without a thought for her chicks. In time, the male bird returned, bringing food, but found that his mate had vanished. Taking pity on his chicks, he looked after them tenderly, not going off to look for food, and so several days passed.

The governor, noticing this, had a man climb the tree and look into the nest. He found the crow still harboring the chicks, but the father and all the chicks were dead. The governor, seeing this, was moved to great pity. With the example of the female crow's infidelity before him, he renounced the world, left his wife and family, gave up his official position, and became a follower of the Most Venerable Gyōgi,[3] practicing good and seeking the Way. His religious name was Shingon. He always declared, "If I die together with the Most Venerable, I am sure to be reborn in the Western Paradise!"

The wife of Shingon was also of the Chinu no agatanushi family. After her husband left her, she remained faithful to him, showing no bitterness but remaining warm and loving. When her son contracted a disease and was on the point of death, he said to her, "If I drink my mother's milk, it will prolong my life!" She accordingly gave her breast to him to suckle. As he suckled it, he lamented, saying, "Alas, I must abandon the sweet milk of my mother to die!" When he died, she too, sorrowing for her son, renounced the world as her husband had done, devoting herself to learning and practicing the good Way.

Meditation Master Shingon, however, did not have good fortune but died before the Most Venerable Gyōgi. Lamenting, the master composed the following poem:

> Are you a crow,
> a big liar,
> promising we'd die together
> but going on ahead?

---

3. Gyōgi (Gyōki, 670–749) was a celebrated Buddhist prelate of the Nara period (710–784). He assisted Emperor Shōmu in completing the great Buddha image of Tōdai-ji.

When we make a fire, we must first have fatty pine wood. When it rains, the slate has been moistened beforehand.[4] Seeing the licentious behavior of the crows, the governor's heart was moved. To show us the right path, the pain of acting otherwise, and then point the Way: Is this not how it is done? The varied creatures in the world of desire have their base ways.[5] Those who hate them turn away from it; those who are foolish follow along.

In appraisal we say: How right it was of the governor, observing the wickedness of the crows, to hate the ways of the world, to turn from the vain flowers of transience and seek for eternal purity. He worked to do good, praying for the righteous commands, his heart yearning for comfort, hoping for release. Such are those who seek a land far different from the one we know.

On the Evil Death Visited Immediately on an Evil and Perverse Son Who, Out of Love for His Wife, Plotted to Kill His Mother (2:3)

Kishi no Homaro was from the village of Kamo in the Tama district of Musashi province. Homaro's mother was Kusakabe no Matoji. In the reign of Emperor Shōmu, Homaro was appointed by Ōtomo (exact name unknown)[6] to serve for three years as a frontier guard in Tsukushi.[7] His mother accompanied him to see to his needs, while his wife remained in Musashi to look after the house.

---

4. The meaning of this sentence is uncertain.
5. The world of desire is the six realms into which unenlightened beings are born and reborn: Hell, hungry ghosts, animals, *asuras* (demons), human beings, and heavenly beings.
6. Throughout the stories, the text in parentheses is Kyōkai's explanations, comments, or interpretations.
7. In Kyushu, Tsukushi was where forces were stationed to guard against possible attacks from China or Korea.

At that time Homaro, separated from his wife, was filled with unbearable longing for her, and hit on a perverse scheme, thinking, "If I murder my mother, I will be obliged to tend to her funeral and will be excused from duty and can go home. Then I can be with my wife!"

His mother by nature thought only of doing good deeds, and so the son said to her, "In the hills east of here, there is to be a meeting devoted to seven days of lectures on the Lotus Sutra. Why don't you go listen to them?" Deceived by these words, the mother set her mind on listening to the sutra. Having bathed in hot water and purified herself, she set off for the mountains in company with her son.

The son, glaring at his mother with ox-like eyes, said to her, "Kneel down on the ground!" Gazing at her son's face, the mother said, "Why do you speak to me like that? Has some demon taken possession of you?" But the son unsheathed a long sword and prepared to cut off his mother's head.

Kneeling before her son, the mother said, "We plant trees in hopes of gathering the fruit and resting in the shade they give. And we raise children in hopes of gaining their help and in time being taken care of by them. But now the tree I have counted on lets the rain leak through! Why has my child turned from his usual thoughts and now wants to do me harm?"

The son, however, paid no heed to her. Then the mother, giving up all hope, took off the clothes she was wearing and put them in three piles. Kneeling before her son, she made this dying request: "Wrap these up as a memento of me. One pile of clothes goes to you, my eldest son. One pile please give to my second son, and one pile to my youngest son."

But when the perverse son stepped forward, preparing to cut off his mother's head, the ground opened and he fell into it. The mother leaped up, ran forward, and seized hold of her son's hair as he fell. Looking up at the heavens, she cried out this plea: "My son is a victim of possession. He does not really mean to do this! Please pardon his offense!" But though she clung to the hair, struggling to save him, in the end he sank into the ground.

The loving mother returned home with the son's hair. Holding a Buddhist service in his memory, she put the hair in a box and placed it before an image of the Buddha, reverently requesting monks to recite scriptures before it.

Because the mother felt profound compassion, she was moved to take pity on her evil and perverse son and to do good on his behalf. Truly one should understand that sins of unfilial conduct meet with immediate requital, and that evil and perverse offenses never go unpunished.

On a Contest Between Two Women of Extraordinary Strength (2:4)

In the reign of Emperor Shōmu, there was a woman of extraordinary strength at Ogawa Market in the Katakata district of Mino province. She was a big woman named Mino Kitsune (the fourth generation of the one whose mother was long ago named Kitsune of Mino province). Her strength equaled that of a hundred men. She lived in the marketplace of Ogawa and took great pride in her strength, making a living by browbeating the merchants who came and went there and seizing their goods.

At that time, there was another woman of great strength in the village of Katawa in the Ayuchi district of Owari province. She was small in size (a granddaughter of the Venerable Dōjō, who once lived at Gangō-ji).

Hearing about how Mino Kitsune forced the people of Ogawa to give up their goods, she thought that she would challenge her. She loaded up fifty *koku* of clams on a boat and anchored it near the market. In addition, she brought along on the boat twenty pliant whips made of vervain fiber.

Kitsune came to the boat, seized all the clams, and began to sell them. "Where did you come from?" she asked the owner of the clams.

The owner did not answer. She asked once more, but still no answer. When she continued and was on her fourth inquiry, the woman replied, "I don't know where I came from."

Kitsune, finding this insulting, got up to hit her. The other woman thereupon seized her with both hands and gave her a lash with one of her whips. The whip cut into the flesh. Then she gave her a lash with another whip, which also cut into the flesh. Before long, she had used ten whips, all of which cut into the flesh.

"That's enough!" said Kitsune. "I was wrong; I've learned my lesson." Thus she admitted that the power of the other woman was greater than her own. The owner of the clams said, "From now on, you can't go on living in this market. If you try it, I'll end up beating you to death!" Kitsune gave in, no longer living in the market and no longer seizing people's goods. All the people in the market delighted in the restoration of safety.

There is always someone who is strong enough to maintain order and keep the peace. Truly we know that it is because of good causes in the life of their ancestors that they have such strength.

On Worshipping Chinese Gods, Killing Oxen as a Sacrifice, but Also Doing Good by Setting Free Living Creatures, He Received Both Good and Evil Rewards (2:5)

Once in the province of Settsu, the district of Himugashinari, in the village of Nadekubo, there lived a master of a rich household. His name is not known, but the time was the reign of Emperor Shōmu. This rich man worshipped Chinese gods and used to pray to them and make offerings. Each year he would slaughter an ox as a sacrifice.[8]

At the end of seven years, having killed seven oxen, he was suddenly seized with a severe illness that lasted for seven years. The doctors tried

---

8. In 791, the government issued an order prohibiting the use of oxen as a sacrifice in the worship of Chinese gods, so the cult was apparently fairly widespread. Animal sacrifice was almost certainly foreign to Japan and was, of course, particularly abhorrent to Buddhists.

various remedies, but to no effect. The rich man summoned diviners and magicians to perform charms and exorcise the evil, but his illness only grew worse. Thinking that his malady had perhaps come about because he had taken life, the man—from the time he first took to his bed—observed without fail the six fast days of each month and set free all his living creatures. When he learned that anyone else was taking the lives of living beings, he immediately ransomed them at whatever price was asked, and he sent men here and there to buy all living creatures in captivity and free them. At the end of seven years, he knew that his time had come and he summoned his wife and children and said to them, "After I die, set my body aside for nineteen days before you cremate it."

Accordingly, his wife and children laid his body away and waited for the end of the nineteen days. But when only nine days had passed, the man returned to life and told them this story:

"There appeared to me seven beings who had the heads of oxen and the bodies of men. They tied ropes to my hair and dragged me along with them. As we went, I saw a palace with tall towers. 'Whose palace is that?' I asked, but the creatures only looked at me with eyes full of hatred and pushed me on, saying, 'Hurry up!'

"When we had entered the gates of the palace, they announced, 'We have summoned him!' and I realized that this was the palace of Yama, the king of Hell. The king asked the demons, 'Is this your enemy, the man who killed you?' 'This is he!' they answered and brought out a carving board and small knives. 'Give your judgment quickly, we pray, for we wish to carve him up and eat him the way he did us!' they said.

"But just then, a host of over a thousand or ten thousand persons appeared and untied the ropes that bound me, saying, 'This man is without blame! He did injury only because of the gods he worshipped.' Then they placed me in the middle, and every day the seven demons and the multitude of men argued and contested back and forth like fire against water. King Yama tried to arrive at a decision but could not determine which side was in the right. The demons pressed their case with fury, saying, 'It is perfectly clear! This man made himself our master, cut off our four legs, and prayed in the hall of worship for his own profit. He chopped us to bits and ate us up. We ask only that now we be allowed to butcher and eat him in the same way!' But then the great multitude would plead with the king, saying, 'We know perfectly well that this man is without blame. The blame rests with the gods and spirits he worshipped!'

"The king pondered and decided that the evidence rested with the majority, and on the evening of the eighth day he issued his royal command: 'Tomorrow come again before me!' On the ninth day, in obedience to his order, we all again came together and King Yama announced his decision: 'Justice has been made clear. We shall abide by the evidence of the majority.'

"When the seven oxen heard this, they began to lick their lips and drool, making motions of chopping something and devouring it. With wrathful looks, they raised their knives and cried, 'Will you give us no recompense for our wrong? We will not forget it, and someday we will have our revenge!'

"Then the great host of people surrounded and protected me and led me out of the palace. They placed me in a carriage and lifted it on their shoulders, raising banners and bearing me onward; they saw me off with shouts of praise and knelt in reverent farewell. All the members of this multitude were alike in appearance, and I said to them, 'Honored sirs, who are you?' They answered, 'We are the living creatures that you ransomed and set free. We have not forgotten your goodness, and now we have come to repay you.'"

After the rich man had returned from the halls of King Yama, he made a vow that he would no longer in any way serve the strange gods and spirits but would put all his faith in the Three Treasures of Buddhism. He tied a holy pennant to his rooftop and converted his house into a temple, placing an image of the Buddha within, practicing the Law, and setting free living creatures. From this time on, his house was known as the Nade Hall. His illness never returned, and he lived to be full of years, dying at the age of over ninety.

The Binaya-kyō says: "Because Karudai was once a priest and sacrificed a sheep, he was killed, even though he had attained arhatship, the revenge being carried out by a Brahmin wife."[9] And the Saishōō-kyō gives the following passage: "Rusui Elder set free ten thousand fish, which were reborn in Heaven and repaid his kindness by presenting him with forty thousand gems."[10] This is what these sutras mean.

ON COPYING THE LOTUS SUTRA WITH UTMOST DEVOTION AND WITNESSING AN EXTRAORDINARY EVENT (2:6)

In the reign of Emperor Shōmu, there was a man in the Sagara district of Yamashiro province who made a vow. His family and personal names are not known. He copied the Lotus Sutra in order to repay the four kinds of blessings[11] and sent messengers to the four quarters in search of white sandalwood and black sandalwood to make a box for the scrolls of the scripture. Eventually, they found some in the capital of Nara, which he purchased for the price of one hundred *kan*.[12] Then he asked a skilled craftsman to measure the new scrolls and fashion a container. But when it was done, he found that the scrolls were too long, the box was too short, and they would not fit together.

He was bitterly disappointed, for he did not see how he could find such materials again. He made a vow, held a service as directed by the scriptures, invited monks to confess offenses for three times seven days, and, wailing, pleaded, "Please let me find such wood again!" After fourteen days had passed, he tried fitting the scrolls into place. The box

---

9. Vinaya-kyō 9, quoted in the *Shokyō yōshū* (*Essential Passages from Various Sutras*) 14. See *Taishō shinshū daizōkyō* 59:53c.

10. Konkōmyō saishōō-kyō 1. See *Taishō* 16:352b–353c.

11. According to one source, the four blessings are indebtedness to mother, father, the Buddha, and monks; another gives indebtedness to parents, all fellow beings, the king, and the Three Treasures of Buddhism.

12. One *kan* is a monetary unit consisting of one thousand *mon* or coins.

seemed to have grown a little bigger, but the scrolls still would not fit in it.

He redoubled his efforts to discipline himself and repent his misdeeds, and at the conclusion of the twenty-one days, he tried again. This time, they fit. Wondering greatly at this, he exclaimed, "Have the scrolls gotten shorter, or has the box gotten bigger?" But when he compared the new scrolls with the old ones, he found that they were no different in length.

Truly we know that this was due to the miraculous power of the Mahayana sutra and a test of the profound faith of the one who made the vow. There can be no doubt about it.

On a Wise Man Who, Out of Envy, Abused an Incarnated Sage and, as an Immediate Penalty, Visited the Palace of King Yama and Underwent Suffering in Hell (2:7)

Shaku Chikō was a monk of Sugita Temple in the Asukabe district of Kawachi province, his native land. His secular name was Sugita no muraji, later changed to Kami no suguri. (His mother was of the Asukabe-no-miyatsuko family.) He was innately intelligent and ranked first in knowledge. He wrote commentaries on the Urabon-kyō, Daihannya-kyō,[13] Hannya Shin-gyō [Heart Sutra], and other works, and lectured on Buddhist teachings to many students.

There was at this time a monk named Gyōgi. His secular name was Koshi no Fubito, and he came from the Kubiki district of Echigo province. His mother was of the Hachida no kusushi of the Ōtori district of Izumi province. He gave up lay life, freed himself from desire, and spread the Law, converting the deluded masses. He was highly intelligent and seemed to be guided by inborn knowledge. Although

13. The Urabon-kyō and Daihannya-kyō are no longer extant.

outwardly he appeared as a monk, on the inside were the workings of a bodhisattva.

Emperor Shōmu was so impressed with his keen virtue that he had great respect for and confidence in Gyōgi, and all the people of the time honored him by calling him a bodhisattva.

In the sixteenth year of the Tenpyō era, the year *kinoe-saru* [744], in the winter, the Eleventh Month, Gyōgi was made great chief executive.[14]

Dharma Master Chikō, envious at heart, spoke ill of him, saying, "I am the wise one; Gyōgi is a mere novice! Why does the emperor ignore my wisdom and put faith only in this novice?" At that time, he retired to Sugita-dera, where he resided, and immediately developed a digestive ailment. After a month, he felt that his end was near and, calling together his disciples, he warned them, "If I die, do not be in a hurry to cremate my body. Wait for a period of nine or ten days. If a student comes asking about me, say that I am away on business. Tell him to wait and serve him meals, but do not let him know that I have departed!"

His disciples did as instructed and closed the door to his death chamber, letting no one know what had happened. Grieving in secret, they guarded the door day and night, waiting for the appointed day to arrive. If students came asking after him, they replied as they had been told, asked them to wait, and provided them with meals.

Meanwhile, two messengers from King Yama came to Master Chikō to escort him, and they set out for the west. Along the way, they saw a golden palace. "Whose palace is that?" asked Chikō. "You are a famous wise man of the country of Ashihara," they said.[15] "How is it that you do not know? You should know that that is where Bodhisattva Gyōgi will reside when he is born here!"

On both sides of the gate were two divine men, their bodies clad in armor, and on their foreheads they wore red bands. The messengers knelt and said to them, "We have brought him." They said to Chikō, "Are you the Venerable Chikō from the land of Mizuho in Toyoashihara?"

---

14. He was named Daisōjō, the highest clerical rank. Other sources give the date as 745.
15. Ashihara and Mizuho in Toyoashihara were old names for Japan.

Chikō replied, "Yes, I am." Then they pointed north and said, "Go along this road!" Accompanied by the messengers, he went along the road. Although he could see no light of a fire, there was intense heat beating down on his body and face. But in spite of the great heat that plagued him, he felt a desire in his heart to go forward. "Where does this heat come from?" he asked. "This is the great heat of Hell that is intended to burn you up!" was the reply.

As they went forward, they came to an extremely hot pillar of iron. "Embrace it!" commanded the messengers. When Chikō embraced the pillar, all his flesh melted away, and he was left with nothing but bare bones. After three days, the messengers swept the pillar with a worn broom, saying, "Let him live, let him live!" With this, his body was restored to its original form.

Again they started northward, and they came to a copper pillar that was much hotter than the one before. But once again, he seemed drawn to it by evil and felt a desire to embrace it. "Embrace it!" commanded the messengers, and he did so, and all his flesh was melted away. After three days, when the messengers brushed the pillar and said, "Let him live, let him live!" his body was restored as before.

Once again, they started northward. The scorching heat was so intense that birds fell out of the sky. As he faced the burning heat, he asked, "What place is this?" "This is the Avichi Hell, which is here to burn you up!" was the reply.[16] And as he went forward, he was seized and dragged into the flames and burned up. Only when he heard temple bells ringing did he feel any cooling, and he found a little rest. After three days, when he heard the messengers knocking at the gates of Hell and saying, "Let him live, let him live!" he came alive again.

Then they led him back to the gate of the palace, where, as before, they said, "We have arrived." The two men at the gate said, "The reason that you were called here was that you spoke ill of Bodhisattva Gyōgi of the country of Ashihara. You have been summoned in order that you

---

16. The Avichi Hell, or the Hell of Incessant Suffering, is the hottest and most terrible of the eight Buddhist Hells.

may atone for your guilt. When his time in the land of Ashihara is finished, the bodhisattva will be born in this palace. Now we are waiting
for him, for the time has almost come. You must not eat any of the food
cooked in the land of the dead. Go back now as quickly as you can!" He
went back east in the company of the messengers, and when he returned,
he realized that it had been exactly nine days.

When he awoke, he called to his disciples. Hearing his voice, they all
gathered around, weeping for joy. But Chikō was deeply grieved, and he
told them exactly what had taken place in the land of Yama. With a look
of profound concern, he said, "I must confess that I spoke slanderously
of a man of great virtue!"

Bodhisattva Gyōgi, in the meantime, had been building bridges, dig-
ging canals, and constructing wharfs for ships in Naniwa. After Chikō
had recovered a little, he went to Gyōgi's place. When the bodhisattva
saw him, he used his divine power of intellect to discover what Chikō
had in mind. Smiling and showing his affection, he said, "I've wondered
why our meetings are so infrequent." Chikō, for his part, frankly confessed his wrongdoing and regret, saying, "Out of a jealous heart, I have
slandered you, saying such things as, 'I am an old monk of great virtue,
whereas Gyōgi is of poor judgment and does not observe the precepts.
Why, then, does the emperor praise only Gyōgi and cast me aside?' For
these sins of my mouth, I was summoned before King Yama and made to
embrace the iron and copper pillars. After nine days, he said that I had
atoned for my offenses of slander. But I am afraid that other sins of mine
will affect my future life, and so I am making this plea. Please help me to
become free of sin!"

At this, the Most Venerable Gyōgi looked compassionate, but said
nothing. Chikō continued speaking, saying, "I saw the place where you
will be reborn. It is in a palace made of gold!" Gyōgi, hearing this, said,
"How delightful! What an honor!"

Truly we know that the mouth is a gate to invite disaster to harm the
body, and the tongue a sharp ax to chop up the good. Thus the Fushigikō
bosatsu-kyō says: "Because he spoke of the faults of Bodhisattva Kenten,
Bodhisattva Nyūzai was destined for ninety-one kalpas to be constantly

born in the womb of loose women, and having been born there, to be cast aside and eaten by foxes and wolves."[17] This is what the passage means.

From this time on, the Venerable Chikō put his faith in Bodhisattva Gyōgi, realizing clearly that he was a sage. As for Gyōgi, he sensed that his time had run out, and in the twenty-first year of the Tenpyō era, the year *tsuchinoto-ushi* [749], in the spring, on the second day of the Second Month, at around six in the evening, he left his clerical form on Mount Ikoma, and his compassionate spirit moved on to the golden palace.[18] As for the Venerable Chikō, he spread the Dharma, passed on the teachings, converted the ignorant, and taught what was right. In the time of Emperor Shirakabe [Kōnin, r. 770–781], this font of wisdom left his shell in the land of Japan, and his wondrous spirit moved on to a world unknown.

ON SAVING THE LIVES OF A CRAB AND A FROG, SETTING THEM FREE, AND RECEIVING AN IMMEDIATE REWARD (2:8)

Okisome no omi Tahime was the daughter of a nun named Hōni, the presiding officer of the nunnery of Tomi in the capital of Nara. She was utterly devoted to the Way and was careful to preserve her chastity, constantly collecting herbs and every day without fail presenting them to the Most Venerable Gyōgi as an offering.

Once, going into the mountains to collect herbs, she saw a large snake about to swallow a large frog. "Please give me that frog!" she pleaded, but the snake went on swallowing the frog. Once more she pleaded, "I will become your wife, so please give me that frog!" The snake, listening this time, raised up its head, peered into her face, and spat out the frog. She said to the snake, "Come to me seven days from now!"

17. Quoted in the Bonmō-kyō koshakki. See *Taishō* 40:706b.
18. Gyōgi was cremated at Mount Ikoma in present-day Osaka prefecture.

When the appointed day came, she shut up the house, plugging up all
the entrances, and waited inside as securely as possible. The snake came
as expected and pounded on the wall. The next day, the woman, terrified, went to the mountain temple of Ikoma, where her master, the Most
Venerable Gyōgi, resided, and reported what had happened. "You cannot go back on your word," he said. "Just make certain that you are faithful to the precepts!" She affirmed her fidelity to the Three Treasures and
the five precepts, and then went home.[19]

On the way, she met an old man she had never seen before who was
holding a large crab. She said to him, "Who are you, old man? Please
give me that crab you are holding." He replied, "I am from the Uhara
district of Settsu province, and my name is Tsukumono Kanimaro. I am
seventy-eight years old and have no sons to look after me. In Naniwa, I
happened to get this crab. But I have promised it to someone, and so I
cannot give it to you."

The woman took off her robe and offered it to him, but he would not
take it. Then she took off her skirt and offered it, too. The old man took it,
exchanging it for the crab.

She brought the crab to the Most Venerable Gyōgi, requesting that he
set it free. "How noble, how good of you!" he exclaimed in admiration.

On the evening of the eighth day, the snake came again, climbing
onto the roof, tearing a hole in the thatch, and coming in. The woman,
frightened, heard something flapping around in front of her bed. When
she looked the following day, she saw a big crab and a big snake that had
been chopped into bits.

Thus we know that the crab that had been set free repaid the debt it
owed. And we also know that this was due to the power of preserving
the precepts. Although she tried to discover just what had happened by
asking the old man, she could never find out who he was. Surely he was
an incarnation of a saintly being. This was a miraculous event!

19. The Three Treasures are the Buddha; the Dharma, or doctrine; and the Order, or com-
    munity of believers. The five precepts are for laypersons to refrain from taking life,
    stealing, engaging in indecent acts, telling lies, and drinking alcoholic beverages.

On Building a Temple and Then Using Its Goods for Private Purposes, He Was Reborn as a Laboring Ox (2:9)

Ōtomo no Akamaro was the governor of the Tama district of Musashi province. On the nineteenth day of the Twelfth Month in the first year of the Tenpyō shōbō era, the year *tsuchinoto-ushi* [749], he died and was reborn on the seventh day of the Fifth Month, in the summer of the second year, the year *kanoe-toru* [750], as a calf with black spots. It had an inscription on its back that said, "Akamaro selfishly used the goods of the temple he himself founded and died without paying for them. In payment for these goods he has been reborn as an ox."

Both his family and his associates felt extremely sorry about this and, reflecting on it in their hearts, declared, "One should beware of doing wrong! How can this sin be atoned for? It is bound to call forth a penalty hereafter!" Therefore, on the first day of the Sixth Month of that year, they announced what had happened to all the people, so that even those who were without fault might see it, have a change of heart, and do good.

Even if you suffer from want and are pressed by need, though you may be forced to drink molten copper, never touch the temple's goods! There is the old folks' saying, "Sweet dew now will bring an iron ball in the future!" This is what it means.

Truly we know that the law of causality never fails to function. Should we not be fearful? Therefore, the Daijuk-kyō says: "Those who steal the goods of the monks commit a sin greater than the five offenses."[20]

---

20. Quoted in the *Shokyō yōshū*. See *Taishō* 13:no. 397. The five offenses are killing one's father, one's mother, or an arhat; injuring the body of a Buddha; and causing dissension in the Order.

❋

On Constantly Stealing Birds' Eggs, and Boiling and Eating Them, He Suffered an Immediate and Evil Penalty (2:10)

In the village of Shimoanashi in the Izumi district of Izumi province, there lived a young man whose name is unknown. He was inherently evil and did not believe in the law of karmic causation, but constantly looked for birds' eggs to boil and eat.

In the sixth year of the Tenpyō shōbō era, in the spring, the Third Month of the year *kinoe-uma* [754], a strange soldier came to him and announced, "I was sent by a provincial official!" He had a formal document four feet long fastened at his waist. They went off together, and when they came to the village of Yamatae in Hitada district, they made their way into a field several acres in size that was filled with wheat more than two feet tall. When the young man looked, he saw that it was all in flames, with no place to put his feet. He began racing around the field, crying out, "I'm burning, I'm burning!"

At that time, one of the villagers had gone up into the hills to collect firewood. Seeing the young man racing around the field and crying, he came down from the hills and tried to drag him out of the fire, but the young man would not move. He struggled with him until he had dragged him out beyond the hedge that bound the field, where the young man fell over on the ground.

He lay on the ground, moaning but saying nothing. Then, after a while, he recovered his senses and began crying, "Oh—my feet!" The villagers asked him why he said that. He replied, "There was a soldier who summoned me and brought me to this fire and forced me to walk in it. My feet felt as though they were being boiled! Wherever I looked, I was surrounded by hills of fire. There was no way out of the flames, and so I was racing around!" When the villagers heard this, they pulled open the garment the young man was wearing and looked at his legs. All the flesh had been burned away, and only the bones were left. The next day he died.

Truly we know that Hell exists in our present world and that we should believe in the law of karmic retribution. We should not be like crows that take loving care of their own chicks but eat those of others. Without compassion, a person is no better than a crow! The Nirvana Sutra says: "Though men and beasts differ in degree of respectability, they are alike in prizing life and regarding death gravely."[21] And the Zen'aku-inga-kyō [Sutra on the Effects of Good and Evil] says: "He who in his present state cooks the little chicks, in death will fall into the Hell of the River of Ashes!"[22] This is what it means!

*

ON CURSING A MONK AND COMMITTING A LUSTFUL ACT, HE SUFFERED AN EVIL RESULT AND DIED (2:11)

In the reign of Emperor Shōmu, the nuns of Sayadera in Kuwahara in the Ito district of Kii province vowed to hold a service and invited a monk of Yakushi-ji on the West Side of Nara, Dharma Master Daie (popularly known as Dharma Master Yosami because his secular name was Yosami no muraji), to perform the rite of repentance before the statue of the Eleven-Headed Kannon.

At that time in the village, there lived a very wicked man. His surname was Fumi no imiki (his popular name was Ueda no Samurō). He was evil by nature and did not believe in the Three Treasures of Buddhism. The wife of this wicked man was a daughter of Kaminotsuke no kimi Ōhashi. She observed the eight precepts for a day and a night,[23] and

---

21. Nirvana Sutra, vol. 20. See *Taishō* 12:484b.
22. Zen'aku-inga-kyō. The Hell of the River of Ashes is one of the sixteen subhells in the eight Hells of Heat.
23. The eight precepts are to refrain from taking life, stealing, committing adultery, telling lies, drinking alcoholic beverages, eating at the wrong hours, engaging in worldly amusements, and wearing ornaments.

went to the temple to participate in the rite of repentance along with the others of the congregation.

When her husband came home, he could not find her. He asked one of the servants where she had gone. The man replied, "She has gone to the rite of repentance." Hearing this, he became very angry and went to the temple to fetch her. The officiating monk saw him and tried to explain, giving reasons of doctrine, but he refused to listen. "It's no use explaining!" he said. "You're trying to seduce my wife! You should be knocked in the head, you worthless monk!" His language was too vile to describe in detail. He called his wife to go home, and when they got there, he violated her. But an ant bit his penis, and he died in great pain.

No penalty was applied, but through his own evil action in using abusive language and daring to misuse his wife, he brought on an immediate punishment.

Although you may have a hundred tongues in your mouth and speak ten thousand words, never abuse a true monk! For you will meet with swift disaster.

On Saving the Lives of Some Crabs and a Frog and Freeing Them, She Gained an Immediate Reward from the Crabs (2:12)

In Yamashiro province, in a community in the district of Kii, there was a young woman whose family and personal names are unknown. Tenderhearted by nature, she believed firmly in the law of karma, observed the five precepts and the ten good deeds,[24] and never deprived any living thing of life. In the reign of Emperor Shōmu, some of the cowherds in the village where she lived caught eight crabs in a mountain stream and

---

24. The ten good deeds are to refrain from taking life, stealing, committing adultery, telling lies, using immoral language, engaging in slander, equivocating, coveting, giving in to anger, and holding false views.

were about to roast and eat them. The young woman, seeing this, pleaded with the herd boys, saying, "Please be so kind as to give me the crabs!" But the boys refused to heed her, replying, "We're going to roast them and eat them!" Earnestly she begged and entreated them, taking off her cloak and offering it in payment, and finally the boys handed over the crabs to her. She then requested Meditation Master Gi to perform prayers asking for merit and set the crabs free.

Sometime later, the young woman went into the mountains and came upon a huge snake about to swallow a large frog. She said to the snake imploringly, "If you will only give me that frog, I will present you with numerous offerings of woven goods!" When the snake ignored her and refused to listen, she promised to gather together even more woven goods and pray to him, saying, "I will worship you like a god if you will heed my pleas and release the frog!" The snake paid no attention, however, and went on swallowing the frog. Then she said to the snake, "If you will give me the frog, I will agree to be your wife, so please let it go!" With this, the snake at last took notice of her, lifting up its head, stretching out its neck, and peering into the young woman's face. Then it spat out the frog and let it go. The woman thereupon arranged an assignation with the snake, saying, "Come to me when seven days have passed."

Later, she told her father and mother all about the incident with the snake. They were distraught and said, "You are our only child! How could you have been so insane as to make impossible promises like that?"

At this time, the Eminent Monk Gyōgi was in residence at the Fuka-osa-dera in the district of Kii, and so the young woman went and reported to him what had happened. When he had listened to her, he said, "Ah, what an astounding story! The only thing to do is to have faith in the Three Treasures!"

Having received his instructions, she returned home, and when the night for the assignation arrived, she shut the house up tight and prepared to defend herself, making various religious vows and placing her trust in the Three Treasures. The snake circled the house, slithering this way and that on its belly and pounding against the wall with its tail. Then it climbed onto the roof, chewed a hole through the thatch, and dropped down in front of the young woman. But before it could approach her, there was a sudden outburst of noise, with sounds of scrambling, biting, and chewing. The next morning when the young woman looked to see what had happened, she found eight large crabs gathered there, and a snake that had been hacked and slashed into little pieces.

Thus we know that if even such lowly and unenlightened creatures know how to repay a debt of gratitude when they have incurred it, how can it be right for human beings to forget the debts they owe? From this time on in Yamashiro province, great honor was paid to the large crabs that live in the mountain streams, and it was considered an act of goodness to set them free.

On Manifesting Love for the Image of Goddess Kichijō, Which Responded with an Extraordinary Sign (2:13)

In a mountain temple of Chinu, in the Izumi district of Izumi province, there was a clay image of Kichijō-tennyo, Goddess Kichijō.[25] In the reign of Emperor Shōmu, a lay brother of Shinano province came to live at the temple. Attracted by the image, he fell in love with it and prayed to it passionately six times a day, saying, "Please send me a woman who is as beautiful as you!"

Once he dreamed that he had relations with the goddess. When he awoke the next morning, he found that the skirt of the image was stained with semen. Seeing this, he was deeply shocked and said, "I wanted a woman like you. But why did you go so far as to give your own self to me?"

He was shamed by what had happened and spoke of it to no one, but one of his disciples happened to learn of it. When the disciple was later

25. Kichijō was the goddess of fortune and beauty, originally a figure in Indian mythology. In Japan, prayers for peace and agricultural fertility were offered to her.

scolded and expelled from the temple for disrespect to his teacher, he spoke ill of the teacher and revealed the whole affair. The villagers, hearing of it, went to the temple to find out if it was true, and they discovered the stain on the statue. The lay brother could not hide his guilt and confessed the whole affair.

Truly we know that deep faith never fails to gain a response. This was a miraculous event. As the Nirvana Sutra says, "A man of many desires feels moved even by a woman in a picture."[26] This is what it means.

ON A DESTITUTE WOMAN WHO PRAYED TO THE IMAGE OF GODDESS KICHIJŌ AND THE IMMEDIATE REWARD IT GAINED HER (2:14)

During the reign of Emperor Shōmu, twenty-three princes and princesses, being one in heart, got together to take turns giving banquets and providing entertainment. But there was one destitute princess among the group. After the other twenty-two had taken their turns in providing food and entertainment, she alone was left with no means of doing so. Filled with shame at her inability to respond, she went to the Hatoribe Hall on the East Side of Nara to pay her respects to the image of Goddess Kichijō, saying, "Because I planted the seeds of poverty in my previous existence, I am now rewarded with a poor fate. I went to the banquets and thoughtlessly ate the food provided by others, but I have no means to provide food in return. I beg you to please send me some wealth!"

At that time, her child came running in haste, saying to her mother, "Good luck! Someone has brought food from the old capital!" Hearing this, the woman ran out and found that it was her old wet nurse who had come. "I heard you had guests, and so I fixed some food and brought it," she said. The food she brought was extravagant, replete with all kinds of

26. *Taishō* 12:515c.

delicious dishes. Nothing at all was lacking, nothing amiss, and it was all served in metal containers carried by thirty men.

All the guests came to the banquet and ate the food with delight. It was twice as delicious as the previous meals, and everyone praised it, saying, "She must be rich—if she were poor, how could she afford so much food? There's even some left over—it's much better than what we offered! And the songs and dances are as marvelous as the music of the gods!" Some doffed their robes in payment; others offered their skirts; while still others handed over coins, silks, cloth, cotton, or other goods. The princess, her joy unbounded, gave the robes and skirts to the wet nurse in thanks. But later, when she went to the temple to worship, she found the robes and skirts draped over the sacred image. Filled with doubt, she questioned her wet nurse. "I know nothing about this!" was her reply.

Truly we know that it was the bodhisattva who did this kind deed. So the princess acquired great wealth and was able to escape from the worries of poverty. This was a miraculous event.

On Copying the Lotus Sutra and Making an Offering of It, He Made Clear Why His Mother Had Been Reborn as a Cow (2:15)

Takahashi no muraji Azumahito was a man of the village of Hamishiro in the Yamada district of Iga province. He was very wealthy and had many possessions. For the sake of his deceased mother, he copied the Lotus Sutra, making a vow, saying, "I want to get a monk to comply with my vow and bring her salvation." He arranged to hold a religious service the next day and gave orders to a servant, saying, "The first monk you meet will do to officiate at the service. If he looks as though he can conduct it, do not bother whether he is an expert or not."

Following these instructions, the servant went out the gate and walked through the village of Mitani in the same district. There, he saw a beggar, whose head was shaved and who had a bag for a begging bowl at his elbow, drunk and sleeping in the road. His name is not known. For a joke, someone had shaved his head and placed a robe around him like a surplice, though, being drunk, he was unaware of this. Seeing him, the servant woke him, greeted him, and asked him to accompany him to his master's house.

When they got there, the master greeted him cordially and kept him secluded for a day and a night, during which time he hastily made a clerical robe and gave it to him to put on. "Why are you doing that?" the man asked. The host replied, "I want you to expound the Lotus Sutra." "I have no learning," the man replied. "I simply recite the Hannya dharani and beg for food, and in that way have managed to stay alive!"[27] The host, however, repeated his request. The man thought that the best way to escape was to sneak away. But the host, aware of his intentions, had him watched.

That night, the man had a dream. A red cow came to him and spoke, saying, "I am the mother of the master of this house. Among his cattle there is a red cow, whose child I am. Once, in a previous existence, I stole goods from my son, and as a result I was reborn as a cow in payment for that deed. Tomorrow, you are going to preach on a Mahayana sutra for my benefit, and therefore with all respect and sincerity I tell you this. If you wish to know whether what I say is true, tomorrow, in the back of the hall where you preach your sermon, prepare a seat for me and I will sit in it."

When the man who had been appointed to speak woke from his dream, he was greatly startled. The following morning, when he ascended the expounder's seat, he said, "I have no knowledge of Buddhism. It is only at the earnest request of the master of this house that I have consented to take this seat. But I want to tell you a revelation that came to me in a dream." He proceeded to relate in detail the dream he had had.

---

27. The Hannya dharani is the brief spell, or *dharani*, in Sanskrit that appears at the end of the similarly brief Hannya Shin-gyō, which means: "Gone, gone, gone beyond, gone entirely beyond—so be it."

The host then stood up, prepared a seat, and called to the cow, which came and lay down in the seat. Bursting into tears, the host said, "This really is my mother! I did not know her in the past, but now I forgive her misdeed!" When the cow heard this, it sighed deeply, and after the service was over, it died. All the members of the congregation cried heartily, the hall echoing with the sound. Since that time, nothing that has happened is stranger then this! The son, for the sake of his mother, continued to do good deeds.

Truly we know that this wonderful event occurred because of the son's deep faith, and that the beggar's efficacious actions were the result of the holy spell that he recited.

✳

ON FREEING CREATURES, BUT GIVING NO ALMS, AND THE GOOD AND BAD RESULTS THAT IMMEDIATELY APPEARED (2:16)

In the reign of Emperor Shōmu, in the village of Sakata in the Kagawa district of Sanuki province, there lived a rich man. Both he and his wife belonged to the Aya no kimi family. Next door to them lived an old man and an old woman who were widowed, having lost their children. They were very poor, possessing only clothes enough to cover their nakedness and no food to keep them alive. They came to the Aya no kimi household day after day without fail to beg for their evening meal. Once, the master of the Aya no kimi household tried getting up late at night and cooking rice for his household to eat, but still they came to beg, which all of his family thought very strange.

The mistress said to her husband, "This old widowed couple are too far along in age to work. Why don't we show them compassion and take them in as members of our family?" The master replied, "Let's share our food with them. From now on, we'll divide our own rations and feed the old widower and widow. Among meritorious actions, to sacrifice your own needs to save the lives of others is the most laudable. Our deeds will call forth merit." Following the master's suggestion, the members of the household divided their rations and fed the old couple.

But there was one servant who, despite the master's words, refused to go along, hating the old couple. And gradually, the other servants came to hate them, too, and begrudge them their share. The mistress, therefore, fed them secretly from her own portion. The troublesome servant, ever discontented, lied to the master, saying, "The mistress reduces our allowance and feeds the old couple. Therefore, we do not have enough to eat and, hungry and exhausted, we cannot do our work and are forced to neglect it!" The mistress continued to feed them, however, in spite of his slanders.

One day, the master[28] and the disgruntled servant went out on the sea to fish with a man who had a creel and fishing tackle. On the fishing line, the master saw ten oysters and said, "I would like to set those oysters free." The fisherman refused to listen. The master pleaded with him, citing the teachings of Buddhism, saying, "People in a position build temples. Why won't you let them go?" The man finally agreed, saying, "Ten oysters— that will cost you five bushels of rice!" The master agreed to this and, inviting a monk to give a blessing, had the oysters returned to the sea.

The master, who had freed the oysters, accompanied by a servant, went one day into the mountains to collect firewood. He climbed a dead pine tree, fell from a branch, and died. His spirit, which took possession of a diviner, said, "Do not cremate my body immediately. Wait until seven days have passed!" Following the diviner's instructions, they carried his body down from the mountains and set it aside to wait for the appointed day.

When seven days had passed, he came back to life and spoke to his family, saying, "There were five monks who went before me and five lay brothers behind. We went along a broad and level road, like one used for transporting goods. Holy banners were ranged to left and right, and in front was a golden palace. I asked, 'What palace is this?' The lay brothers whispered among themselves and then said, 'This is where your mistress will be reborn. It has been built because of her merit in taking care of the

---

28. The text appears corrupt at this point, as the word "master" must have dropped out.

old widowed couple. And do you know who we are?' I replied, 'No, I don't.' 'You should know us. We ten men, monks and lay brothers, are the ten oysters that you set free.'

"On either side of the palace door stood men with a single horn on their heads. They carried huge swords and threatened to cut off my head. But the monks and lay brothers pleaded with them not to do so.

"Delicious food was served to the gatekeepers on either side of the gate, everyone feasting happily. But during my seven days among them, I was so hungry and thirsty that my mouth was in flames. I was told, 'This is the penalty you pay for the sin of refusing food for the hungry old widow and widower!' Then the monks and lay brothers escorted me back, and in an instant I came alive again."

After that, the man was as generous in freeing living creatures as a fountain spouting water. The reward for saving living beings returns to the doer, while that of failing to do so appears in the form of hunger and thirst. Good and evil never fail to have their reward.

On Bronze Images of Kannon That Showed, by Their Transformation into the Form of a Heron, an Extraordinary Sign (2:17)

In the nunnery of Okamoto, in the village of Ikaruga in the Heguri district of Yamato province, there were twelve bronze images of Kannon. (In the past, in the reign of the empress at the Owarida Palace,[29] it had been the residence of Prince Regent Kamitsumiya, who made a vow and turned it into a nunnery.) During the reign of Emperor Shōmu, six of the bronzes were stolen. A search was made, but they could not be found, after which many days and months passed.

To the west of the stage house in Heguri, there was a small pond. One summer, in the Sixth Month, some men were herding cows in the vicinity

29. Empress Suiko (r. 592–628).

of the pond when they noticed something like a wooden stake sticking up in the pond. On top of the stake, a heron had alighted. Seeing it, they gathered rocks and stones and tried throwing them at it, but it did not fly away. Tired of that, they waded into the pond to catch it, but they had barely reached it when it dove into the water. Looking closely at the stake on which it had been seated, they saw that it had golden fingers. When the stake was pulled out of the water, it turned out to be the bronze images of Kannon. Because of Kannon, the pond was thus named Pond of the Bodhisattva.

The herdsmen told everyone about their find, and eventually word of it reached the nunnery. Hearing of it, the nuns came and found that they were in fact their images, though the gilt had come off in the water. Surrounding the images and weeping with pity, the nuns said, "We lost our precious images, and mourned day and night. And now they have by chance come back to us. What sin were our Masters guilty of, that they should have met with the fate of being stolen?" Then they prepared a palanquin, placed the images in it, and returned them to the temple. Clergymen and lay believers agreed that they must have been stolen by men who forged coins, but finding them of no use, had abandoned them.

Truly we know that the heron, though it looked like a real heron, was an incarnation of Kannon. There can be no doubt of it! The Nirvana Sutra states, "Although the Buddha may pass away, his Dharma body remains."[30] This is what it means.

On Speaking Ill of a Monk Reciting the Lotus Sutra and Gaining the Immediate Penalty of an Evil Death (2:18)

In the Tenpyō era [729–749] in the Sagaraka district of Yamashiro province, there once lived a layman whose name is unknown. At Koma

---

30. *Taishō* 12:901c.

Temple in the same district, there was a monk named Yōjō[31] who used to recite the Lotus Sutra constantly. It happened that the monk and the layman had been playing *go* for some time.[32] Whenever the monk put down a stone, he said, "This is the Venerable Yōjō's game of *go*." When he did so, the layman would mock him, deliberately twisting his mouth and saying, "This is the Venerable Yōjō's game of *go*." He went on and on in this way, never stopping. Suddenly, the layman's mouth became distorted. In fear, he left the temple, holding his chin in his hands. He had not gone any distance when he fell over on his back and immediately died.

People observing this said, "Though he did not actually persecute the monk, mocking him got him a twisted mouth and sudden death. If one with a vengeful heart actually persecuted a monk, how much greater must the penalty be!"

The Lotus Sutra says: "A wise monk and a foolish monk cannot be compared in standing. Further, a long-haired monk is to be counted wiser than a layman who does not shave his head. They must not be served the same dishes. If one does so, he will be forced to swallow an iron ball that has been heated on red-hot copper and ashes and will fall into Hell."[33] This is what the passage refers to.

ON A WOMAN DEVOTEE OF THE SHIN-GYŌ VISITING THE PALACE OF KING YAMA AND THE FOLLOWING EXTRAORDINARY EVENT (2:19)

The laywoman Tokari no ubai was from Kawachi province. Her surname was Tokari no suguri, and hence she was called the laywoman Tokari. She was innately pure of heart and put her faith in the Three Treasures of Buddhism. She constantly chanted the Shin-gyō as a form of religious

---

31. The name may also be read as Eijō.
32. Most games were forbidden to monks, but an exception was made for *go*.
33. No such passage is found in present texts of the Lotus Sutra.

devotion. Her chanting of the Shin-gyō was so beautiful that she was beloved by both clergy and laity.

In the reign of Emperor Shōmu, this laywoman went to sleep one night and, without being ill, died suddenly and went to the palace of King Yama. The king, seeing her, stood up and spread a seat for her, saying, "I have heard of how fine is your recitation of the Shin-gyō. I thought that I would like to hear it for myself, and so I brought you here for a little while. Please let me hear your recitation. I long to hear it!" She complied, and, hearing it, the king rose from his seat, knelt down, and said, "How wonderful—just as I had heard it was!"

When three days had passed, the king said, "Now it is time you went back home!" and he escorted her out of the palace. At the gate were three men dressed in yellow clothes. They greeted her delightedly, saying, "We met only once before and have not met since. Therefore, we thought of you with longing. How lucky, that we meet again! Hurry on home, and three days from today we will without fail see you again at the east market of the capital of Nara!" Then she left them, returned home, and suddenly woke up.

On the morning of the third day, in accordance with what she had been told, she went to the east market of the city. There she waited all day, but the men did not come. Only a poor-looking man came into the market from the east gate, walking around and selling Buddhist scriptures, saying, "Who will buy my sacred texts?" He passed by her and was about to go out the west gate, when she decided that she wanted to buy some scriptures and sent for him to come back. When she opened the texts, she discovered that they were the two volumes of the Bonmō-kyō and the one volume of the Shin-gyō, both of which she had copied in the past. Before she even had a chance to use them, she had lost them and, for many years, had searched for them unsuccessfully. Now, with joy in her heart, she knew that this man had stolen them, and, with an attitude of forgiveness, she asked, "How much are they?" When he replied, "Each scroll is five hundred *mon*," she bought them at that price.

Then she realized that the three scrolls were the three men who had promised to meet her at the market. She held a service for the reading of

the scriptures and deepened her faith in the law of causality. Day and
night without ceasing, she recited the texts devotedly.

Ah, what a miracle! As the Nirvana Sutra says: "If a person does good
works, his name will be noted among heavenly beings; if he does evil, his
name will be noted in Hell."[34] This is what it means.

On a Mother Who, Having Had a Bad Dream, Had Scriptures Recited with True Faith and Saved Her Daughter by an Extraordinary Sign (2:20)

In the village of Yamamura in the Sou upper district of Yamato province, there lived an aged mother whose name is unknown. She had a
married daughter who had two children. Her son-in-law was appointed
provincial magistrate, and accordingly he took his family to his post.
Several years passed.

The wife's mother had stayed in the village to look after the household. Suddenly, she had a dream that portended ill for her daughter.
She was greatly disturbed and thought, "I must have a sutra recited for
my daughter!" But, being very poor, she had no money to do so. Having
no other course, she took off her robe, washed it clean, and offered it
in payment for the recitation of a scripture. But the evil signs continued, more sinister than before. Growing more fearful, the mother took
off her skirt and, washing it too and offering it in payment, had another
scripture recited.

Meanwhile, her daughter was living in the official residence of the
provincial magistrate at her husband's post. Her two children were playing in the courtyard, while she was in the back quarters. The children
saw seven monks sitting on the roof and reciting a scripture. The children said, "There are seven monks sitting on the roof and reciting a

34. Nirvana Sutra, vol. 12. See *Taishō* 12:434c.

scripture. Hurry—come out and see them!" The monks' chanting sounded like bees humming all together. The mother, wondering at this, got up and came out of the rear building. She had no sooner done so than the wall of the building collapsed. At the same moment, the seven monks suddenly disappeared.

The woman was terrified, thinking to herself, "Heaven and Earth have saved me from being crushed by the falling wall!" Later, however, she received word from her mother, who sent to tell her about the evil omens that had appeared and that she had had scriptures recited to avert them. When she learned this, she was deeply frightened and impressed with her mother's faith, and believed more firmly than ever in the Three Treasures of Buddhism.

Thus we know that the sequence of events was due to the power of reciting scriptures and the protective force of the Three Treasures.

On the Clay Image of a God-King from Whose Legs Emanated a Light, and Whose Supplicant Received an Immediate Reward (2:21)

On the hill east of the city of Nara, there was a temple named Konjū-ji.[35] In that mountain temple lived a man who was called Konjū because he made his residence there.[36] That temple later became known as Tōdai-ji. During the reign of Emperor Shōmu, the practitioner Konjū constantly lived there and followed the ways of Buddhism. In the temple was enshrined a clay image of Vajradhara Shūkon.[37] The practitioner took hold

35. Konjū-ji was the old name of the Hokke-dō of Tōdai-ji.
36. Konjū is better known as Rōben (689–773). In 733, Emperor Shōmu founded Konshō-ji for him, and later expanded it into Tōdai-ji. He was put in charge of Tōdai-ji and became one of the most distinguished monks of the Nara period.
37. Originally a Vedic deity, Vajradhara Shūkon was taken over and worshipped as a protector of Buddhism.

of a rope tied to the legs of the image and prayed to it day and night without ceasing.

It happened that light emanating from its legs reached the palace of the emperor. In surprise and wonder, he dispatched a messenger to discover its origin. The messenger traced the light back to the temple, where he found practitioner Konjū. Grasping the rope tied to the legs of the image, the layman paid honor to the Buddha and confessed his sins. The messenger quickly returned and reported what he had found.

The emperor summoned the practitioner and asked, "What are you praying for?" He replied, "I am praying that I may become a monk and may study and practice the Law of the Buddha." He was accordingly granted permission to join the clergy and given the name Konjū. The emperor praised his practice of the teachings and provided him with a generous amount of money to cover the four necessities.[38] The people of the time, praising his discipline, called him Bodhisattva Konjū. The image of Vajradhara Shūkon that sent forth the light still stands by the north door of the Kensaku Hall of Tōdai-ji.

In appraisal we say: How good he was—the practitioner Konjū! He kindled the flame in spring in the east, and it burned brightly in autumn in the west.[39] The light from the legs helped the fire to burn, and the emperor reverently displayed the sign of his faith.

Truly we know that there is no vow that goes unanswered. This is what it means.

---

38. The four necessities are shelter, clothing, food and drink, and flowers and incense.
39. In Konjū's youth, the light of his Buddhism in the east part of Nara kindled the flame of faith; in Konjū's later years, the emperor in the west part of the city responded to it with fervor.

On a Bronze Image of the Buddha That Was Stolen by a Thief and Revealed His Identity by a Marvelous Sign (2:22)

In a part of the Hine district of Izumi province, there was a thief. He lived near the highway, but his name is unknown. He was inherently evil, killing and stealing for a living, and did not believe in the law of karmic causation. Constantly, he stole metal from temples, made it into strips, and sold it.

In the reign of Emperor Shōmu, he stole a metal image of the Buddha from a temple named Jin'e-ji in the district. At that time, there happened to be a man passing along the road. When his horse passed the north side of the temple, he heard a voice crying and saying, "It hurts, it hurts!" Hearing the voice, the man supposed that someone was being attacked and spurred his horse ahead, but as he did so, the voice gradually died out. Halting his horse and listening, all he could hear was the sound of metal being hammered. He accordingly spurred his horse past the place. As he went farther along, however, he heard the same sound as before. He could not simply ride on, but turned around again. Once more, the cries ceased and there was only the sound of hammering. Suspecting that there had been a murder or some foul scheme, he wandered around for some time and sent his servant to peer into the building. The servant saw a man cutting off the arms and legs of a bronze Buddha image that had been laid on its back and using a chisel to pry off its head.

He seized the culprit at once and asked, "What temple does this Buddha image belong to?" "This is the Buddha of Jin'e-ji," was the reply. He sent a message to the temple and found that, indeed, its Buddha had been stolen. The messenger reported the whole affair in detail. The monks and parishioners, hearing of this, came to the spot and, surrounding the broken Buddha, wailed and lamented, crying, "How pitiful, how terrible! Our Master! What fault has he committed, to be treated by a thief like this? If the sacred image were still at the temple, we would honor it as Our Master! Now that it is broken, what shall we revere as Our Master?"

The monks purified a palanquin, placed the broken image in it, and, weeping, held a ceremony at the temple. The thief they let go without inflicting any penalty. But the man who caught him had him turned over to the authorities, who put him in prison.

Truly we know that the Buddha performed this miracle to put a stop to evil. Utter sincerity is a fearful thing—the Buddha's spirit cannot but respond to it. Thus in chapter 12 of the Nirvana Sutra, the Buddha tells us: "I have a high regard for the Mahayana scriptures. If I hear the Brahmins speak slanderously of them, I will cut off their lives. And for doing so, I will not as a consequence fall into Hell." And in chapter 33 of the sutra, it says: "Those of the category of *icchantika* [persons of incorrigible evil] shall perish forever. If you kill so much as an ant, you will be accused of the sin of killing. But if you kill an *icchantika*, you will not be accused of the sin of killing." This is what it means. (Because these persons slander the Buddha, the doctrine, and the community of monks; fail to preach the Law for all living beings; and lack a sense of gratitude, killing them is not a sin.)

On a Bronze Image of Bodhisattva Miroku That Was Stolen and Revealed the Thief Through a Miraculous Sign (2:23)

In the reign of Emperor Shōmu, an imperial messenger went around the city at night. At midnight, he heard wailing emanating from the field of smartweed south of the Kazuraki nunnery in the capital of Nara. It made a sound like "It hurts, it hurts!" Hearing the sound, the messenger proceeded in the direction of the cries. He found a thief breaking up a bronze image of Bodhisattva Miroku,[40] using a stone. When he caught and questioned the thief, he replied, "Yes—this is the bronze image of the Kazuraki nunnery." The image was returned to the nunnery, and the thief was handed over to the authorities, who put him in prison.

The Buddha in his Dharma body has no flesh or blood. Why, then, did it suffer pain? This took place only to show that Dharma exists constant and unchanging. It, too, is a miraculous event!

On the Devils, Messengers of King Yama, Who Accepted the Hospitality of the One for Whom They Had Been Sent and Repaid It (2:24)

Nara no Iwashima lived on Fifth Avenue and Sixth Street, on the East Side of Nara—that is, in the village west of Daian-ji. During the reign of Emperor Shōmu, he borrowed thirty *kan*[41] from the Shutara fund of Daian-ji, went to the port of Tsuruga in Echizen, purchased goods, and loaded them on a ship he had bought to bring them home. On the way home, he was suddenly taken ill. Leaving the ship, he decided to go on alone and hired a horse to do so.

When he reached Shiga-no-karasaki in the Takashima district of Ōmi province, he saw three men running after him. They were about half a furlong away. By the time he reached the Uji Bridge in Yamashiro, they had caught up and went along with him. Iwashima asked them, "Where are you going?" They replied, "We are messengers from King Yama who have been sent to summon Nara no Iwashima." "That's me!" said Iwashima. "But what am I summoned for?" The devil messengers

---

40. Bodhisattva Miroku is Maitreya, who resides in the Tuṣita Heaven and will descend to Earth to teach the Law at the end of the world.
41. This was a considerable sum of money.

said, "We went looking for you at your home, but were told, 'He has gone on a business trip and has not yet returned.' So we went to the port, hoping to catch you there. But the messenger from the Four Guardian Kings[42] asked us to desist, saying, 'Leave him be, since he has a loan from the temple and is on temple business!' Therefore, we let you go free for a time. We've spent so many days trying to catch you that we're hungry and exhausted. Do you have any food?" Iwashima replied, "All I have is dried rice," and he gave that to them. The devil messengers said, "You'll be made sick by our spirits, so don't come any closer to us. Otherwise, you have nothing to fear."

When he at last reached home, he fixed a feast for the devil messengers. They said, "We are very fond of the taste of beef. Therefore, if you would fix beef, that would be fine. We are the devils who catch cows." Iwashima told them, "I have two brindled cows. If I serve you these, will you let me go?" The devils replied, "We have eaten a great deal of your food. But if in exchange for that we let you go free, we will be accused of a grave sin and beaten a hundred times with an iron rod. Do you know anyone who was born in the same year as you?" "No, I don't," replied Iwashima. Then one of the devils asked, "What year were you born in?" Iwashima replied, "I was born in the year *tsuchinoe-tora* [678]." The devil said, "I have heard that there is a diviner at the shrine of Izagawa who was born in the same year as you. He can be your substitute. We will call him instead. However, so that we may escape whipping for the sin of accepting your offer of a cow, you must recite the Diamond Sutra one hundred times, invoking our names. The first name is Takasamaro, the second name is Nakachimaro, and the third name is Tsuchimaro." With that, they left at midnight.

The next day, when Iwashima looked, he found that one of his cows had died. He went to the Nantō-in of Daian-ji and asked Novice Nin'yō (at that time not yet ordained) to recite the Diamond Sutra one hundred times. According to his request, Nin'yō spent two mornings reciting it.

---

42. The Four Guardian Kings are the four deities who guard the four quarters of the world; in Japanese they are Tokkoku (east), Zōchō (south), Kōmoku (west), and Tamon (north).

After three days had passed, the devil messengers appeared and said, "Due to the power of the Mahayana scriptures, we escaped the penalty of one hundred strokes, and in addition we were given half a bushel more rice than the usual ration. How happy and wonderful! From today on, on every holy day, practice virtue and hold a service for our sake!" Then they suddenly disappeared.

Iwashima was over ninety when he died.

Just as Dou Dexuan of Tang China,[43] because of the power of the Diamond Sutra, escaped from the messenger of King Yama, so did Iwashima of Japan, because he was engaged in business with a loan from the temple fund, escape the summons of the devil messengers from King Yama. The same moral will be found in the story of a woman who sold flowers who was born in the Trāyastrimśa Heaven or of Kikuta, who had once wanted to poison the Buddha but whose good heart was restored by the Buddha's omniscience.

On the Devil, Messenger of King Yama, Who Accepted the Hospitality Offered Him and Repaid the Kindness (2:25)

In the Yamada district of Sanuki province, there lived a woman named Nunoshi no omi Kinume. In the reign of Emperor Shōmu, this woman suddenly fell ill. At the time, she prepared a splendid feast and placed it to the left and right of her doorway as an offering for the god of the dead.

A demon messenger came from King Yama to summon her. The messenger was tired, and, casting a covetous look at all the delicacies, he accordingly helped himself. Then he said to the woman, "I have accepted your delicious meal, and hence owe you some reward. Is there anyone

43. Dou Dexuan was a high minister who lived in the reign of Gaozong (650–683).

who has the same name as you?" The woman replied, "Yes—there is. She, too, is named Kinume and lives in the Utari district of the same province." Thereupon, he took the first Kinume to the house of the second Kinume in Utari and confronted her. Taking out a one-foot-long chisel from his red bag, he drove it into the forehead of the second Kinume and summoned her to King Yama. He secretly dismissed the first Kinume and allowed her to return home.[44]

When King Yama had had a chance to examine the action, he said, "This is not the person I sent you to summon! There's been as mistake! However, leave things as they are for now, and go and summon the Kinume of Yamada district!"

As his attempt to hide her had failed, the devil's messenger then went to the house of the first Kinume to summon her as well. When King Yama saw her, he said, "This is the Kinume I summoned!" With this, he allowed the second Kinume to return to her home.

But three days had elapsed, and Kinume of Utari found that her body had already been cremated. Returning to the court of King Yama, she complained bitterly, saying, "I have no body to return to!" King Yama asked, "Is the body of the Kinume of Yamada district in existence?" "It is," he was told. "In that case, take that for your body!" he replied. Accordingly, Kinume of Utari came back to life in the body of Kinume of Yamada.

But she said, "This is not my home! My home is in Utari!" Her father and mother said, "You are our child—why do you say such things?" But the woman would not listen, and, going to the home of the woman of Utari, she declared, "This is my real home!" Her father and mother disclaimed her, saying, "This is not our child! Our child has been cremated!" Then she explained to them in detail the orders that King Yama had given to her. The parents of the two families, having listened sincerely to her words, allowed her to inherit the fortune of both houses. This is how this one Kinume came to have two sets of parents and to possess two inheritances.

---

44. As is often the case, the heading covers only the first part of the action.

Fix a feast for the devil messenger of the dead—it will not be in vain.[45] If you have something on hand, offer it as a bribe. This, too, was a miraculous event!

※

On a Log, Intended for Buddha Images, That Was Abandoned but Showed an Extraordinary Sign (2:26)

Meditation Master Kōdachi, whose secular name was Shimotsukeno no asomi, was a man of the Muza district of Kazusa province. (Some say that he was from Ahiru district.) During the reign of Emperor Shōmu, he went to the mountain called Kane-no-mitake in Yoshino, where he walked around underneath the trees, reciting scriptures and seeking to practice the Way of Buddhism.

At that time, there was a horse-chestnut tree in the village of Tsuki in Yoshino district. This tree was cut down with the intention of making Buddha images, but was abandoned for many years. At that place, there was a river called Akikawa. The log that had been cut for Buddha images had been placed across this river so that men and beasts could go back and forth over the river.

Once Kōdachi had occasion to go to that village, and he crossed over the log. As he did so, it made a sound, saying, "Ah, don't tread so heavily on me!" Kōdachi, hearing this, looked to see if someone had spoken, but there was no one there. He hesitated for a long time, unwilling to try crossing it again, and then he picked up the log and examined it. He saw that the log had been intended for use in making Buddha images, but that this had never been done. Greatly startled, Kōdachi enshrined the log in a sacred area, wept tears of contrition,

---

45. Although the text says to fix a feast for the messenger, the one who did so, Kinume of Yamada, lost her body, whereas the one who did not ended up with two sets of parents and two inheritances. This is one of the puzzles of the *Nihon ryōiki*.

and paid homage to it, giving voice to this vow, "I have come upon this as a result of dependent causation. Therefore, I will see to it that you are made into images!"

He took the log to an appointed place, called on the people to gather around, and had images of Amida Buddha, Bodhisattva Miroku, and Bodhisattva Kannon made from it. They are now enshrined in the Oka-dō in the village of Koshibe in Yoshino district.

A log such as this does not have a mind. How, then, can it cry out? This was nothing but the work of the Buddha's holy spirit! There can be no doubt about it.

On a Woman of Great Strength (2:27)

Owari no sukune Kukuri was the governor of the Nakashima district of Owari province in the reign of Emperor Shōmu. His wife came from the village of Katawa in the Aichi district of the same province (a granddaughter of the Venerable Dōjō of Gangō-ji). She was faithful to her husband and as gentle and compliant as silk cloth that has been glossed. Once, she wove fine hemp for her husband's sake. Its color and pattern were beyond compare.

At that time, the ruler of that province was Wakasakurabe no Tau. When he saw the beauty of the robe the governor was wearing, he took it away from him, saying, "It is too good for you to wear!" and refused to return it. When the district governor's wife asked what had happened to it, he replied, "The ruler of the province took it away!" "And do you miss that robe?" asked his wife. "Very much indeed!" he replied.

Thereupon, the wife went to see the ruler of the province and begged him, saying, "Give me that robe!" The ruler of the province said, "What a woman! Get her out of here!" Then, with only two fingers, she picked up the bench the ruler was sitting on and carried it outside the ruler's office with the ruler on it. She tore the hem of his robe into pieces, all the time crying, "Give me back the robe!" The ruler was so frightened and embarrassed that he returned the robe. She took it back home, washed and cleaned it, and folded and put it away. She could crush a piece of bamboo into strips as fine as silk thread.

The parents of the governor, seeing this, were greatly afraid and said to their son, "Because of your wife, you have aroused the enmity of the ruler of the province, and we fear that you are headed for big trouble! If she treats even the ruler in such a way, where will it end? What shall we do? We can't even sleep in peace or go about our business!" Then they sent her back to her own parents and had nothing further to do with her.

After that, she went back to her native village. There, she was once washing clothes in the Kayatsu River when a merchant happened to pass by in a large boat loaded with merchandise. The captain of the boat, seeing her, began to banter with her in a provocative manner. "Be quiet, you!" she said. "Those who are rude to others get a swift slap on the cheek!" The captain, hearing this, grew angry, stopped the boat, and hit her. She did not feel the blow, but pulled the boat halfway up on the beach, leaving its stern sunk in the water. Hiring some men from the neighborhood of the ferry to unload the boat, he then had it reloaded.

The woman, for her part, said, "Because he spoke to me in such a rude manner, I pulled the boat up! Why do people always treat a poor woman in a mean manner like this?" She then proceeded to drag the boat, fully loaded, for half a furlong. At this, the men in the boat, thoroughly frightened, knelt down and said, "We were wrong—we admit our fault!"

Therefore, she forgave them. As a matter of fact, five hundred men all pulling could not have moved the boat, so it is obvious that she had the strength of over five hundred men!

As it is said in a certain sutra, "If you make rice cakes and offer them to the Three Treasures of Buddhism, you will gain the strength of a god like Narayana!"[46] And so we know it is true. Because in her previous existence she made a big rice cake for the ruler of the Three Treasures and the monks and communion of believers, she was able to acquire extraordinary strength such as this!

---

46. Narayana is an Indian deity noted for his great strength.

ON A VERY POOR WOMAN WHO TRUSTED TO THE BENEFICENCE OF THE SIXTEEN-FOOT BUDDHA AND WON AN EXTRAORDINARY SIGN AND GREAT GOOD FORTUNE (2:28)

During the reign of Emperor Shōmu, there was a woman living in the village west of Daian-ji in the capital of Nara. She was extremely poor, having nothing with which to sustain life and, in fact, was starving.

Having heard that the Sixteen-Foot Buddha of Daian-ji responded to the vows of the community, she went as quickly as possible to present her pleas. She brought flowers, incense, and lamp oil and presented them before the Buddha, voicing her pleas, saying, "I did not plant the seeds of good fortune in my past existence, and hence I am rewarded with extreme poverty now in my present one. Therefore, please grant me some wealth so that I may escape my dire want!" Such were her prayers day after day, month after month.

Once, she went as usual to pray for good fortune, offering flowers, incense, and oil, and then returned home to sleep. The next morning when she got up and looked, she found four *kan* of coins by the gate bridge.[47] There was a note attached that said, "This money is from the Dai-shutaraku fund of Daian-ji."[48] The woman, frightened, sent the money back to the temple immediately. The monks of the Dai-shutaraku group checked the treasury and found that the seal had not been broken but that four *kan* of coins were missing. So they put them back in the safe.

The woman then went to pray to the Sixteen-Foot Buddha as before, offering flowers, incense, and oil, and then went back home to sleep. The following day, when she got up and looked in the garden, there were four

---

47. One *kan* is a monetary unit consisting of one thousand *mon* or coins.
48. At Daian-ji, there were five seminar groups: Shutara, Sanron, Betsusanron, Ritsu, and Shōron. Each had its own office, treasury, and officers.

kan of coins there, along with a note saying, "These are from the Daian-ji Jō-shutaraku fund." The woman took them back to the temple.

When the monks in charge of the fund checked, they found that it had not been opened, but when they opened it, it was missing exactly four *kan* of coins. Wondering, they sealed it again.

As had been her practice, the woman once more went to pray for good fortune, and then returned home to sleep. The next day when she awoke, she found four *kan* of coins on her threshold, with a note attached to it saying, "This is money from the Jōjitsuron seminar of Daian-ji."

When she returned the money to the temple, the monks of the seminar, checking their fund, found no sign that anything had been touched, but when they opened it, they discovered that four *kan* of coins were missing.

The monks in charge of all five seminars' funds got together, wondering, and questioned the woman, saying, "What did you do?" She replied, "I did not do anything. But as I was very poor and had no money to live on, nowhere to turn, no one to look to, I came to this temple; offered flowers, incense, and oil; and prayed to the Sixteen-Foot Buddha for a share of good fortune."

The community of monks, hearing this, pondered and then announced, "This is money that the Buddha has granted to her. Therefore, we will not continue to withhold it." Accordingly, they gave her the money. She used the four *kan* of coins as a means to advance in the world, becoming very wealthy, living in ease, and enjoying a long life.

Truly we know that this was a demonstration of the wonderful power of the Sixteen-Foot Buddha and the sincerity of the woman. It was a miraculous affair.

On How the Most Venerable Gyōgi Used His Divine Insight to Examine a Woman's Hair and Scold Her for Applying Animal Oil (2:29)

In the village of Gangō-ji in the old capital,[49] there was once held a splendid Dharma meeting at which, before the gathering of monks and lay members, the Most Venerable Gyōgi was invited to preach for seven days. Among those assembled to listen to the preaching of the Law was a young woman whose hair had been smeared with animal oil. When the Most Venerable Gyōgi saw her, he spoke admonishingly, saying, "This smell is highly offensive to me. Her hair smells of blood! Take her far away from here!" The woman was greatly astonished and left the congregation.

We ordinary mortals with our human eyes see only the color of the oil. But a saint with his penetrating eyesight can see the actual blood of the animal. This was the work of a sage who, a manifestation of the Buddha body, appeared in Japan. It was the Buddha in disguise!

On the Most Venerable Gyōgi Examining the Child of a Woman, Perceiving That It Was an Enemy from Past Ages, and Recommending That She Throw It Away, Resulting in an Extraordinary Sign (2:30)

The Most Venerable Monk Gyōgi opened up the Naniwa River Canal, set up ferry crossings, preached the Way, and converted people. Monks and laymen, eminent and humble, all gathered about him to listen to the

---

49. That is, in the period before the meeting moved to the capital at Nara.

Dharma. On one such occasion in the province of Kawachi, the district of Wakae, in the village of Kawamata, there was a woman who, carrying her child in her arms, went to take part in the religious meeting and listen to the Dharma. But the child began to wail and complain, so she could not hear the sermon. The child was already more than ten years old but had never learned to walk and did nothing all day but wail and scold, suck the mother's milk, and eat.

The Most Venerable Monk Gyōgi addressed the woman, saying, "Fie, young lady! You must take your child and throw it in the depths of the river!" When the crowd heard this, they put their heads together and began to whisper, saying, "The holy man is usually so compassionate— what possible reason would he have for making a pronouncement like that!" The woman, being of a loving nature, did not throw away the child but continued to hold it in her arms and listen to the sermon.

The following day, she came once more with the child in her arms to hear the Dharma, but this time the child wailed so vociferously that the entire crowd was prevented from hearing the sermon. The Most Venerable Monk Gyōgi berated the woman, saying, "Throw that child in the river!" The woman began to grow suspicious and, unable to put her doubts out of her mind, finally threw the child into the deepest part of the river. The child floated to the surface of the water, where it kicked its feet, flailed its arms, glared with wide staring eyes, and said in a tone of great disappointment, "What a pity! I wanted to keep on eating off you for three years more!"

The mother, more suspicious than ever, returned to the meeting to listen to the Dharma. "Have you thrown the child away?" the Most Venerable Gyōgi asked. The woman, in reply, told him all that had happened. "In a past existence," he explained to her, "you borrowed something from that person and failed to pay it back, and so the person took on the form of a child and was trying to get back at you by eating so much. That child was none other than the owner of the goods!"

Alas, how shameful for the woman! One should never die without paying back one's debts to others, for if one does, one will surely meet with some reprisal in a future existence.

Truly it says in the Shutchō-gyō: "Because of a penny's worth of salt owed to the driver, he was reborn as an ox and driven hard to repay that debt to the driver."[50] This refers to the same kind of thing.

On the Birth of a Girl with *Shari* in Her Hand, Owing to Her Parents' Vow to Build a Pagoda (2:31)

Niu no atai Otokami was a man of the Iwata district of Tōtōmi province. He made a vow to build a pagoda, but a number of years had gone by and he still had not done so. He always looked on this with regret.

In the reign of Emperor Shōmu, Otokami, who was seventy years old, and his wife, who was sixty-two, gave birth to a girl baby. At the time of birth, her left hand was clenched tight. Her father and mother, lamenting, wondering at this, tried to make her unclench her fist, but it was clenched tight and refused to open. Her father and mother, lamenting, said, "It is a shame that, at a wholly unlucky time, a defective child is born to us. We regard it as a source of great regret. But the karmic conditions were such, and therefore we gave birth to you." They therefore did not neglect her, but raised her with loving care.

She grew into a very handsome child, and when she was seven years old, her hand unfolded and she showed it to her mother, exclaiming, "Look at this!" In the palm of her hand were two *shari*.[51] In joy and wonder, the mother relayed the news to all the people around. Soon the rejoicing had spread until it reached to the government officials. The local

---

50. This is not an exact quotation but a summary of a passage in the Shutchō-gyō. See *Taishō* 6:425. The passage tells of two brothers, one who chose to become an arhat, and the other, to remain a layman who would never listen to his brother's preaching. Once, the arhat met his brother, who had been reborn as an ox and loaded with a burden. The arhat told the driver of the ox that his brother had been reborn as an ox because of his debt of salt to the driver.

51. *Shari*, from the Sanskrit *śarira*, refers to relics of the Buddha's body, which were believed to be the source of miraculous power.

officials, all delighting, banded together to form a group and proceeded to build a seven-story pagoda and place the two *shari* in it for proper recognition. This is the pagoda of Iwata Temple, which stands now in Iwata district. After the pagoda had been built, the child suddenly died.

Truly we know that no vow is ever left unfulfilled. Once the vow has been made, it will surely be fulfilled. This is what it means.

On Borrowing Money from the Temple Rice-Wine Fund, Failing to Repay It, and Being Reborn as an Ox as a Result (2:32)

In the reign of Emperor Shōmu, villagers of Mikami in the Nagusa district of Kii province organized a devotees' association to rotate the fund of Yakuō-ji (now called Seta Temple). At the home of Okada no suguri Obame, this medical fund was used to earn profits in a brewery.[52]

One day, a spotted calf came onto the grounds of Yakuō-ji and lay down at the base of the pagoda. The men of the temple chased it away, but it came back again and lay down, refusing to be shooed away. The men, wondering at this, said, "Who does this calf belong to?" But no one admitted that it was his. The monks then caught it, tied it up, and proceeded to raise it. In time, it grew big and was driven into the fields and used in the temple work.

When five years had gone by, Okada no suguri Iwahito, a patron of that temple, had a dream. He said, "I dreamed that that calf chased me, butted me over, and trampled me with its feet. I was frightened and cried out. The calf then said to me, 'Do you know who I am?' I answered, 'No, I don't.' The calf then released me, stepped back, and in tears said to me, 'I am Mononobe no Maro of the village of Sakura.' (He was popularly called Shiozuki. When he was alive, he shot at a boar and thought that

---

52. The temple made loans of rice and had people brew rice wine, which was lent again to gain interest for medical expenses.

he had made a hit, though in fact he had missed. However, thinking that he had made a hit, he ground salt and took it to the spot,[53] to find not a boar but only an arrow stuck in the ground. The villagers laughed at him and called him *shiozuki* [ground salt], which became his popular name.) 'In my previous existence I borrowed ten gallons of rice wine from the medical fund of the temple, but died without ever repaying it. Therefore, in my present existence I have been reborn as an ox and am driven hard to pay for my debt. The date of my service was set at eight years. I have already served for five years, so that leaves three years still to go. The temple people are merciless, beating me on the back and driving me on, and I have suffered greatly. But you are not without pity like the others, and so I am telling you this.'

"Iwahito asked, 'How can I tell if your story is true?' The ox replied, 'Please ask Big Sister of Sakura village if it is true or not.'" (Ōomine [Big Sister] was Iwahito's younger sister, a woman who was in charge of the rice-wine brewery.)

Wondering all the while, Iwahito visited his younger sister and related the details. She replied, "It's just as he said. He borrowed ten gallons of rice wine from the fund but died without ever repaying it."

When Jōdachi, a monk in charge of the temple household, and other patrons of the temple heard the story, they recognized that it was based on the law of causality. Their hearts overflowed with pity. They arranged for sutras to be read on his behalf. After eight years had passed and its term of service had ended, the ox disappeared and no one knew what became of it.

Hence we know that debts must be repaid, or there will be a penalty. Dare we forget that? Therefore, it says in the *Jōjitsuron*: "Those who borrow things and do not repay them will in their next existence fall among oxen, sheep, *kujika* deer, donkeys, horses, and such like. Such will be the reward for their deeds."[54] This is what it means.

---

53. Salt was used to cure the boar's flesh.
54. Harivarmin, *Jōjitsu-ron* (*Treatise on the Establishment of Truth*), chap. 6. See *Taishō* 32:301.

On a Woman Devoured by an Evil Demon (2:33)

During the reign of Emperor Shōmu, a popular song spread all over the country:

> Who asked you to be a bride,
> Yorozu-no-ko of Amuchi-no komuchi?
> *Namu, namu.*
> Mountain ascetics chanting formulas,
> Bring us wine
> Lots and lots of it![55]

At that time, there was a wealthy man who lived in the eastern part of the village of Amuchi in the Tōchi district of Yamato province. His surname was Kagamitsukuri no miyatsuko. He had a daughter named Yorozu-no-ko. She was unmarried, a virgin, and of beautiful appearance. But although men of high rank proposed to her, she refused them all, and so the years went by.

There was one man who repeatedly sent presents, including three wagonloads of dyed goods. Seeing these, her heart was moved and she agreed to be friendly with him. Eventually she accepted his proposal, and they entered the bedroom and became husband and wife.

That night, there was a voice heard from the bedroom, saying three times over, "It hurts!" Her father and mother, hearing this, talked it over, but said, "It hurts because she's not used to it yet!" They decided to ignore it and went back to sleep.

The next day at dawn, the mother knocked on the door but surprisingly got no answer. Wondering at this, she opened the door—to find only the woman's skull and the bones of one finger remaining, all the

---

55. The interpretation of the song, particularly the latter part, is highly tentative.

rest of her having been eaten. Her father and mother stared, shocked and grieved at what they saw. When they looked at the dyed goods sent to the bride, they found them all turned into animal bones, and the three wagons that had brought them had changed into silverberry wood. People from all quarters, learning of what had happened, gathered around to stare, and there were none who were not filled with wonder. Her skull was placed in a beautiful Korean box and put in front of the Three Treasures of Buddhism, where on the first of the seventh-day mornings it was served a vegetarian feast.

We suspect, therefore, that an omen must have preceded the calamity. The song was the omen. Some say that it was the mysterious work of a deity, while others say that she fell foul of a demon. On reflection, however, we know that this was payment for some deed in her past. This was a miraculous event.

On an Orphan Girl Who Paid Respects to a Bronze Statue of Kannon and Received Recompense in a Miraculous Manner (2:34)

In a village near the Uetsuki Temple in the western sector of the capital of Nara there lived an orphan girl who was as yet unmarried; her family and given names are unknown. When her father and mother were alive, the family possessed great wealth, built numerous houses and storerooms, and cast a bronze image of Bodhisattva Kannon, two feet five inches in height, erecting a sanctuary some distance from the main house in which the statue was enshrined and worshipped. But in the time of Emperor Shōmu, the young woman's parents passed away, the servants ran off, and the horses and oxen died. The former wealth vanished, the household was reduced to poverty, and the young woman, all alone in her empty mansion, did nothing but sigh and shed sorrowful tears day and night. Hearing that pleas addressed to Bodhisattva Kannon were likely to be answered, she tied a cord to the arm of the bronze statue, and, taking it in her hand and making offerings of flowers, incense, and lamps, she prayed for good fortune, saying, "I am an only child, an orphan without father or mother, living alone in a poor house without wealth or means to support myself. I pray you to grant me a happy lot! Grant it quickly, send it soon!" she said, weeping and imploring day and night.

In the same village, there lived a rich man who had lost his wife. Seeing the girl, he dispatched a matchmaker to arrange for her to become his bride. But the girl said to the matchmaker, "I am now impoverished and do not have so much as a cloak to cover my naked body! Where would I get a veil for my face so that I could appear before him and speak in his presence?"

The matchmaker returned and reported this to the man, who, on hearing it, replied, "I am perfectly aware that she is poor and has no proper clothes. But will she marry me or not?" The matchmaker conveyed his words to the girl. She persisted in her refusals, but the man went and forced his way into the house, coaxing her until her heart softened and she consented to sleep with him.

The following day, it rained, and the rain continued so that the man was unable to return to his own home and had to remain at the young woman's house for three days. Growing very hungry, he said, "I'm starving! Bring me something to eat!"

"I will prepare something at once," his bride replied. She built a fire in the stove, set the empty rice steamer on it, and crouched beside it, pressing her hands to her cheeks; she wandered this way and that through the empty rooms, sighing loudly. Then she rinsed her mouth, washed her hands, went to the statue, wept, and said, "Do not let me be put to shame! Send me some wealth right away!" When she had finished speaking, she left the sanctuary and returned to the kitchen, squatting before the empty stove as before, her hands pressed to her cheeks.

The same day, around four in the afternoon, there was a sudden rapping at the gate and the voice of someone calling. When the young woman went to see who it was, she found the wet nurse from the rich family next door. The nurse was carrying a large wooden box filled with a hundred different things to eat and drink, every conceivable delicious flavor and aroma, all in vessels of metal or lacquer. Handing the box to the young woman, she said, "We heard that you had a guest, and so the mistress next door fixed these things to bring to you. Just be good enough to return the dishes when you're finished."

The young woman was delighted beyond measure, and, her heart overflowing with gratitude, she took off the black cloak she was wearing and gave it to the nurse, saying, "I have nothing but this grimy cloak to offer, but I hope you will be kind enough to accept it." The nurse took the cloak, put it on, and hurried off home. When the young woman served the dishes to her husband, he looked at the food in astonishment and then, taking his eyes from the food, stared at the face of his bride.

The following day, the man took his leave and later sent his wife ten bolts of silk and ten bales of rice, saying, "Sew the silk into robes as soon as you can and quickly make some wine from the rice." The young woman went to the rich house next door to tell them of the happiness in her heart and express her thanks and respect, but the mistress of the house said, "Have you gone mad, child, or are you perhaps possessed by devils? I have no idea what you are talking about!" The nurse added, "Neither have I!"

Scolded thus, the young woman returned to her house and, as was her custom, went to the sanctuary to pay her respects. There she saw the black cloak that she had given to the nurse draped over the bronze statue, and for the first time realized that it was Kannon who had aided her. As a result, she came to believe in the law of karmic retribution and, doubling her devotions, treated the statue with even greater respect and reverence than before. Thereafter, she regained the wealth that her family had once possessed and was freed from hunger and fret. She and her husband, spared from illness, lived in health to a great old age.

This, indeed, was a wondrous affair.

On Hitting a Monk and Incurring the Immediate Penalty of Death (2:35)

Prince Uji was innately evil and put no faith in the Three Treasures of Buddhism. During the reign of Emperor Shōmu, this prince happened to be traveling through Yamashiro, accompanied by eight men, on his way to Nara. It chanced that the monk Taikyō of the Shimotsuke Temple was traveling on foot from Nara to Yamashiro, and was passing through the district of Tsuzuki. He chanced to come upon the prince so suddenly that there was no place for him to move out of the way. He lowered his hat, hiding his face, and stood at the side of the road.[56] Seeing this, the prince halted his horse and prepared to administer punishment. Although the monk and his attendants ran into the rice paddies to escape, the men followed them there, administering blows, and broke open the sutra boxes they were carrying and scattered the contents. Seeing this, Taikyō cried out, "Is there no protection for the Dharma?"

The prince had not had time to proceed far on his way when he was suddenly seized by a serious illness. He let out a loud cry and leaped two or three feet off the ground. His attendants, observing the prince's distress, begged the monk Taikyō to lend his aid, but he refused. Two or three times they repeated their request, all in vain. "Is he in pain?" asked the monk. "Yes, very great pain!" was the answer. To which the monk said, "Let the miserable prince suffer a thousand times, ten thousand times the pain!"

At that time, the relatives of the prince submitted a report to the emperor, stating, "Monk Taikyō has put a curse on Prince Uji. He should be seized and put to death!" But the emperor did not allow this to happen.

56. According to article 19 of the Sōni-ryō (Articles for Monks and Nuns), monks and nuns are equal to persons of the Sixth Rank. When meeting with someone of the Fifth Rank or higher, if mounted, they are to dismount, salute, and retire; if on foot, they are to retire. Since the prince belonged to the Fifth Rank, a rank higher than the monk Taikyō, who was on foot, Taikō was required to retire or hide himself.

Three days later, Prince Uji died, his body turning as black as ink. Once more, the relatives appealed to the emperor, saying, "One suffered death, so the other must die! Since Prince Uji is already dead, Taikyō should be arrested and pay the penalty of death!" But the emperor issued a decree, saying, "I am a monk, and Taikyō is a monk. How can a monk inflict death on a monk? Taikyō is not responsible for the disaster that befell Prince Uji." The emperor himself had shaved his head, received the precepts, and become a follower of the Way. Therefore, he showed special favor and refused to kill Taikyō.[57]

The insane Prince Uji was extremely evil in nature and was punished by the guardian of the Dharma. The guardian of the Dharma is ever at hand. How can you not believe this?

On the Wooden Image of Kannon That Revealed Godlike Power (2:36)

In the reign of Retired Emperor Shōmu,[58] the head of the image of Kannon, the attendant image on the east side of the Amida in the Shimotsuke Temple in the capital of Nara, fell off for no apparent reason.

The patron of the temple, observing this, decided that he would repair it on the following day and, meanwhile, left it as it was for a day and a night. On the morning of the following day, however, when he looked, he found that the head had returned to its original position on its own. Not only that, but now it gave off a light.

Truly we know that the Dharma body of wisdom always exists.[59] This is a miraculous sign to bring the unbelieving to a realization of this.

---

57. Emperor Shōmu received the Mahayana bodhisattva precepts from the Chinese Buddhist monk Ganjin (Jianzhen, 688–763) and retired from the throne in 749.
58. The meaning is the same as "In the reign of Emperor Shōmu."
59. The *dharmakāya*, or world of the Dharma as the embodiment of truth and wisdom.

✳

ON A WOODEN IMAGE OF KANNON
THAT SURVIVED FIRE AND REVEALED
GODLIKE POWER (2:37)

In the reign of Emperor Shōmu, in the Izumi district of Izumi province, in a mountain temple, there was a wooden image of Bodhisattva Shōkanjizai that was enshrined and venerated.[60] Once, a fire broke out and consumed the entire hall. But the wooden image of this bodhisattva moved about thirty steps out of the burning hall, and then lay down without sustaining any damage.

Truly we know that the Three Treasures of Buddhism, although they have no visible form or mind and cannot be seen by the eye, yet possess divine power. This is the first of all wonders!

✳

ON REBIRTH AS A HUGE SNAKE
BECAUSE OF AVARICE (2:38)

In the reign of Emperor Shōmu, there was a monk who always lived in a mountain temple in Maniwa in the capital of Nara. When he was on the verge of death, he said to his disciples, "After I die, you must not open the door to my room until three years have passed!"

But after he died, when only seven times seven days had gone by, a huge snake appeared, lying at the door to the room. The disciples, knowing the reason it had come, obtained its permission and then opened the door. They found thirty *kan* of coins that had been secretly stored away there. They took the money, used it to commission the recitation of sutras, practiced good, and secured great benefit for the dead man.

---

60. Bodhisattva Shōkanjizai is the Kannon of the Lotus Sutra and many other Mahayana sutras, in contrast to various Tantric variations of Kannon.

Truly we know that, because of his deep attachment to his store of hidden money, he was reborn in the form of a huge snake that had come to guard it. There is a saying, "Even though you may see the top of Mount Sumeru,[61] you cannot see the top of Mount Desire!" This is what it refers to.

ON THE WOODEN IMAGE OF YAKUSHI BUDDHA, WASHED AWAY IN WATER AND BURIED IN SAND, THAT SHOWED AN EXTRAORDINARY SIGN (2:39)

Between Suruga province and Tōtōmi province, there flows a river called Ōigawa. Beside the river is the village of Uda, which is in the Harihara district of Tōtōmi province. In the second year of the Tenpyō hōji era of the reign of Emperor Ōhi [Junnin, r. 758–764], who reigned at the Nara Palace, the year *tsuchinoe-inu* [758], in the spring, the Third Month, a voice was heard coming from the sand on the beach at the village of Uda, crying, "Get me out! Get me out!"

At that time, a monk was traveling through Tōtōmi province, and when he passed the spot he heard these ceaseless cries of "Get me out!" He responded to the cries from the sand, and, supposing that some dead person buried there had come back to life, he dug down to see. He found a wooden statue of Yakushi Buddha,[62] six feet five inches in length, with both ears missing. Weeping, he paid homage to it, saying, "My Great Master, what caused you to fall victim to the flood? Since I have been destined by karma to find you, please allow me to repair you."

He invited his friends to join him, enlisted a sculptor to make a new pair of ears, and installed the statue in a hall in the village of Uda, where it was properly venerated. This is what is now called Uda Hall. This statue of the Buddha gave miraculous signs, giving off light and responding to the requests of those who appealed to it.

---

61. Sumeru is the lofty mountain that stands at the center of the Buddhist universe.
62. Yakushi Buddha is Bhaiṣajyaguru, or the Medicine Master Buddha.

In this respect, it resembles the sandalwood statue made by Uten,[63] which stood up to pay homage to Buddha, or the wooden image of Ding Lan's mother,[64] which was said to have moved as though alive. This is what it means.

On an Evil-Loving Man Who Got an Immediate Penalty, Being Killed by Sharp Swords and Suffering an Evil Death (2:40)

Tachibana no asomi Naramaro was a son of Prince Kazuraki [d. 757]. With overweening ambition, he plotted to usurp the throne, gathering around him a band of disaffected persons for that purpose. He had a monk's figure painted and used it as a target, trying to shoot out its eyes. He loved to do evil deeds, none more evil than this.

Once a lackey of Naramaro went to the Nara Hills with a hawk to hunt birds. Finding many foxes there, he caught one and skewered it with a stick, leaving it stuck in the ground at the opening to the fox hole.

This man had a baby child. The mother fox, seeking revenge, changed herself into the likeness of the baby's grandmother. Taking the baby in her arms, she carried it to the entrance to the fox hole, where she threaded it on a skewer. She left it stuck at the entrance to the hole as the man had done to her child.

Even humble animals know how to take revenge for an evil deed! Immediate penalty lies close at hand. You must never do heartless acts, for if you do, you will call down heartless punishment. Not long after, Naramaro roused the ire of the emperor and suffered the extreme penalty.

Thus we know that the death inflicted earlier on the baby was an omen of the fate that awaited Naramaro. This, too, was a miraculous event!

---

63. Uten is Udayana, king of Kushan and patron of Buddhism.
64. *Shokyō yōshū* 15. See *Taishō* 54:74.

ON A WOMAN WHO WAS VIOLATED BY A LARGE SNAKE BUT SURVIVED, DUE TO THE POWER OF DRUGS (2:41)

In the village of Umakai in the Sarara district of Kawachi province, there lived a daughter of a wealthy family. In Emperor Ōhi's reign, in the third year of the Tenpyō hōji era, in the summer, the Fourth Month of the year *tsuchinoto-i* [759], the girl climbed a mulberry tree in order to pick the leaves. A large snake crawled up the tree after her. A passerby, seeing this, warned her, whereupon, frightened, she fell to the ground. The snake, too, fell to the ground and, taking advantage of her unconscious state, entered her vagina.

Her father and mother, seeing this, sent for a doctor and, placing her on some bedding, with the snake inside her, brought her home. There the doctor burned three sheaves (this means a bundle three feet high) of millet stalks and put the ashes into hot water to get fourteen gallons of liquid. This he then boiled down to nine gallons and added ten bunches of chopped boar's hair. Then the people hung her on stakes by her head and two feet, and poured the mixture into the vaginal opening. When they had poured in five gallons of the brew, the snake came out and was killed and thrown away. The snake's eggs were white, like frogs' eggs, and had boar's hair stuck to them. About two and a half gallons of them came out of her opening. By the time the people had poured in nine gallons of brew, all the snakes' eggs had come out.

The girl, who had fainted, woke up and began to speak. Replying to her parents' inquiries, she said, "I felt as though I were dreaming, but now I am awake and all right." Since drugs can have an effect like this, we cannot but be cautious in their use. As for the girl, three years later she was again violated by a snake and died.

If there is deep affection between husband and wife or between parents and their child, when the time for death comes, one will speak in a loving way, saying, "When I die, I know we will be together again in a future life!" But the spirit of that person, following the dictates of karmic causality, may in fact be reborn as a snake or a horse, a cow, a dog, or a bird. If the conditions are unfavorable, one may be loved by a snake or may be reborn as a mere creature. Love and affection do not ensure a favorable form of rebirth.

A sutra describes it like this: "Long ago, when the Buddha and Ānanda were walking through a graveyard, a man and his wife were presenting offerings of food and drink at a tomb and bewailing the dead. The man was lamenting the loss of his mother, while the wife was bewailing the death of a little child. The Buddha, hearing the cries of the wife, joined in the sound of lamentation. Ānanda asked him, 'Why are you lamenting?' The Buddha replied to Ānanda, 'This woman in a previous existence bore a male child whom she dearly loved. She was so attached to him that she kissed his penis. After three years, she suddenly contracted a disease. As she was dying, she caressed him, kissing his penis and saying, "In my future existences, I will always be born with you!" She was reborn as the daughter of a neighbor and eventually became the wife of her own son. She is now lamenting over the ashes of her husband. Since I understand the chain of causation that brings these things about, I am lamenting.'"65 This is what the passage means.

And in another sutra it is written: "Long ago, there was a child who was very light in body and could run as fast as a flying bird. His father constantly loved and cared for him, as though he were his own pair of eyes. Once, observing the child's agility, he exclaimed, 'Excellent, my son! You are as swift as a fox!' Then the child died and later was reborn as a fox. You should think only of good analogies! For if you think of bad ones, your words may come true."66

65. The source of this quotation has not been identified.
66. The source of this quotation has not been identified.

On an Extremely Poor Woman
Who Implored the Thousand-Armed
Kannon, Asking for Aid, and Received
Great Good Fortune (2:42)

Amanotsukai Minome lived at the juncture of Ninth Street and Second Avenue on the East Side of the capital of Nara. She had given birth to nine children and, being extremely poor and having no means to support them, was having great difficulties. She had been praying for nearly a year to the Thousand-Armed Kannon of Hozumi Temple for a share of good fortune.[67]

In the reign of Emperor Ōhi, in the seventh year of the Tenpyō hōji era, in the winter, on the tenth day of the Tenth Month of the year *mizunoto-u* [763], quite unexpectedly her younger sister happened to visit her and left a chest made of leather. Its legs were soiled with horse manure. Her sister said, "I will come again soon. Meanwhile, would you please keep this for me?" But the sister did not come again. The woman asked her younger brother about it, but he said, "I know nothing of the matter!"

Wondering what was in it, she opened it and found that it contained a hundred *kan* in coins. When, as usual, she bought flowers and incense and oil and went to pay her respects to the Thousand-Armed Kannon, she noticed that its feet were soiled with horse manure. Then she began to wonder if the chest had not been a gift from the bodhisattva. Three years later, it was discovered that the sum of a hundred *kan* in cash was missing from the construction fund donated to the Thousand-Armed Kannon. Thus it became evident that the money had been the work of Kannon.

67. The Thousand-Armed Kannon has forty arms in addition to the regular two, each with twenty-five spheres of existence; hence the figure of one thousand.

In appraisal we say: How good was the longtime mother of the Amanotsukai family! In the morning, looking at her starving children, she wept tears of blood, while in the evening she burned incense and lights, imploring Kannon's aid. In response, she was given money, putting an end to the trials of poverty. She was blessed with the enjoyment of the holy one's favor, a font of riches that flowed down to her. She was given all that was needed to raise her children, and when the clothes were removed,[68] its source became known. She loved her children and brought them good fortune; buying incense truly had its merits.

As the Nirvana Sutra puts it, "The mother loved her children and she was therefore reborn in the Brahma Heaven."[69] This is what it means. This was a miraculous happening!

---

68. The "clothes" refer to the cloth covering the feet of the statue.
69. The Heaven of the god Brahma is the lowest of the four *dhyana* (meditation) heavens.

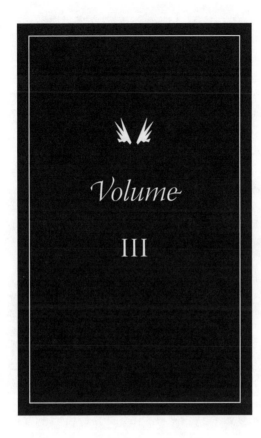

Volume

III

The root causes of good and evil are revealed in the scriptures of Buddhism, while the workings of good luck and bad are recorded in the outer writings, those of a non-Buddhist nature. Studying all the teachings of Śākyamuni made in the course of his lifetime, we learn that these fall into three periods. First is the 500 years of the Correct Law, second is the 1,000 years of the Counterfeit Law, and third is the 10,000 years of the Latter Day of the Law. Since the date when the Buddha entered nirvana, 1,722 years have elapsed by the time we come to the sixth year of the Enryaku era, the year with the cyclical sign *hinoto-u* [787]. The two periods of the Correct Law and the Counterfeit Law have already passed, and we have entered that of the Latter Day of the Law. From the time when Buddhism was first introduced to Japan up to the sixth year of the Enryaku era is a period of 236 years.[1]

Flowers bloom, but they have no voice; cocks crow, but they have no tears.[2] If we observe the age, we see that those who practice good are as rare as blossoms on a rocky peak, while those who do evil are like the grasses on a fertile hill. Without consideration for the law of karmic retribution, people commit sins. Enticed by fame, gain, and killing, they

---

1. Kyōkai, or whoever wrote this section of the text, evidently accepted 552 as the date when Buddhism first entered Japan.
2. That is, things no longer follow their natural order.

are doubtful of the consequences (like blind men stepping on a tiger's tail and ignoring the consequences, or like devils entwined with poisonous snakes but thinking to be free from harm). But to those who do evil, recompense comes as inevitably as a mirror of water reflects a form. And to the power of goodness, the return is as sure as the echo from a valley. Such is the immediate response that these acts engender. How, then, can we fail to act with caution? If we pass this life in vain, it is useless to repent afterward. Since our lifetime is limited, who can challenge its limitations? How can we count on anything as frail as one mortal being? Already we have entered the final age—what can we do but practice good?

Alas, alas, how can we escape the fate that goes with the age? But if one donates as much as one meal to the congregation of monks, one will elicit the good fortune of practicing alms giving and escape the fate of encountering starvation. And if for one day one observes the injunction to avoid taking life, one can wield the power of the Way in combat with the force of this baleful age and never meet with harm in the shape of its swords or arms.[3]

Once there was a monk who lived on a mountain and practiced meditation. Whenever he ate his frugal meal, he would set aside a portion of it to feed to a crow. The crow would always peck at it, coming each day to get its share. After finishing his vegetarian fare, the monk would pick his teeth, rinse out his mouth, wash his hands, and then play with a stone. The crow would go over to the other side of the hedge. Once this monk, unaware that the crow was on the other side of the hedge, threw the stone and hit the crow in the head. The stone crushed its skull, and it died and was reborn as a boar. The boar, living in that mountain, went to the area above the monk's cell, rooting among the stones and searching for food. It happened to dislodge one of the stones, which rolled down on the monk and struck and killed him. The boar had no intention of

---

3. The opening section, down to the words "swords or arms," is found only in the Maeda manuscript of the preface, which has led many commentators to question whether it is by Kyōkai or a later hand.

killing him—the stone just rolled down, hit him, and he died. When one commits a fault unintentionally, there is no penalty exacted. Why should there be? But if the killing is done with evil intention, how can there not be a penalty? An evil intention produces the fruit of a dire penalty, which is the product of a deluded mind, while good intentions lead to enlightenment, which is the goal of a striving mind.

I, the miserable monk Kyōkai, have not studied enough to rival the Learned One Tiantai.[4] My understanding does not grasp the subtleties known to holy and eloquent men. I am one who wields a mere seashell to dip up the ocean, who looks through a straw to measure the sky. Although I am not an expert who transmits the light of the Dharma, I do my best to meditate on such matters. The pure wheel tracks I follow as far as I am able; I hasten along the road toward the mind of understanding. I repent of my misdeeds committed long ago, and pray that I may gain the good after lengthy striving, depending, as it were, on a miracle. My aim has been to gather and transmit the stories told to me, to hasten the feet of those who are on the Way. My prayer is that they may quickly accomplish their journey and be reborn in the Western Paradise, leaving none of us behind, but all to dwell in the jeweled halls of Heaven.

4. The Learned One Tiantai is Zhiyi (538–597) of China, the founder of the Tiantai, or Tendai, school of Buddhism.

✳

On the Tongues of the Reciters of the Lotus Sutra That Did Not Decay, Although Exposed to the Elements (3:1)

In the reign of Empress Abe,[1] who ruled over the Eight Great Islands at the Nara Palace, there was a monk, Meditation Master Yōgō, in the village of Kumano in the Muro district of Kii province. The people of the time, highly esteeming his activities, honored him with the title of bodhisattva. And because he lived south of the imperial city, he was called the Bodhisattva of the South.

At that time, there was a meditation master who came to the bodhisattva's place, bringing with him a copy of the Lotus Sutra (it was written in very small characters in one scroll),[2] along with a pewter pitcher and a seating platform made of rope. He would constantly recite the Lotus Sutra, this being his main religious act.

After a year or more had passed, he prepared to take leave of Meditation Master Yōgō and, bowing in honor, presented him with the stool, saying, "I am leaving you to go into the mountains and cross over to the province of Ise." Hearing this, the master gave him one bushel of ground dry glutinous rice to take with him. And he assigned two lay brothers to accompany him and see him on his way. After having been escorted for a day, he gave them his Lotus Sutra, along with the bowl and ground dry rice, and sent them back. He continued on his way with only twenty yards of hemp rope and the pewter pitcher.

---

1. Empress Abe has two posthumous names: Empress Kōken (r. 749–758) and Shōtoku (r. 764–770). It is difficult to know whether this incident dates from her first or her second reign.
2. Throughout the stories, the text in parentheses is Kyōkai's explanations, comments, or interpretations.

After two years had passed, the villagers of Kumano, following the stream of the Kumano River, went up the mountains to cut trees in order to build a boat. Listening, they heard a voice reciting the Lotus Sutra. The voice did not stop, though the days grew into months. The boat builders, listening to the voice reciting the sutra, were moved in their hearts and felt faith arising. And with their rationed food as an offering, they looked everywhere, but could find no trace of the reciter. Although they prepared to leave, however, the voice reciting the sutra went on as before.

After half a year, they returned to the mountain to pick up their boat and, listening, found that the sutra recitation was still going on. Wondering at this, they reported to Meditation Master Yōgō. He, too, wondering, went and found that it was in fact quite true. Looking for the source, he discovered a corpse, its feet tied together with a hemp rope, hanging from a cliff—that of a man who had jumped to his death. Beside the body was a pewter pitcher. Thus he knew it was that of the meditation master who had left him. Viewing this, Yōgō lamented in sorrow and went back home.

After three years had passed, the villagers came to him, reporting that the sutra recitation constantly continued as before, never ceasing. Yōgō went to the mountain once more to collect the bones. Examining the skeleton, he found that, although three years had passed, the tongue was still alive and showed no sign of decay.

Truly we know that this came about through the mysterious power of the Mahayana sutra and the merits of the monk who recited it.

In appraisal we say: How noble of the meditation master to have used his flesh-and-blood body to constantly recite the Lotus Sutra, revealing the miraculous power of the Mahayana. Although he flung himself from the cliff, exposing his body to the elements, his tongue alone did not decay. This was a sacred happening, not an ordinary one!

～

Also, on Kane-no-mitake peak in Yoshino there was a meditation master who went around from peak to peak. Once, when he was preparing to go around, he heard a voice reciting the Lotus and Diamond sutras. He stopped to listen and, in searching the branches, found a skull. Although it had been exposed to the elements for a long time, its tongue had not decayed but was still alive. The meditation master placed it in a purified place, paying it honor and praying to the skull in these words, "Through the law of karmic causation, I have come upon you!" He fashioned a shelter for it out of grass, living beside it to recite the sutra and hold services six times a day. As he recited the Lotus Sutra, the skull joined in, reciting with him. When we observe the motion of its tongue, we know that this, too, was a miraculous happening!

ON KILLING LIVING CREATURES AND SUFFERING REVENGE, BEING REBORN AS A FOX AND A DOG, HATING EACH OTHER, AND INCURRING A PENALTY (3:2)

Meditation Master Yōgō was a monk of Kōfuku-ji on the East Side of the capital of Nara. His secular name showed that he belonged to the Ashiya-no-kimi or the Ichiyuki family. He came originally from the Teshima district of Settsu province, and lived in the village of Kumano in the Muro district of Kii province, observing a disciplined way of life.

Once, a sick man came to the temple where he lived, asking him to cure him of a disease. As long as he recited a sacred formula, the disease was cured, but when he stopped reciting, the disease would immediately return. Thus, strange as it was, many days passed but the disease was not cured. Vowing to gain success, Yōgō continued to chant the formula, whereupon the sufferer, possessed, said, "I am a fox, so it is useless to chant. Don't try to force me!" "Why?" Yōgō asked. The spirit answered, "He killed me in his previous life, and so I am taking revenge on him. If he eventually dies, he will be reborn as a dog and will kill me." Hearing this, Yōgō, surprised, tried to instruct him, but he would not cease and finally the patient died.

A year later, one of Yōgō's disciples lay sick in the same room where the man had died. At that time, a visitor tied up his dog at the master's room and came to see him. The dog barked and tried to break free from his leash. The master, wondering at this, said, "Set him free so we can tell what's the matter!" As soon as he was freed, he ran into the room where the sick disciple lay and came out with a fox in his mouth. Although the master tried to stop him, he would not stop but chewed the fox to death.

It was evident that the dead person had been reborn as a dog to take revenge on the fox. Ah—thus we can see that revenge knows no limits! Why do I say this? King Virūdhaka killed 99,900,000 persons of the Śākya tribe to revenge the past.[3] If one requites revenge with revenge, vengeance will never cease, but will go on like a rolling wheel. But if a man has forbearance, when he sees vengeance, he will react like our master and display mercy.

He will not seek vengeance, but will react with forbearance, for forbearance is the teacher of vengeance. Thus it is written in the scriptures: "If one had no respect for forbearance, one would think even of killing one's own mother!"[4] This is what it means.

ON A MONK WHO, DEVOTING HIMSELF TO AN ELEVEN-HEADED KANNON IMAGE, RECEIVED AN IMMEDIATE REWARD (3:3)

The monk Bensō was a clergyman of Daian-ji temple. He was innately eloquent and, acting as representative of the congregation, addressed the Buddha, gaining numerous devotees and expressing the wishes of the mass of believers.

---

3. King Virūdhaka was the son of King Prasenajit. While still a prince, he was humiliated at Kapilavastu, the city of the Śākya clan, because of his mother's low status. Later, when he became king, he took revenge by wiping out a large number of the members of the Śākya clan.
4. The source of this quotation has not been identified.

During the reign of Empress Abe, Bensō borrowed thirty *kan* from the Shutaraku fund of the temple for his private use and was unable to repay it. The official of the temple who handled such matters pressed for repayment, but he was unable to do so. He therefore went up to the mountain temple of Hatsuse to confront the image of the Eleven-Headed Kannon and ask for help. Taking the rope tied to the hand of the image in his own hand, he prayed, saying, "I have spent the money I borrowed from the Shutaraku fund of the temple, but I cannot repay it. Please give me some money!" He called the image by its name and pleaded his request, saying, "Please wait a moment. I am praying for the money now—it won't take long!"

At that time, Prince Fune,[5] acting out of righteous motives, had come to the mountain temple to hold a service. He heard Bensō's words as he held the robe tied to the image and repeated, "Please send money—send it quickly so I can return it!" He asked Bensō's disciple, "Why does the master say that?" The disciple explained the circumstances to him. Hearing the explanation, the prince handed over the money to repay the temple.

Truly we know that this was due to the great mercy of the bodhisattva and the deep faith of the master Bensō.

On a Monk Who Was Thrown into the Sea, but Was Saved from Drowning by Reciting a Mahayana Sutra (3:4)

In the capital of Nara, there was a fully qualified monk, whose family and personal names are unknown. This monk constantly recited a Mahayana sutra, but he lived as a secular person and lent money to support his wife and family. He had one daughter who was married and lived separately with her husband.

---

5. Prince Fune was a son of Prince Toneri and a grandson of Emperor Tenmu.

During the reign of Empress Abe, his son-in-law was appointed an official in Mutsu province. He accordingly borrowed twenty *kan* from his father-in-law to cover expenses and went off to his new post in the province. After a year and more had passed, he had repaid the principal but had not repaid the interest, which in the course of time had become as much as the principal. As the months and years went by, the father-in-law requested repayment. The son-in-law developed a secret hatred for him, thinking to himself that he would like to find some chance to kill him. The father-in-law, unaware of this, continued to press for repayment.

The young man then said to his father-in-law, "I would like to take you on a trip to Mutsu!" The father-in-law, agreeing with this, got on board a ship and set out for Mutsu. The son-in-law, plotting with the sailors to carry out his scheme, tied up his father-in-law's four limbs and threw him into the sea. Then, lying to his wife, he said, "Your father longed to see your face, and so I invited him to come along on the trip. But then the waves suddenly rose up, the ship sank into the sea, and your father, fine gentleman that he was, was washed away—there was no way to save him. In the end, he sank out of sight! I alone barely managed to escape." The daughter, hearing this, was deeply grieved, and said, "So there was no way to save my father! Without intending to, I've lost my treasure! Now I know that it would be easier to find a jewel on the bottom of the sea than to see him and gather up his bones! Alas, how pitiful!"

The father-in-law, meanwhile, sinking into the sea, thought to begin reciting his Mahayana sutra, whereupon the ocean waters opened around him and he crouched on the bottom without drowning. After two days and two nights had passed, another ship bound for Mutsu happened to sail by. When the sailors saw the tail end of a rope drifting on the sea, they stopped the ship, hauled on the rope, and pulled the man to the surface. In shape and color, he was just the same as usual. The men on the ship, greatly startled at this, asked him, saying, "Who are you?" He replied, "I am So-and-so. I met up with some robbers and was bound with a rope and thrown into the sea!" They continued to ask, saying,

"Master, what magic did you use to allow you to sink into the water and not drown?" He replied, "I always recite a great Mahayana sutra. And what happened is due to its wonderful spiritual powers!" But he did not reveal the name of his son-in-law. Then he said that he wanted to go to a port in Mutsu, and the sailors, complying with that, took him to Mutsu. Meanwhile, in Mutsu, the son-in-law held a service for his father-in-law and made offerings to the Three Treasures. The father-in-law, who had been wandering and begging for food there, happened to attend the service with a group of self-ordained monks. His face was covered when he came forward to receive his share. When the son-in-law in person held out his hands to dispense the food to the congregation of monks, the supposedly drowned father-in-law put out his hands to receive it. The son-in-law, his eyes staring, his face flushed, drew back in terror and tried to hide. But the father-in-law only smiled benignly, hiding all signs of anger, and in the end no reference was made to the evil deed. Thus although he had sunk into the sea and been surrounded by water, he did not drown, nor was he eaten by poisonous fish. He escaped with no harm to his body or life. Truly we know that this was due to the efficacy of the sutra and the protection of the various Buddhas.

In appraisal we say: How splendid! He did not show his anger, but was able to act with forgiveness. In fact, this was due to the vast mercy displayed by this reverend monk, a lofty act of forbearance. As it says in the Jō-agon-gyō: "To requite vengeance with vengeance is like trying to put out a fire with hay. But to requite vengeance with mercy is like putting out a fire with water."[6] This is what this refers to.

---

6. This is not in the Jō-agon-gyō, but in the Bonmō-kyō koshakki 3. See *Taishō shinshū daizōkyō* 40:712.

On How Bodhisattva Myōken Assumed
a Strange Form in Order to Detect
a Thief (3:5)

In the Asuka district of Kawachi province, there was a mountain temple in Shidehara. It was a place to offer lamps to Bodhisattva Myōken.[7] Every year, lamps were offered from the provinces around the capital.

In the reign of Empress Abe, the devotees' association held the usual celebration, offering lamps to the bodhisattva and making offerings of money and valuables to the monk in charge of the temple. At that time, his disciple stole five *kan* of the money for the offerings and hid it. Later the disciple went to get the money, but could not find it. All he found was a dead deer with an arrow in it. In order to carry away the deer, he went to the village of Inoe-dera near the town of Kawachi to get men to help him. When he led them to the spot, however, there was no deer to be seen, but only five *kan* in coins. In this way, the identity of the thief was made clear.

Thus we know that it was not a real deer, but a manifestation of the bodhisattva. This was a miraculous event!

On the Fish That a Meditation Master
Wanted to Eat, Which Turned into
the Lotus Sutra to Defend Him from
Popular Abuse (3:6)

On Mount Yoshino, there was a mountain temple called Amabe-no-mine. In the reign of Empress Abe, a fully qualified monk was living there who

---

7. Myōken originated in Chinese worship of the North Star, which was believed to control the lives and fortunes of people. In Japan, the cult was celebrated at both Buddhist temples and Shinto shrines.

was ardent in his actions and diligently followed the Way. But he was physically weak and lacking in strength, and when he could no longer move around freely, he conceived a desire to eat some fish, saying to his disciple, "I have a longing for fish. Get me some so I can replenish my strength!" Since his master had requested it, he went to the seacoast of Kii province, where he bought eight fresh gray mullet and, putting them in a small chest, returned with them.

On his way back, he happened to meet three familiar patrons of the temple. They asked, "What is that you are carrying?" The acolyte disciple answered, "This is the Lotus Sutra." But water leaked out of the chest, and it gave off an odor like that of fish. Laymen though they were, they knew that it was not the sutra. Presently, they reached the neighborhood of the market at Uchi in Yamato province. They all sat down to rest when the laymen pressed their inquiry, saying, "What you are carrying is not the sutra—it's fish!" The acolyte denied this, saying, "There is no fish—just the sutra!" But they forced him to open the chest. Unable to deny their request, he opened it. Inside were the eight scrolls of the Lotus Sutra.

Two of the patrons, awe-struck and wondering, went on their way. But there was one who, thinking to himself, "Strange—let's follow him and see!" secretly went along behind the acolyte. When the latter returned to the temple, he reported in detail to his master what had taken place. The master, hearing this, was at once both surprised and joyful, for he knew that Heaven had protected him. Thus when it came time to eat the fish, the patron, who had seen what had gone on, prostrated himself on the ground, stretching out his limbs, and said to the master, "Although you eat fish, when a holy man eats it, it turns into the Lotus Sutra! But because of my ignorant and deluded mind, I did not understand the law of causality, and needlessly accused you, causing you worry. Please forgive my sins! From now on, I will regard you as our great teacher, and will honor and serve you!" After that, he became a major supporter of the temple, serving the meditation master.

Truly we know that the master saved his life for the sake of the Dharma. As to food, although you might mix poison with it, it would still be as sweet as dew! Thus eating the flesh of fish is not a sin, since the flesh turns into a sutra and Heaven in approval sanctions the Way. This, too, was a miraculous event!

ON RECEIVING THE HELP OF A WOODEN KANNON AND NARROWLY ESCAPING THE KING'S PUNISHMENT (3:7)

Hasetsukaibe no atai Yamatsugu of the Senior Sixth Rank, Upper Grade, came from the village of Ogawa in the Tama district of Musashi province. His wife was of the Shirakabe family. Yamatsugu became a soldier and was sent to the frontier to fight against the hairy men.[8] While he was away, his wife, praying for her husband's safety, made a wooden image of Kannon and worshipped it with great devotion and reverence. When the husband returned, having escaped harm in his mission, he joined his wife in paying honor to it, only too delighted to do so, and continued for a number of years.

In the reign of Empress Abe, in the eighth year of the Tenpyō hōji era, the year with the cyclical sign *kinoe-tatsu* [764], in the Twelfth Month, Yamatsugu was involved in the rebellion of Ōmi Nakamaro and sentenced to death.[9] Thirteen men were sentenced, and twelve of them had already been executed by having their heads cut off.

Yamatsugu, greatly disturbed, had a strange vision. The wooden Kannon, which he had prayed to and honored, accused him, saying, "Ah, why do you linger in such a filthy land as this?" Then it raised its leg and encircled his body from the head on down.

---

8. The term "hairy men" refers to the indigenous people of northeastern Japan, who were ethnically different from those of the Yamato court.

9. The rebellion was led by Fujiwara no Nakamaro (716–764), known in later life by the name Emi no Oshikatsu, who joined Emperor Junnin against former Empress Kōken. After this event, Kōken was re-enthroned as Empress Shōtoku.

When he was ordered to stretch out his neck in preparation for his beheading, an imperial messenger suddenly appeared and said, "Is there someone here named Hasetsukaibe no atai Yamatsugu?" "Yes," was the reply. "He's about to be beheaded!" "Don't kill him!" said the messenger. "He's been ordered into exile instead!" Thus he was sent into exile in Shinano province.

Not long after, he was recalled from exile and appointed to the post of assistant governor of Tama district. But he retained on his neck the scar that remained from the time when he stretched it forth to receive the executioner's blade. That he escaped death and remained alive was due wholly to the help of Kannon. Therefore, if in addition to your own good works, you will believe and nourish a heart of faith, you will experience great joy. For you will be saved from all disasters!

On the Miraculous Appearance of Bodhisattva Miroku in Response to a Vow (3:8)

In the village of Tōe in the Sakata district of Ōmi province, there lived a wealthy man whose name is unknown. He made a vow to copy the Yuga-ron,[10] but although many years passed the vow was still unfulfilled. Finally, the man fell on hard times and lost his means of livelihood. He left home, abandoned his wife and family, and practiced the Buddhist Way, hoping for good luck. But when he thought of his unfulfilled vow, it was a constant weight on his mind.

In the reign of Empress Abe, in the second year of the Tenpyō jingo era, the year *hinoe-uma* [766], in the autumn, the Ninth Month, he had arrived at a mountain temple and was spending some time there. In its

---

10. The Yogācāra-bhumi (Discourse on the Stages of Concentration Practice), translated into Chinese by Xuanzang, is a major text of the Hossō, or Dharma Characteristics, school of Buddhism. See *Taishō* 30:no. 1579.

precincts there grew a bush that in its bark suddenly produced an image of Bodhisattva Miroku.[11] Seeing it, the man, now a Buddhist practitioner, viewed it with devotion and proceeded to circumambulate the bark and grieve over his unfulfilled vow.

Hearing of this, people gathered around to view the image. Some bound together sheaves of rice stalks as an offering, while others contributed money or clothing. With these offerings of wealth, he was able to complete the copying of the entire hundred scrolls of the Yuga-ron and hold a presentation ceremony. By this time, the image had already disappeared.

Truly we know that Miroku, dwelling on high in the Tuṣita Heaven,[12] responded to his vow and came down to the place where the man lived in the land of sufferings, to ensure that he would enjoy deep faith and good fortune. How can there be any doubt of it?

On King Yama Sending Out a Strange Order and Encouraging a Man to Do Good (3:9)

During the reign of Empress Abe, Fujiwara no asomi Hirotari was suddenly stricken with illness. In order to cure his sickness, in the second year of the Jingo keiun era [768], on the seventeenth day of the Second Month, he went to a mountain temple at Makihara in the Uda district of Yamato province to live and observe the eight precepts. He took up a brush, as though to practice his calligraphy, but leaned on his desk without moving until evening came. His attendant, thinking that he must have fallen asleep, shook him, trying to wake him, saying, "The sun has set now. Therefore, it is time to pay respects to the Buddha." But he did not wake. When the attendant struck him more forcefully, his hand

---

11. Also known as Maitreya, the deity is worshipped by the Hossō school of Buddhism.
12. Tuṣita is the fourth of the six Heavens of the world of desire, from which Maitreya will descend to Earth to teach the Law at the end of the world.

dropped the writing brush, his four limbs folded up, and he fell down lifeless. The attendant, assuming him to be dead, was greatly flurried, and hastened to his house to inform his family and relatives of his death. They knew nothing of the matter, but, receiving the news, began to make preparations for the funeral. After three days had passed, however, they went to the temple and found him restored to life.

In reply to their inquiries, he said, "There were men whose beards stood straight up, wearing red robes, clad in armor, and carrying swords and halberds. They called my name, Hirotari, and said, 'The Office has suddenly summoned you!' With halberds prodding me in the back, they forced me to accompany them. One man went in front of me, and two men came behind. Thus, with myself in the middle, they forced me to hurry along.

"Ahead of us was a deep river. The water was black as ink and stretched deep and quiet, not flowing along. A limb was placed in the middle of the stream, but its branches did not reach the sides of the stream. The man standing in front of me said, 'You must plunge into the stream. Do it by following in my footsteps!' I followed him across.

"In front of us on the road stood a tall building, gleaming and glittering. Its four sides were hidden by a curtain of beads, so I could not see the face of the person inside. One of the messengers ran inside and said to him, 'He has answered your summons!' In reply he said, 'Bring him in!'

"In response to the order, I went in. The curtain of beads was parted, and he said, 'Do you know the woman standing behind you?' When I turned and looked, I saw that it was my wife, who had died in giving birth to my child. I replied, 'Yes—this is my wife.' Then he spoke again, saying, 'It is because of this woman's grievance that I have summoned you. She has been condemned to suffer for six years. She has already spent three years here and has three years to go. Now she has implored me, saying that when she bore your child, it died in infancy. Therefore, she wishes to share the rest of her suffering along with you.'

"I answered, 'For her sake, I will copy the Lotus Sutra, read and expound it, and thus help to alleviate her suffering.' My wife then addressed the king, saying, 'If he will truly undertake this duty as he says, then free him at once and let him go back to life!' Heeding her words, the king then said, 'Return to the land of the living and quickly carry out this task!'

"Having received his order, I went back to the entrance to the palace. There, wishing to know who had summoned me, I asked, 'What is your name, Sir?' He replied, 'If you wish to know, I am King Yama. In your country, I am called Bodhisattva Jizō.'[13] Then he stretched out his right hand, stroked my neck, and said, 'I have placed my seal on you. Therefore, you will never meet with distress. Now hurry on back!' One finger of his hand was around ten yards long."

Such, then, is the story of the asomi Hirotari. For the sake of his deceased wife, he copied the Lotus Sutra and read it, expounding it as his offering and gathering together many merits to atone for her sufferings and to bring her salvation. This was a miraculous event!

On the Lotus Sutra, Copied in Accordance with the Law, That Survived a Fire (3:10)

The Muro no shami, or novice of Muro, was of the Enomoto family. He was self-ordained and had no clerical name. Because he was a native of the Muro district of Kii province, he was called by the name of Muro. He lived in the village of Arata in Ate district, shaved his head, and wore a surplice, but he lived a householder's life and followed a vocation to earn his living. He made a vow to copy the Lotus Sutra, reverently and in accordance with the rules of the Law, doing the copying himself. After every major or minor toilet function, he purified himself by bathing before returning to the task of copying; after six months had passed, he had completed his work. Once the work was done, he put the sutra in a lacquered leather container that he placed not outside but in a high

---

13. Known in Sanskrit as Kṣitigarbha (Earth Repository), Jizō is a bodhisattva who saves suffering beings, especially the souls of dead children.

niche in his living room, where he could read it over at certain specific times.

In the third year of the Jingo keiun era, the year *tsuchinoto-tori* [769], in the summer, on the twenty-third day of the Fifth Month, around noon, a fire broke out and destroyed his entire house. Only the container with the copy of the sutra was spared, it alone suffering no damage from the flames. When he opened the container, he found the color of the sutra as brilliant as before and all its characters unharmed. People came from all directions to see it, and there were none who did not wonder at it.

Truly we know that it was just as in the case of the highly disciplined nun of Hedong in China, whose sutra was copied in accordance with the Law, or in the case of that read by the daughter of Wang Yu in the time of the Chen dynasty, whose pages, too, escaped the power of the flames.[14]

In appraisal we say: How admirable! Mr. Enomoto, deeply faithful, piled up merit by copying a single-vehicle sutra.[15] Guarded by the deities who protect the Law, the flames testified to his miraculous power! This tale has the power to change the hearts of those who lack faith; it is a superb teacher, correcting the evils of persons of mistaken belief.

ON A WOMAN, BLIND IN BOTH EYES, WHOSE SIGHT WAS RESTORED THROUGH HER DEVOTION TO THE WOODEN IMAGE OF YAKUSHI BUDDHA (3:11)

In the Tadehara Hall in the village of Tadehara, south of the pond of Koshide in the capital of Nara, there was a wooden image of Yakushi Nyorai, or the Buddha of Healing.[16]

---

14. For the story of the nun of Hedong, see *Mingbaoji* (Jp. *Myōhōki; Record of Invisible Works of Karmic Retribution*), chap. 1, story 4. The source of the story of the daughter of Wang Yu has not been identified. See *Taishō* 51:789.
15. A single-vehicle sutra teaches that there is only one vehicle, or way, to salvation.
16. Yakushi Buddha is Bhaiṣajyaguru, or the Medicine Master Buddha.

During the reign of Empress Abe, a woman blind in both eyes lived in the village. She was a widow whose only daughter was seven years old. Having no husband and being so poor, she had great difficulty living. Lacking any way to acquire food, she was on the verge of starvation. She said to herself, "This is due to the deeds of my past lives. It is not a penalty from those of my present life alone. Rather than die of hunger in vain, it is better to practice goodness!"

Taking her daughter's hand, she went to the hall, where she prayed to the image of Yakushi Buddha for the restoration of her eyesight, saying, "I do not care about my own life, but that of my daughter depends on me—two lives dependent on one! Please restore the sight to my eyes!" A patron of the temple who happened to be present opened the door and let her in, so she could pay her respects to the image.

Two days later, the daughter, who had accompanied her, saw something like sap from a peach tree oozing from the breast of the image. The daughter told her mother, who expressed a desire to eat it, saying, "Put some of it in my mouth, please!" When the daughter did so, she ate it and found it sweet. And with that, her eyes were opened.

Truly we know that with all her heart she voiced her wish, and when such a wish is expressed, it can never be denied. This was a miraculous event!

On a Man, Blind in Both Eyes, Who Paid Reverence to the Name of Nichimani-no-mite of the Thousand-Armed Kannon and Was Rewarded by Having His Eyesight Restored (3:12)

In the village east of Yakushi-ji in the capital of Nara, there lived a blind man. Both his eyes were open, but he could not see out of them. He was devoted to Kannon and meditated on Nichimani-no-mite in hope of restoring his sight.[17] During the day, he would sit at the eastern gate of Yakushi-ji, spread a handkerchief, and chant the name of Nichimani-no-mite. Passersby, sympathizing with him, would put money, rice, or other types of grain on top of the handkerchief. Or at other times, he would sit in the marketplace doing the same thing. When the temple bell sounded at noon, he would go into the temple to beg for food from the congregation of monks. In this way, he lived for many years.

In the reign of Empress Abe, two strangers came to him, saying, "With regard to your case, we two have come to cure your eyes." After treating both his left and right eyes, they said, "We will be back without fail after two days have passed. Be sure to be here, don't forget!" Not long after, his eyes suddenly regained their power of vision, and he could see as he had originally. But although he waited until the promised two-day period was over, the two never returned.

In appraisal we say: How excellent! This man, blind in both eyes, in his present lifetime regained his sight and was able to practice the great Way of Buddhism. He threw away his walking stick, for now he was able to walk without it!

Truly we know the power of Kannon's virtue and the deep faith of this blind man.

On a Man Who Vowed to Copy the Lotus Sutra and Was Saved from a Pit Devoid of Sunlight by the Power of His Vow (3:13)

In the Aita district of Mimasaka province, there was an iron mine owned by the state. In the reign of Empress Abe, a provincial magistrate commanded ten workmen to enter the mine to dig out the ore. At that

17. The Thousand-Armed Kannon has forty arms in addition to the regular two, each with twenty-five spheres of existence; hence the figure of one thousand. Nichimani-no-mite is the eighth right arm of the forty, which holds the jewel of the sun, a symbol of Kannon's cosmic significance.

time, the entrance to the mine suddenly caved in. The workmen, surprised and terrified, made a rush for the exit. Nine of them barely managed to escape, but one was left behind and could not get out. Before he could do so, the entrance was blocked. The magistrate and the other people, supposing that he had been crushed to death, grieved for him. His wife and family, waiting in sorrow, painted an image of Kannon, copied sutras, and put their trust in the power of good fortune. Thus the seven-days services came to an end.[18]

Meanwhile, the man, sealed in the pit, thought to himself, "Formerly I vowed to copy the Lotus Sutra, but I have not yet done so. Please save my life, so I will be able to do so!" In the dark pit, he wailed and grieved, for in the long days of his life he had never experienced such sorrow as he felt at that time.

Then he noticed that the door of the pit opened a little, and a ray of sunlight came in. Through the opening a novice entered, bringing with him a bowl filled with splendid food. Handing it to him, he said, "Your wife and family made offerings of food and drink and asked me to save you. You have been weeping piteously, and therefore I have come." Then he went out by the way he had come. He had not been gone long when a hole opened above the man's head, and sunlight flooded in. The opening was something over two feet square and was situated fifty feet above his head.

At that time, some thirty or more men who had come into the mountains to collect vines passed near the hole. The man at the bottom of the hole, seeing them pass, called out, "Lend me a hand!" The workmen heard what sounded like the hum of a mosquito. Wondering at this, they fastened a stone to the end of a vine and dropped it down the hole. The man at the bottom took hold of it and pulled. Thus they knew that there was someone at the bottom. They wove vines to make a basket, tied vines at the four corners of the basket, and, setting up a pulley at the entrance, lowered it bit by bit down to the bottom. There the man at the

---

18. The seven-day services represent the period during which a dead person's future existence is decided.

bottom got into the basket and was pulled up. Thus the man was able to go back to his family.

When his family and relatives saw him, they were moved and delighted beyond words. The magistrate asked him, "What good did you do to deserve this?" He replied by describing what had happened. Greatly moved, the magistrate organized a group of devotees to cooperate in copying the Lotus Sutra and held a dedication ceremony when it was completed.

This took place owing to the divine power of the Lotus Sutra and the favor of Kannon. There can be no doubt about it!

On Striking the Reciter of the *Dharani* of the Thousand-Armed Kannon and Receiving the Immediate Penalty of a Violent Death (3:14)

In the Kaga district of Koshi-no-michi province,[19] there was an official in charge of vagrants.[20] He tracked them down and made them pay production and labor taxes. At that time, there was a man registered in the capital of Nara whose name was Ono no asomi Niwamaro. He became a lay brother and constantly recited the *dharani* of the Thousand-Armed Kannon.[21] He wandered here and there in the mountains of the Kaga district, carrying out his religious practice.

In the third year of the Jingo keiun era, the year *tsuchinoto-tori* [769], in the spring, on the twenty-sixth day of the Third Month, around noon, the official was in the village of Mimakawa in that district. He came

---

19. In 823, Kaga district became Kaga province, so this story offers evidence for dating the compilation of the *Nihon ryōiki*, or at least this volume of it, before that year.
20. The term "vagrants" refers to those who left their registered place of residence to evade taxation.
21. A *dharani* is a spell or short religious text that expresses devotion to a Buddhist deity and ensures the deity's protection.

across the lay brother, or practitioner, and said to him, "What province do you come from?" The man answered, "I am a religious practitioner, not a layman." The official accused him angrily, saying, "You are a vagrant! Why don't you pay your taxes?" He bound and hit him to force him to work, but the man refused and resisted him, earnestly quoting the proverb that says, "'When lice from the clothes climb up to the head, they turn black; when those from the head climb down to the clothes, they turn white.' So the proverb says. I carry the *dharani* on the top of my head and the sutra on my back, in order to avoid trouble from laypeople. Why do you hit and humiliate someone who upholds the Mahayana teachings? If they truly have miraculous power, you will see it exercised now!" Meanwhile, the official took the Senju-kyō,[22] bound it up, and dragged it along the ground.

The official's house was about half a mile from the place where he hit the practitioner. When he reached the gate of his house and tried to get down from his horse, he found that he was fastened tight and could not move. Then he and his horse flew through the sky to the place where he had been when he hit the practitioner. He remained hanging in the sky for a day and a night, and the next day, at noon, he fell from the sky and was killed. His body was broken into bits, like a bag full of little blocks.

Of those who witnessed it, none but were filled with terror.

It is just as the Senju-kyō says: "If you recite this great divine *dharani*, even a dead tree will bring forth limbs, branches, flowers, and fruit." And a Mahayana scripture says: "But he who derides these *dharanis* will be comparable to one who destroys pagodas and temples in eighty-four thousand countries."[23] This is what it means.

---

22. Senju sengan Kanzeon Bosatsu kōdai enman muge daihishin darani kyō. See *Taishō* 20:111.
23. The source of this quotation has not been identified.

On Hitting a Novice Who Was Begging for Food and Receiving the Immediate Penalty of a Violent Death (3:15)

Inukai no sukune Maoi lived in the village of Saki, north of the imperial mausoleum of Ikume in the capital of Nara. He was innately evil in nature and hated beggars. In the reign of Empress Abe, a novice came to Maoi begging for food. Maoi, far from offering him anything, stripped him of his surplice and abused him, saying, "What kind of monk are you?" The novice replied, "I am a self-ordained monk!" Maoi chased him away and, deeply offended, he left.

That evening, Maoi cooked some carp in soup and set it aside to chill and set. The next morning around eight o'clock, he got out of bed and tasted the carp. He was about to take a drink of rice wine when black blood came pouring out of his mouth, and he fell on his side as though in a trance; as though he had gone to sleep, his life came to an end.

Truly we know that an evil mind is a sharp sword that cuts the body of the bearer; an angry heart is a speedy devil that calls down disaster; greed and covetousness are the malady that summon the devil starvation; avarice is an impenetrable thicket that blocks the show of compassion. When someone comes to you begging, you should display compassion and greet him with a smiling face and a joyful manner, offering spiritual and material assistance. Thus the Jōbu-ron says: "Those greedy at heart will value even mud, hording it like gold and jewels, while those compassionate at heart treat gold and jewels as less valuable even than grass or trees. At the sight of someone begging, they cannot bear to say, 'Nothing!' They wail with pity until their tears fall down."[24]

24. *Shokyō yōshū (Essential Passages from Various Sutras)* 10. See *Taishō* 59:93.

✳

ON A LICENTIOUS WOMAN WHOSE CHILDREN
CRIED FOR MILK AND WHO RECEIVED AN
IMMEDIATE PENALTY (3:16)

Yokoe no omi Naritojime was from the Kaga district of Koshi no Michi province.[25] She was innately licentious and used to keep company with many men. Before she had completed the best years of her life,[26] she died, and many years passed.

Dharma Master Jakuren, who was from the village of No-no-o in the Nagusa district of Kii province, left his home and traveled to other provinces, practicing the teachings and seeking the Way. He came to the village of Uneda in Kaga district and stayed there for some years.

In the reign of Emperor Shirakabe [Kōnin, r. 770–781], who governed the Eight Great Islands at the Nara Palace, in the first year of the Hōki era, the year *kanoe-inu* [770], in the Twelfth Month, the night of the twenty-third day, he dreamed that he was heading eastward along the path in front of Prince Shōtoku's palace at Ikaruga in Yamato province.[27] The path was like a mirror, about half a furlong in width and straight as a plumb line, with groves of trees on one side. When he looked into the grove of trees, he saw a large plump woman, completely naked, crouching there. Her two breasts were swollen as big as an oven for baking metal objects, hanging down with pus oozing out of them. Kneeling down, she grasped her knees with her hands, looked at her sick breasts, and said, "How they hurt!" She moaned in pain over them.

Jakusen asked, "Who are you, woman?" She replied, "I am the mother of Yokoe no omi Narihito from the village of Uneda in Ōno township in the Kaga district of Koshi no Michi province. During my best years, I went off on licentious affairs, abandoning my little ones day after day to

---

25. In 823, Koshi no Michi province became part of Echizen province.
26. The best years are those from twenty-one to sixty.
27. See "On Imperial Prince Shōtoku's Showing Unusual Signs" (1.4).

go and sleep with young men, so that they hungered for my breasts. And Narihito was the hungriest of them all. Because of this sin of causing them hunger, I am now repaid with this sickness in my breasts!" Jakuren asked, "How can you be freed from this sin?" She replied, "If Narihito learns of it, he will surely pardon my sin!"

Awaking from his dream, Jakuren, wondering, went around the village making inquiries. There he came upon a man who said, "Yes—I am that man." When Jakuren told him of his dream, he replied, "When I was young, I was separated from her and did not know my mother. But I have an older sister who may know of how things were." He then asked his older sister, who replied, "It is just as you said. When I was young, my mother was very beautiful in appearance. She was loved by men and gave herself to them. So she did not want to give her breasts to us." Then all the children joined in grieving, saying, "We bear her no ill will. Why does our dear mother have to suffer for this sin?" They made Buddhist images, recited sutras, and atoned for their mother's sin. After the ceremony was over, she appeared once more in an enlightenment dream, saying, "Now my sin has been pardoned!"

Truly we know that the sweet milk from a mother's two breasts, although capable of bestowing benefit, if denied to those little ones, can on the contrary become a source of sin! Why, then, should she refuse it to them?

ON CLAY IMAGES, HALF FINISHED, WHOSE GROANS PRODUCED AN EXTRAORDINARY SIGN (3:17)

Novice Shingyō came from the village of Mike in the Naga district of Kii province. His secular name was Ōtomo no muraji Oya. He renounced his secular status, ordained himself, shaved his head, and wore a surplice, looking for anything that would bring good fortune. In that village was a sacred place, called the Mikeyamamuro Hall, built by the villagers themselves. (Its formal Buddhist name was Jishi zenjū-dō

[Maitreya's Meditation Hall].) Inside were two unfinished images of the attendants of Bodhisattva Miroku. Their arms, which were broken off, were kept in the bell hall. The patrons of the temple, discussing the matter, said, "We should keep these images in some pure place in the mountain!" Novice Shingyō lived in the hall and tended to the striking of its bell. Looking at the unfinished images, he was constantly distressed. Tying the fallen arms to the images with thread, he always used to stroke their limbs and make a vow, saying, "I hope that some saint will come and complete you!"

Many years went by, and in the reign of Emperor Shirakabe, in the second year of the Hōki era, in the autumn, the Seventh Month of the year *kanoto-i* [771], around midnight, voices were heard groaning and saying, "It hurts! It hurts!" They were very feeble, sounding like women's voices, giving long-drawn-out groans. At first, Shingyō thought that some traveler, crossing the mountains, had been suddenly taken ill and had stopped there. But when he got out of bed and went around inspecting, he could find no ailing person. This puzzled him, but he said nothing about it. The groans of people in pain, however, continued night after night. Unable to endure it any longer, he got up again and made another search. He found that the groans issued from the bell tower and were, in fact, coming from the images. Seeing this, Shingyō was both surprised and troubled.

At that time, the monk Bukyō from Gangō-ji temple on the East Side of Nara was staying regularly at the temple. Shingyō surprised him by knocking on his door and saying, "Ah, venerable master, please get up and listen!" Then he told him about the groans. Bukyō and Shingyō, the two of them wondering and grieving, formed a devotees' association and completed the two images for dedication, holding a service to enshrine them. They are at present in the Mike Hall, the attendants of Bodhisattva Miroku. (The one on the left is Bodhisattva Daimyōshō, and the one on the right is Bodhisattva Hōonrin.)

Truly we know that there is no vow that goes unfulfilled. This is proof of that fact. This, too, was an extraordinary event!

On a Sutra Master Who Copied the Lotus Sutra but, Because of Licentiousness, Incurred the Immediate Penalty of a Violent Death (3:18)

Tajihi the sutra master came from the Tajihi district of Kawachi province. His surname was Tajihi, and so he was called by that name.

In that district, there was a temple called Nonaka Hall and a person who made a vow there. In the second year of the Hōki era, the year with the sign *kanoto-i* [771], in the summer, the Sixth Month, he went to the sutra master and requested him to make a copy of the Lotus Sutra, gathering the women members of the congregation to provide pure water to add to the copier's ink. The time was that from around one o'clock to five, when dark clouds appeared and rain began to fall. To escape the rain, they moved inside the temple. But the hall of the temple was very small, and so the copier and the women attendants were forced to occupy the same space. The sutra master, being seized with lustful desire, placed himself in back of one of the women, lifted her skirt, and entered her. As his organ entered her body, they clasped hands and both of them died. But the woman died with foam coming out of her mouth.

Truly we know that this was punishment inflicted by the guardian of the Law. Although desire may burn your body and heart, you must never give in to the licentious thoughts and commit an unclean act! A fool acting in lust is like a moth leaping into a flame. Therefore, the text on the precepts says, "An untrained youth naturally commits deeds that would shame the mouth." And the Nirvana Sutra says, "If you understand the Law of the five desires, you will not find pleasure in them, nor will you indulge in them even for a moment. They are like a dog chewing on a bone that has gone dry—there is no pleasure in them!"[28] This is what it means.

---

28. Nirvana Sutra, vol. 22. See *Taishō* 12:496.

❋

ON A GIRL BORN OF A FLESH BALL WHO
PRACTICED GOOD AND CONVERTED PEOPLE (3:19)

The wife of Toyobuku no Hirogimi of the village of Toyobuku in the Ya-tsushiro district of Higo province became pregnant. In the second year of the Hōki era, the year *kanoto-i* [771], in the winter, on the fifteenth day of the Eleventh Month, about four o'clock in the morning, she gave birth to a flesh ball. It looked like an egg. Both husband and wife, considering this inauspicious, put it in a container and stored it in a cave in the mountains. After seven days had passed, they went to look at it and found that the ball had broken open and a girl child had emerged. The father and mother took her home and nursed and raised her. Of those who saw or heard of this, there was no one in the province who did not think it amazing.

After eight months had passed, she suddenly grew very large. But her head and neck were joined together, without any chin as in an ordinary person. She was three and a half feet in height and could speak very clearly, being endowed with natural intelligence. Before she was even seven years old, she could recite the Lotus Sutra and the eighty-volume Flower Garland Sutra perfectly without flaw. In the end, she decided to renounce the world, shaving her head and wearing a surplice, practicing good and converting others. There were none who did not have faith in her. She spoke in a loud voice, which overawed her listeners. In her body, she differed from others; she had no vagina or any way of coupling, only an opening for urine. Ignorant people laughed at her, calling her a Saru Hijiri [Monkey Sage].

At one time, a monk of the provincial temple of Kokubun-ji in the Takuma district and a monk of the Daijin-ji in Yahata in the Usa district of Michinoku province of Toyokuni, the two of them, joined in denouncing the nun, saying, "You are a follower of non-Buddhist teachings!" They criticized her in very harsh terms. A divine man flew down from the sky, bearing a halberd, and made as though to strike them. They screamed in terror and eventually died.

When the Most Reverend Kaimyō, a monk of Daian-ji, was appointed as superior provincial preceptor of Tsukushi province, about the seventh or eighth year of the Hōki era [776 or 777], Sagano kimi Kogimi, of the Senior Seventh Rank, Upper Grade, governor of the Saga district of Hizen province, held a retreat and invited Dharma Master Kaimyō to lecture on the eighty-volume Flower Garland Sutra. The nun was among those in the congregation, always present. Seeing her, Kaimyō said, accusingly, "What is that nun doing seated there?" The nun replied, "The Buddha, out of his compassion, promulgated the correct teachings for the sake of all living beings. Why do you single me out for discriminatory treatment?" Then she asked a question, quoting a verse from the sutra, and the lecturer was unable to explain it. All the eminent and wise persons present, amazed at this, questioned and examined her, but she never failed to answer them. Thus they knew that she had the understanding of a sage. The clergy and lay believers alike revered her and made her their teacher.

Long ago, when the Buddha was in the world, Sumanā, a daughter of Sudatta, a wealthy man of the city of Śrāvasti, gave birth to ten eggs. They opened to produce ten men, all of whom renounced the world and became arhats.[29] And the wife of a wealthy man of Kapilavastu became pregnant and gave birth to a flesh ball. After seven days, it opened to produce a hundred children, all of whom renounced the world at the same time and became arhats.[30] Even in a country as paltry as ours, we, too, have a similar case. This also is an extraordinary event!

29. Kengu-kyō 13. See Taishō 4:440.
30. Senjū hyakuen-gyō 7. See Taishō 4:237a–b.

ON SPEAKING ILL OF A WOMAN COPYING THE LOTUS SUTRA AND IMMEDIATELY GETTING A TWISTED MOUTH (3:20)

In the village of Hani in the Nakata district of Awa province, there was a woman whose surname was Imube no obito. (Her given name was Tayasuko.) In the reign of Emperor Shirakabe, she was copying the Lotus Sutra at Sonoyama-dera in Oe district. At that time, Imube no muraji Itaya of the same Oe district spoke ill of her, slandering her, and for that reason his mouth became twisted and did not mend, remaining always that way.

In the Lotus Sutra it says: "If one speaks ill of the reciter of this sutra, his faculties will be impaired; he will be squat and ugly, crooked, lame, blind, deaf, his body all hunched over."[31] And it also says: "If anyone sees a person who accepts and upholds this sutra and tries to express the faults and evils of that person, whether what he speaks is true or not, he will in his present existence be afflicted with white leprosy."[32] This is what these passages mean. Therefore, be careful, speak with a heart of faith, and praise the person's virtue. For if you censure his faults, you will encounter great disaster!

ON A BLIND MONK WHO HAD THE DIAMOND SUTRA RECITED AND WAS CURED (3:21)

The novice Jōgi was a monk of Yakushi-ji on the West Side of the capital of Nara. In the third year of the Hōki era [772], he lost the sight in one of

31. This is not a direct quote from, but a summary of the meaning of, Lotus Sutra, end of chap. 3, "Simile and Parable."
32. The Lotus Sutra, trans. Burton Watson (New York: Columbia University Press, 1993), chap. 28, "Encouragements of the Bodhisattva Universal Worthy," 324.

his eyes. Five months went by, and day and night he was ashamed and grieved. He invited a number of monks to recite the Diamond Sutra for three days and nights. As a result, his eye was then cured, and he could see as he had in the past.

How great is the power of the Diamond Sutra! Therefore, make your vow in a spirit of faith. For it will never fail to be fulfilled.

On Using Heavy Scales to Cheat Others, but Copying the Lotus Sutra, and the Immediate Good and Bad Rewards He Got (3:22)

Osada no toneri Ebisu was a man of the village of Atome in the Chiisakata district of Shinano province. He had great wealth and used to lend money and rice to others. He copied the Lotus Sutra twice, and each time held a ceremony to recite it. After thinking it over further, he was not satisfied with this, so reverently copied it once more, but held no ceremony when it was done.

In the fourth year of the Hōki era, the year *mizunoto-ushi* [773], in the summer, the last week of the Fourth Month, Ebisu suddenly died. His wife and family conferred, saying, "He was born in the year of *hinoe* [fire]; therefore, we will not cremate him." Hence they consecrated the ground on which to build a tomb, while providing temporary burial.

After seven days had passed, he returned to life and told them the following story: "There were four men accompanying me and guiding me. At first, we crossed a broad field and then came to a steep slope. When we had climbed the slope, we could see a tall building. Standing there and looking over the path ahead, I could see many men sweeping the road with brooms and heard them saying, 'A man who copied the Lotus Sutra will pass along this road. Therefore, we are sweeping it to make it clean.' When I got to where they were, they stood and bowed to me. In front of me was a deep river, about 120 yards wide. This river had a bridge over it. Many men were repairing it, saying, 'A man who copied the

Lotus Sutra will pass over this bridge. Therefore, we are repairing it.'
When I got there, they stood and bowed to me.

"When I had crossed the bridge and reached the other side, I saw
a golden palace with a king inside. There were three roads leading from
the edge of the bridge. The first was broad and level, the second was
somewhat overgrown with grass, and the third was covered with thick
bushes. While we stood looking at the three roads, a man in the palace
said, 'We have brought him!' The king, seeing me, said, 'This man has
copied the Lotus Sutra.' Pointing to the second road, somewhat overgrown with grass, he said, 'Let him come by that road.'

"The four men accompanying me, we went to a place where there was
a hot pillar coated with iron. I was made to hug it while they put a burning
iron net over my back and pressed it there. After three days and nights
of this, I was made to embrace a copper-coated pillar, while they pressed
a burning copper net over my back. Again, three days passed, but the objects were still as hot as burning charcoal. But although both the iron and
the copper were hot, they were not unbearably so. And although the iron
coating was heavy, it was not unbearably so, but it was not light either. I
was drawn by my evil karma and just longed to clasp them.

"When six days had passed, I left the palace. Three monks questioned me, saying, 'Do you understand the meaning of all this?' 'No,
I don't,' I replied. Then they asked me, 'What did you do that was good?'
I answered, 'I made three copies of the Lotus Sutra. But one of them has
not yet been dedicated.' Then they took out three writing tablets, two of
them of gold and one of iron. And they took out two scales; one of them
weighed on the heavy side, making one measure of rice look like two,
and the other on the light side, making a measure of rice look much
lighter. Then they said, 'Checking our tablets, we find that you have told
the truth. You reverently made three copies of the Lotus Sutra. But
though you copied a Mahayana text, you are also guilty of a serious
crime. Why do we say this? Because you used the lighter-weight scale
when weighing out rice, but used the heavier one when you collected
the return. Therefore, we have summoned you here. Now go home
quickly!'

"As I went home, I saw the same thing as before. Many men swept the road with brooms and repaired the bridge, saying, 'The man who copied the Lotus Sutra is coming home from the palace of King Yama!' And when I had finished crossing the bridge, I realized that I had returned to life."

Thereafter, he paid homage to the sutra that he had copied, his faith grew ever deeper, and he read and recited it with devotion. Truly we know that doing good brings good fortune, while doing evil brings disaster. The effects of good and evil never decay and disappear; one will receive the rewards of both of them. Therefore, one should practice only good and never evil.

On Using Temple Property, but Vowing to Copy the Great Perfection of Wisdom Sutra, and the Immediate Good and Bad Rewards He Got (3:23)

Ōtomo no muraji Oshikatsu was a man of the village of Omuna in the Chiisakata district of Shinano province. The Ōtomo family, being all of like mind, got together to build a hall in the village to serve as a family temple. Oshikatsu, in order to provide it with a copy of the Great Perfection of Wisdom Sutra, made a vow, gathered contributions, shaved his head, put on a surplice, and, accepting the precepts, became a follower of the Way, constantly living in the hall.

In the fifth year of the Hōki era, the year *kinoe-tora* [774], in the spring, the Third Month, he suddenly became a victim of slander, was attacked by the patrons of the hall, and killed. (All the patrons of the hall were members of the same family as Oshikatsu.) The family members conferred and said, "Since this is a case of murder, we will wait for a judgment." Accordingly, they did not cremate him immediately but made a tomb and arranged for the corpse to undergo a temporary burial. After five days had passed, however, he returned to life.

He told this story to his family: "Five messengers had come, accompanying me and hurrying us along. Ahead on the road was a very steep slope. When I reached the top of the slope and looked around, I saw that there were three big roads ahead. One of them was level and broad, one was rather overgrown with grass, and one was clogged with bushes. In the center of the roads sat the king. The messengers reported, saying, 'We have brought him.' The king, indicating the level road, said, 'Bring him by this road!' Surrounding me, the messengers took me over that road.

"At the end of the road was a large cauldron, steaming with hot water. It bubbled as though with waves and made a roaring sound like thunder. But when they seized me and threw me in, the cauldron turned cold, broke apart, and fell into four pieces.

"Then three monks appeared and questioned me, saying, 'What good deed have you done?' I answered, 'I have done nothing good. But I did intend just to make a copy of the six hundred chapters of the Great Perfection of Wisdom Sutra. I vowed to do that, but the actual work has not yet been done.'

"They then brought out three iron writing tablets and appeared to be examining them. The monks said to me, 'It is true, as you say, that you made a vow, renounced the world, and practiced the Way. All this was good. But you made frequent use of things that belonged to the temple where you lived. In that way, you brought destruction on yourself. Now go back and carry out your vow, and then make restitution for the temple property you used!' Then, having been suddenly released, I passed over the three big roads, came down the slope, and found myself restored to life. This came about because of the power of the vow I made regarding the sutra, and the disaster I brought about by using the temple property—this was a sin that caused me to be summoned. Hell has nothing to be blamed for!"

The Great Perfection of Wisdom Sutra says: "One *mon* if multiplied for twenty days will make 1,740,003,968 *mon*.[33] Therefore, never steal or use even one *mon*." This is what it means.

---

33. There is something faulty in the text, as the calculation indicated comes to 524,288, not the more than 1 billion given here.

ON PREVENTING PEOPLE FROM PRACTICING THE WAY AND BEING REBORN AS A MONKEY IN PENALTY (3:24)

In the Yasu district of Ōmi province, on the mountain called Mikamu-no-take, there was a shrine named the home of Taga no Ōkami. It had the holdings of six families as its endowment. Near the shrine was a temple.

In the reign of Emperor Shirakabe, during the Hōki era [770–781], there was a monk living in the temple, Eshō of Daian-ji, who was carrying out a retreat. In a dream, a man appeared to him, saying, "Please recite a sutra for me!" He was surprised, and after he awoke, he wondered and pondered the matter.

The next day, a little white monkey appeared and said to him, "Since you are living in this temple, please recite the Lotus Sutra for me." "Who are you?" he asked the monkey. The monkey replied, "I was a great king in eastern India. In the state, there were monks carrying out religious practices, and they had several thousand followers, who neglected their agricultural duties. (This means about one thousand men, not thousands.) Therefore, I ordered them suppressed, saying, 'There should not be so many followers!' At that time, I forbade there being so many followers, saying that it was a hindrance to the observance of the Way. I did not actually prohibit them from practicing the Way. But in limiting the number who could follow it, I committed a sin that called forth a penalty. So in my present existence, I have been condemned to take on a monkey's body and become the god of this shrine. Therefore, in order that I may put off this present body, please stay in this temple and recite the Lotus Sutra for me!"

The monk said, "In that case, you must make an offering." But the monkey replied, "I have nothing to give as an offering!" The monk said, "This village produces lots of unhulled rice. You can give me some of that as my fee for the service, and I will recite the sutra for you."

The monkey said, "The government officials have given it to me. But there is someone who has charge of it, and he considers it his personal possession. He would never let me use it. I cannot dispose of it as I would like." (By "someone who has charge of it," he means the official at the shrine.) "Then, if you have no offering, how do you expect to have the sutra read?" said the monk. The monkey answered, "You are right. But there are many monks in this district of Asai, and they are going to recite the Rokkan-shō [Six-Volume Writings]. I will ask them to let me join their group." (Asai is one of the districts in the same province. The Rokkan-shō is the name of a work on the precepts.)

The monk thought this very strange, but he went along with the monkey's words. He told all this to the Very Reverend Manyo of Yamashina Temple, who was a patron. Manyo rejected it, saying, "That's what the monkey said, but I don't believe it! I would never accept it or listen to it."

When he was preparing for the reading of the Rokkan-shō, an acolyte and a lay brother came rushing to him in haste, saying, "There was a little white monkey in the hall. And when we looked, the whole hall, nine spans of it, all fell down into a heap of dust! Everything was crushed and broken, all the Buddhist statues were ruined, and the monks' quarters were destroyed."

When Manyo went to look, he found that it was just as they had said. Since all had been destroyed, he and the monk built a new hall seven spans in size, and, accepting the words of the monkey that he was Taga no Ōkami, allowed him to join in with the other celebrants. He listened to the recitation of the Rokkan-shō, according to the request of the god of the shrine. After that, until the vow was fulfilled, there was no further trouble.

You must not prevent anyone from practicing the Way, or that person, as we have seen, will receive the penalty of being reborn as a monkey. Therefore, monks must be allowed to hold services. If not, then someone may suffer an evil penalty.

Long ago in the past, when Rahula was a king in a previous existence,[34] he stopped a self-enlightened monk from begging, barring him from

34. Rahula was the Buddha's son, born before the Buddha had entered religious practice. The story derives from the *Dazhidu-lun* (*The Treatise on the Great Perfection of Wisdom*), 28. See *Taishō* 25:182.

entrance into the borders of his kingdom. Within seven days, the man died of starvation. As a penalty for this offense, Rahula spent six years in his mother's womb before he was finally born. This is the lesson this story teaches us.

On Being Put Adrift on the Ocean, Reverently Reciting Śākyamuni Buddha's Name, and Preserving Their Lives (3:25)

Ki no omi Umakai was a man from the village of Kibi in the Ate district of Kii province. Nakatomi no muraji Ōjimaro was a boy from the village of Hamanaka in the Ama district of the same province. Kinomaro no asomi lived in a port in the Hidaka district of the same province, using a net to catch fish. Umakai and Ōjimaro were paid annually for their labor by Kinomaro no asomi. Regardless of whether day or night, they went with him, trying to catch fish with a net.

In the reign of Emperor Shirakabe, the sixth year of the Hōki era, the year *kinoto-u* [775], on the sixteenth day of the Sixth Month, a strong wind was blowing and drenching rain came down. The surf rose in high waves and washed out much loose timber. Kinomaro no asomi sent the two to try to catch the drifting timber. The man and boy, the two of them, collected the logs and fitted them together to form a raft and, riding on the raft, tried to row against the current. But the waves were extremely rough, breaking the ties holding the raft together and carrying it out to sea. The two of them, each straddling a single log, were set adrift on the sea. Both of them, ignorant as they were, again and again recited the words "Hail Śākyamuni Buddha, deliver us from all grave danger!" their cries never ceasing.

After five days, in the evening, the boy was finally cast by the waves onto a beach at a salt makers' village, Tano-no-ura in the Tsuna district in the southern part of Awaji province. The man, Umakai, around four in the morning of the sixth day, was washed ashore in the same place. The local people asked them where they were from and, learning of their plight, took pity on them and gave them help. They also informed the government official, who, feeling sorry for them, gave them some of the rations under his command.

The boy, lamenting, said, "I have been following a man who kills living creatures, and therefore I have met with endless disaster. And if I go back home, I will be in his employ again, and when will there be an end to this business of killing?" Therefore, he stayed in the provincial temple of Awaji province, becoming a follower of the monk there.

After two months had gone by, Umakai returned home. His wife and family, seeing him, were surprised and shocked at his face and eyes all puffed and changed by the effects of the water. They exclaimed in wonder, "He was carried out to sea and drowned. After seven days, we held a vegetarian feast for him. We have already done all that is needed to thank the Buddha for saving him from a worse fate. Now what does he mean, coming back to life again? Is this a dream, or is he a ghost?" He then told his wife and family all that had happened to him. When they heard his story, they responded with pity and joy. He himself was moved in his heart, renounced the world, and went to the mountains to practice the Way. All who saw him or heard of him could not help but marvel at this story.

Those who go to sea meet with many strange events, but they manage to stay alive and preserve themselves. This is due entirely to the wonderful protection of Śākyamuni Nyorai, and the deep faith of those who drift on its surface. They meet with immediate rewards, as we have seen, and how much more will they be rewarded in their future existence!

ON COLLECTING DEBTS BY FORCE AND WITH HIGH INTEREST, AND RECEIVING THE IMMEDIATE PENALTY OF A VIOLENT DEATH (3:26)

Tanaka no mahito Hiromushime was the wife of Oya no agatanushi Miyate of Outer Junior Sixth Rank, Upper Grade, a governor of the Miki district of Sanuki province. She gave birth to eight children and was very rich, possessing heaps of wealth. Her riches included horses, cattle, male and female slaves, money, rice, rice fields, other kinds of fields, and more. But by nature, she lacked any feeling for the Way and was so greedy that she never gave anything away. By selling rice wine diluted with a lot of water, she managed to make a big profit. When she made a loan, she used a small measuring cup, but when she collected the loan, she used a big cup. On the day she lent rice, she used a light-weight scale, but when she collected it, she used a heavy-weight scale. She showed no mercy in forcibly collecting interest, sometimes ten times and sometimes a hundred times the original loan. Her ears were deaf to the pleas of those in trouble, and her heart knew no generosity. Because of this, many people, greatly worried, abandoned their homes to escape from her, wandering to other provinces. There has never been anyone so greedy!

In the seventh year of the Hōki era [776], on the first day of the Sixth Month, Hiromushime took to her bed and remained there for a number of days. Then, on the twentieth day of the Seventh Month, she called her husband and her eight sons to gather around, and she told them of a dream she had had. "I was summoned before King Yama," she said, "and he showed me in the dream my three kinds of sins. One was the sin of using much of the property of the Three Treasures and not repaying it.[35] The second was of selling wine diluted with a lot of water. The third was of using two kinds of measuring cups and scales, giving seven-tenths of a

---

35. The Three Treasures are the Buddha; the Dharma, or doctrine; and the Order, or community of believers.

loan and collecting twelve-tenths in return. 'I have summoned you because of these sins. You must pay an immediate penalty, as I shall show you!' said the king." Then, having told of her dream, she died on the very same day.

Seven days passed, but they did not cremate her. They called together thirty-two meditation monks and lay brothers for nine days to make vows and to pray for her good fortune. On the evening of the seventh day, she came back to life. The lid of her coffin opened by itself, and when they looked inside, they were overpowered by a terrible stench that was beyond description. From the waist up, she had already turned into a cow, with horns on her head measuring four inches in length. Her two hands had become two cow's feet, with the nails cracked like the instep of a cow. The lower part of her body retained its human form. She was naked, no clothes on her, and lay in her filth.

People from east and west all gathered around to look at her, gazing in wonder, no end to them. Her husband and children, filled with shame and pity, threw themselves to the ground, making endless vows. To atone for her sins, they offered various household treasures to Miki temple, and to Tōdai-ji temple in Nara: seventy oxen, thirty horses, fifty acres of fields, and four thousand bundles of rice. And they cancelled all her debts. After the district and provincial officials had seen her and were about to send a report to the central government, at the end of five days she died. All the people in that district and province who had seen or heard of her worried over her fate.

She did not understand the law of karmic retribution, but lacked reason and a sense of righteousness. Thus we know for certain that there is an immediate penalty for unrighteousness and evil. And since the immediate penalty comes as surely as this, how much more so will be that in a future life!

One sutra says: "Those who fail to pay their debts will be reborn as horses or cattle as a consequence."[36] The debtor is compared to a slave;

---

36. This is a summary of a passage from Harivarmin, *Jōjitsu-ron* (*Treatise on the Establishment of Truth*).

the creditor, to a master. The debtor is like a pheasant; the creditor, like a hawk. Thus although you may make a loan, do not use excessive force in collecting the debt. For if you do, you will be reborn as a horse or a cow and made to work for your debtor. Avoid this mistake!

On a Man Who Removed a Bamboo Shoot from the Eye of a Skull and Prayed for It, Receiving an Extraordinary Sign (3:27)

In the reign of Emperor Shirakabe, the ninth year of the Hōki era, the year *tsuchinoe-uma* [778], in the winter, the latter part of the Twelfth Month, Homuchi no Makihito of the village of Ōyama in the Ashida district of Bingo province went to the Fukatsu market in the Fukatsu district of the same province to buy things in honor of the New Year. Evening overtook him while he was still on the road, so he spent the night in the bamboo grove at Ashida in Ashida district.

In the place where he spent the night, he heard a voice saying, "My eye—how it hurts!" Hearing this, he crouched down, but was unable to sleep all night. The next day when he looked, he saw that there was a skull with a bamboo shoot growing out of its eye socket. He pulled it out of the eye, relieving the eye of pain, and offered the skull some of his dried rice, saying, "May I hereby get some good luck!"

When he reached the market, he bought various things, his shopping going as he wished. Then he began to wonder if the skull would actually repay him for the kindness he had done. On his way back from the market, he stopped once more in the same bamboo grove in the province. This time, the skull had returned to the form it had had in life, and said to him, "I am Ananokimi no Otogimi of Anakuni village in Ashida district. I was killed by my wicked uncle Akimaro. When the wind blew and moved the shoot, it hurt my eye terribly! But thanks to your generous kindness, I have been freed of my pain. Now I have attained a state of great joy, and I will never forget your help. My parents' home is in the village of Anakuni. Please go there on the evening of the last night of this month. Because if I do not repay you on that night, I will have no other opportunity to do so."

As he listened, Makihito wondered more and more, but he spoke of it to no one. On the eve of the last day, he went to the house of the parents. The spirit took his hand and guided him inside, where they helped themselves to the goods prepared and together ate their share of them. What was left over, the spirit wrapped up and, along with some treasures of the house, gave to Makihito. Then, after some time had passed, he suddenly disappeared.

The parents had come to the house to pay their respects to the various spirits there. When they saw Makihito, they were surprised and asked him why he had come. He then told them in detail all that had happened. They seized Akimaro and asked him why he had killed Otogimi, saying, "You told us earlier that you went to the market with our son. There you said you met someone you owed money to and had not yet paid. On the way, he pressed you for payment, so you left Otogimi. Later you asked if he had come home yet, and we replied, 'No, not yet. We haven't seen him!' Why does the story we have heard differ from yours?"

The evil Akimaro, completely shaken by what he heard, could not deny the facts. Eventually, he said, "At the latter part of last year, I went to the market with Otogimi to buy things for the New Year. He brought with him a horse, some cloth, some cotton, and some salt. Night came on while we were still on the way, so we stopped for the night at the bamboo grove. There I secretly killed him and took his belongings. I went on to the Fukatsu market, where I sold the horse to a man from Sanuki province. I am now using the rest of his things myself."

When they heard this, the parents exclaimed, "Alas! Our beloved son was killed by you, not by robbers!" But since the parents and the uncle were as close as reeds are to the rushes, they concealed the fact that he was the murderer and only banished him from the place. They thanked Makihito and gave him more food and drink. When he returned from their place, he related what had happened there.

Even a skull bleached by the sun is like this! It repays an offering of food with good fortune and goodness with goodness. Therefore, how could a man forget a deed of goodness? The Nirvana Sutra says: "Goodness received calls forth goodness."[37] This is what it means.

On a Sixteen-Foot Image of Miroku Whose Neck Was Bitten by Ants and the Extraordinary Sign It Showed (3:28)

In the village of Kishi in the Nagusa district of Kii province, there was a temple called Kishi-dera. It was so called because the villagers of Kishi had built it with their donations.

In the reign of Emperor Shirakabe, there was a lay believer who lived in the temple. Once, when he was in the temple, he heard a voice crying, "It hurts! It hurts!" It sounded like the voice of an old man.

At first, he thought that someone, having been taken ill, had come to the temple in the early part of the evening and was staying there. But when he got up and walked around the hall to see, he could find no one there. At that time, there was a pile of timber for a pagoda, but it had not been built yet and had lain on the ground for a long time, rotting away. He wondered if it was the spirit of the pagoda that had spoken. The ailing voice continued night after night. But when he could endure the sound no longer and got up to search for the sick person, he could find no one. And then, toward the end of the night, he heard the voice wailing twice as loud as before, the sound echoing throughout the land. Once more, he wondered if it could be the spirit of the pagoda.

The following day, when he got up early and went to the hall, he found that the head of the sixteen-foot statue of Miroku had fallen off and lay on the dirt floor. Thousands of big ants had swarmed over it, chewing the head right off. He reported it to the patrons of the temple.

37. *Taishō* 12:539c.

Feeling sorry for the statue, they had it repaired and, with due reverence, held a dedication ceremony.

They say that the Buddha does not have a live body, but if so, how could it feel pain? Truly we know that even after the Buddha himself has died, his Dharma body continues to exist, eternally and without change. Never doubt this!

ON A VILLAGE BOY WHO IN PLAY MADE A WOODEN BUDDHA AND A FOOLISH MAN WHO BROKE IT, INCURRING THE IMMEDIATE PENALTY OF A VIOLENT DEATH (3:29)

In the village of Hamanaka in Niki, in the Ama district of Kii province, there lived an ignorant man whose name is unknown. He was ignorant by birth and had no understanding of the law of karmic retribution.

For people going back and forth between Ama and Ate, there was a little mountain trail called Tamasaka. If one climbs the mountains from Hamanaka and travels south, he will come out in the village of Hata. One time, a child of the village went into the mountains to collect firewood. He played along the way, collecting wood and fashioning a Buddha figure. He piled up stones to make a pagoda and placed the Buddha he had fashioned in the stone temple, from time to time playing there.

In the reign of Emperor Shirakabe, the ignorant man, coming on the Buddha fashioned in play by the boy and laughing in derision, took his ax and chopped it to pieces, completely destroying it. He had not gone far before he fell to the ground, blood spurting from his mouth and nose, his two eyes blinded, and, as though in a dream, he suddenly died.

Truly we know that this was due to the protector of the Way, do we not? How could we not revere it? Thus in the Lotus Sutra it says: "Even if little boys in play should use a piece of grass or wood or a brush, or perhaps a fingernail, to draw an image of the Buddha, such persons as these . . . will all attain the Buddha way. . . . Or even should [they] raise a single hand or give no more than a slight nod of the head, and if this were done in offering to an image . . . [they] would attain the unsurpassed Way."[38] For this reason, be reverent and believe!

On a Monk Who Accumulated Merit by Making Buddhist Images and, When His Life Ended, Showed an Extraordinary Sign (3:30)

Elder Master Kanki's secular name was Mimana no Kanuki. He was from the Nagusa district of Kii province. By nature, he was a highly learned man. He had completed the usual Buddhist ceremonies, as well as being accomplished in secular matters. He lived the life of a layman, pursuing agricultural occupations and thereby supporting his wife and family.

In the village of No-no-o, there was a temple built by his ancestors, called Miroku-dera but popularly referred to as No-no-o-dera. In the reign of Emperor Shōmu [r. 724–749], Kanki made a vow to carve a sixteen-foot image of Śākya, along with its attendant figures. In the reign of Emperor Shirakabe, the tenth year of the Hōki era, the year *tsuchinoto-hitsuji* [779], he completed the task, and placed them in the golden hall of No-no-o-dera, holding a dedication ceremony. Then he made another vow to carve a ten-foot image of the Eleven-Headed Bodhisattva Kannon. It was to have been ten feet in height, but he got only halfway through the work and failed to complete it. Having few helpers and spending years at the work, he had become too old and weak to finish the task. When he was over eighty, in the reign of Emperor Yamabe [Kanmu, r. 781–796], in the first year of the Enryaku era, the year *mizunoto-i* [782],

---

38. *Lotus Sutra*, trans. Watson, chap. 2, "Expedient Means," 39–40.

on the eleventh day of the Second Month, he passed away in bed in No-no-o-dera.

After two days, he returned to life again. He called his disciple Myōki to him and said, "I forgot to tell you something. And because I could not bear that, I've come to life again!" Then he had an elevated seat built on the floor, with a mat spread over it, and food served there. This was for Musashi no suguri Tarimaro, a patron of the temple. He had him sit on the seat, served him a meal, and sat opposite him. When the meal was over, he rose from his seat, leading Myōki and all his relatives, and knelt to pay homage to Tarimaro, saying, "My years having run out, my life came to an end. Without completing the statue of Kannon, I suddenly departed. But now I have been given this fortunate opportunity, and so I will state my hope. It is that, imposing on your great benevolence, I may persuade you to bring the sacred image to completion. If this wish of my heart is granted, I will be the recipient of immediate benefit. Because of my most sincere desire, I have been permitted to return to life. Unreasonable as is my request, I make bold to state it here."

Thereupon, Tarimaro, Myōki, and the others, weeping in pity, replied, "We beg to accept your plea. We will without fail complete the statue." Hearing this, Kanki rose to his feet and clapped his hands in joy.

After two days had passed, on the fifteenth day of the same month, Kanki summoned Myōki and said, "Today is the anniversary of the Buddha's entry into nirvana. And I, too, will end my life today." Myōki was about to second his master's announcement. But, being moved by feelings of devotion, he could not in his deep attachment bear to do so. Instead, he lied and said, "No—it is not that day yet!" His master, glancing at the calendar, said, "Today is the fifteenth day! Why do you lie to me, my child, and say, 'It is not that day yet!'"

Having asked for hot water, he bathed, changed his surplice, knelt, clasped his hands, burned incense, and faced west. At around four in the afternoon, his life came to an end.[39] The Buddhist artist Tarimaro, hav-

---

39. This is typical of the manner in which those who have faith in rebirth in the Western Pure Land die.

ing agreed to carry out his wishes, completed the statue of the Eleven-Headed Kannon and finished the dedicatory ceremony. It was placed in No-no-o-dera, where it is now.

In appraisal we say: How admirable was the great virtue of Mimana no Kanuki! He hid his sacred Buddha heart within himself, and on the outside showed only the form of a layman. He went along with secular manners, following the ordinary, and yet did not stain the jewel of the precepts. When he faced death, he turned to the west, followed in the footsteps of the gods, and showed an extraordinary sign.

Truly we know this was saintly, not of a mundane nature.

On a Woman Who Gave Birth to Stones and Honored Them as Gods (3:31)

In the village of Kusumi in Mizuno, in the Katakata district of Mino province, there was a woman whose surname was Agata. She was over twenty when, being unmarried, she became pregnant without any sexual intercourse. Three years went by, and in the reign of Emperor Yamabe, the first year of the Enryaku era, the year *mizunoto-i* [782], in the spring, the latter part of the Second Month, she gave birth to two stones. They measured five inches in diameter. One was mixed blue and white in color, while the other was pure blue. They grew larger year by year. In Atsumi, the district next to Katakata, there was a great god who was called Inaba. Conveying his words through a diviner, he said, "These two stones she has given birth to are my sons." Accordingly, they were enshrined at the woman's residence, being placed in a sacred spot surrounded by a hedge.

From the distant past down to the present, we have never heard a story like this in our sacred land. This is an extraordinary event.

✳

ON TAKING A NET, GOING TO SEA TO FISH, AND MEETING TROUBLE, BUT DUE TO DEVOTION TO BODHISATTVA MYŌKEN, HE WAS SAVED (3:32)

Kurehara no imiki Naguhashimaro was from the village of Hata in the Takechi district of Yamato province. From the time he was little, he used to make nets and catch fish for a living. In the second year of the Enryaku era, the year *kinoe-ne* [783], in the autumn, on the night of the nineteenth day of the Eighth Month, he went out on the sea between Iwataki Island, in the Ama district of Kii province, and Awaji province to cast his net for fish. There were three boats fishing, with a total of nine men. Suddenly a great wind blew up, capsizing the three boats and drowning eight of the men.

At that time, Naguhashimaro, floating on the waves, devoted all the thoughts of his heart to Bodhisattva Myōken, making a vow and saying, "If you will save my life, I will make a statue of Myōken as tall as I am!" He floated on the sea, battling the waves, exhausted in body and downcast at heart. He was as if in a dream, without any waking consciousness. Then he awoke to a bright moonlit night, to find himself lying on the grass on the beach of Kadanoura. He was the only one who was saved. In gratitude, he made a statue as tall as himself.

Ah, how miraculous! When the gale blew and overturned the boats, they were all cast on the waves and were lost! He was the only one to survive. So he made a statue as tall as himself. Thus we know that this was due to Myōken's great assistance and the powerful faith of one cast on the waters.

ON PERSECUTING A HUMBLE BEGGING NOVICE
AND RECEIVING THE IMMEDIATE PENALTY
OF A VIOLENT DEATH (3:33)

Ki no atai Yoshitari, popularly known as Master Hashi-no-iegimi, was from the village of Wake in the Hitaka district of Kii province. He was evil by nature and did not believe in the law of karmic causation. In the fourth year of the Enryaku era, the year *kinoto-ushi* [785], in the summer, the Fifth Month, a provincial official who was making the rounds of the district to hand out loans of government rice came to that district to distribute them to all the peasants.

There was a self-ordained monk who was called Ise no shami, or the novice of Ise. Reciting the divine names of the Twelve Generals of the Yakushi-gyō,[40] he went around the village begging for food. Following the official who was distributing rice, he came to the gate of the evil man. At the sight of the novice, the man offered nothing, instead scattering the rice he was carrying and stripping him of his surplice, behaving in an overbearing manner. The novice fled, hiding himself in the residential quarters of Wake temple. The evil man chased him, caught him, and brought him back to his own door. There he picked up a big stone, took aim at the novice's head, and said, "Recite the divine names of the Twelve Generals and bind me with a charm!" The novice refused, but the evil man only pressed him harder. Unable to bear the abuse, the novice recited them once and then ran away. Not long after, the evil man fell to the ground and died.

There can be no doubt that the man was punished by the guardian of the Dharma! Although the other man was only a self-ordained monk, he deserved to be treated with a heart of compassion, for there are sages who live hidden among the mass of men. When one is not guilty of any

---

40. Yakushi rurikō nyorai hongan kudoku-gyō (Medicine Master Sutra). See *Taishō* 14:no. 450.

flagrant error, do not "blow back the hair, searching for hidden defects!"
If you are looking for shortcomings, even among those in the three preliminary stages or the ten stages in the bodhisattva's ascent, there are
those who have some.⁴¹ And if you are looking for virtue, even those who
speak ill of the Dharma or block the good have things that are worthy of
praise.

Thus the Jurin-gyō says: "As a gardenia, even when withered, excels
other flowers, so monks, though they break the precepts, are superior to
non-Buddhist believers. To speak of a monk's faults, whether he violates
the precepts or keeps them, whether he even recognizes the precepts or
does not, whether he has faults or does not, is worse than causing the
bodies of countless Buddhas to bleed!"⁴²

(According to the commentaries, this means: "Even if you cause the
Buddha-body to bleed, this does not hinder the Buddha's teachings. But
when you speak of a monk's faults, you destroy the faith of many persons, cause them to have cravings, and block the Way of the Buddha.
Therefore, the bodhisattva seeks to delight in virtue and does not seek to
expose error.")

The Zōbō kechigi-kyō says: "In the world of the future, secular officials should not make monks pay taxes. If they do, they will be committing an immeasurable sin. Ordinary secular persons should not ride on
the horses or cattle belonging to the Three Treasures of Buddhism. They
should not whip slaves or any of the six kinds of animals belonging
to the samgha.⁴³ And they should not accept the greetings of the slaves
of the Three Treasures. If they violate these rules they will all suffer
punishment."

Or another commentary puts it like this: "People who are stingy at
heart value mud more than gold or jewels, and misers, even when asked
for dirt, will begrudge the gift. Stingy of their wealth, they will never make
offerings, fearing that their accumulated wealth will become known to

41. In the Mahayana tradition, three preliminary stages precede the ten stages in the practice of bodhisattvas.
42. Daijō daizu Jizō jurin-gyō. See Taishō 24:no. 1485.
43. The six domestic animals are the horse, ox, sheep, dog, pig, and fowl.

others. When they pass away, leaving their bodies, empty-handed, they join the group of hungry demons who in their hearts lament their hunger and cold."[44]

Speaking of wealth, it is shared by five parties. What are the five parties? First, government officials, who might come and demand it unreasonably. Second, robbers, who might come to steal it. Third, water, which might wash it away. Fourth, fire, which might burn it up suddenly. And fifth, evil children, who might waste it unreasonably and use it up.[45] Therefore, a bodhisattva is delighted to make offerings.

ON CONTRACTING A FOUL DISEASE BUT EMBRACING THE PRECEPTS, PRACTICING GOODNESS, AND GAINING AN IMMEDIATE CURE (3:34)

Kosebe no Azame was a woman from the village of Haniu in the district of Nagusa in Kii province. In the fifth year of the Tenpyō hōji era, the year *kanoto-ushi* [761], she contracted a foul disease, which caused a growth to form on her neck as big as a melon. It was extremely painful and did not go away with the years. She said to herself, "My past deeds have brought this on, not those of my present existence only. If I am to wipe out those sins and cure my sickness, nothing is more effective than doing good!" Accordingly, she cut off her hair, accepted the precepts, donned a surplice, and took up residence in the Ōtani Hall in the village. There she recited the Shin-gyō [Heart Sutra] and devoted herself to the practice of the Way.

Fifteen years had gone by when a practitioner named Chūsen joined her in residence at the hall. Observing her affliction, he took pity on her, recited a spell over it, and took a vow, saying, "In order to cure your

---

44. *Daijōbu-ron*. See *Taishō* 30:260b.
45. The source of this paragraph is uncertain.

affliction, I vow to recite the Yakushi-gyō and the Kongō hannya-gyō ten thousand times, and the Kannon sanmai-gyō one hundred times.[46] Fourteen years later, he finished reciting the Yakushi-gyō twenty-five hundred times, the Kongō hannya-gyō one thousand times, and the Kannon sanmai-gyō two hundred times, and he was always chanting the Senju dharani. The scriptures had not yet been recited the promised number of times, even though twenty-eight years had passed from the time she contracted the disease. Then, in the sixth year of the Enryaku era, the year *hinoto-u* [787], in the winter, on the twenty-seventh day of the Eleventh Month, about eight o'clock in the morning, her growth opened of its own accord, discharged its pus, and was healed in accordance with her prayers.

Thus do we learn of the miraculous power of the Mahayana's divine spells, and of the virtues accumulated from a career practiced by an ailing woman. "To those aware of the incalculably great mercy of the Buddha is revealed a miraculous sign; to those with deep faith in his unseen wisdom is shown a token in bright colors." This is what this passage means.

ON BORROWING AN OFFICIAL'S AUTHORITY, RULING UNRIGHTEOUSLY, AND THUS GAINING AN IMMEDIATE PENALTY (3:35)

In the reign of Emperor Shirakabe, there was a man of the district of Matsura in the province of Hizen in Tsukushi named Hi no kimi, who died suddenly and went to the land of King Yama. When the king checked, however, it was found that his death was premature, and he accordingly was sent home.

---

46. The Yakushi-gyō is the Yakushi ruriko nyorai hongan kudoku-gyō (Medicine Master Sutra), the Kongō hannya-gyō is the Diamond Sutra, and the Kannon sanmai-gyō is the Kanzeon bosatsu juki-kyō.

On his way back, he saw a Hell that looked like a boiling kettle in the ocean. In it was something that looked like a black stump rising and sinking, and as it rose, it spoke to him, saying, "Wait—I have something to tell you!" It sank out of sight, but then, as the water boiled, it came up again and said, "Wait—I have something to tell you!"

This was spoken three times, and on the fourth, it said, "I am Mono-nobe no Furumaro of the Harihara district of Tōtōmi province. When I was alive, I had charge of handing out hulled rice, working for many years and taking other people's property unrightfully. And in requital for those sins, I am now suffering. I beg you for my sake to copy the Lotus Sutra and offer it, so I may be pardoned from these sins!"

Seeing this, when Hi no kimi came back from the land of the dead, he submitted a detailed report to the local government officials in Dazaifu. They, receiving it, sent it on to the central government. But the latter did not take it seriously, and therefore the grand secretary did not bother to report it to the emperor, ignoring it for twenty years.

When Sugano no asomi Mamichi of the Junior Fourth Rank, Upper Grade, was appointed head secretary, he reported it to Emperor Yamabe. The emperor, apprised of this, consulted with Assistant Executive Monk Sekyō,[47] saying, "We living beings in the world—after we suffer for twenty years in hell, are we then released from our suffering?" But Sekyō answered, "That is only the beginning of their suffering! Why do I say this? Because one hundred years in the world equals only one day and one night in Hell. That is why he has not yet been released!"

On hearing this, the emperor clicked with his thumb, indicating dis-satisfaction, and sent his messenger to Tōtōmi province to look into Furumaro's activities there. Thus he discovered that the report was true. The emperor was grieved at this, and in the fifteenth year of the Enryaku era [796], the Third Month, on the seventeenth day, he summoned four sutra copiers to copy the Lotus Sutra for the sake of Furumaro. He ap-pointed a devotees' association to support this work, inviting the prince regent, ministers, and officials in number equal to the 69,384 characters

47. Sekyō was appointed junior assistant executive in 797.

of the sutra. The emperor also requested the Most Venerable Zenjū to be lecturer,[48] and Assistant Executive Monk Sekyō to be reciter, holding a great service at a private temple in the capital of Nara to recite the sutra, the Lotus, and requesting that its merits be applied to release the spirit of Furumaro from suffering.

Ah, how foolish Furumaro was, like a fox who borrows a tiger's skin! In conducting government affairs, to exercise his power unrighteously and thus bring on an evil recompense! He lacked an understanding of the law of karmic causation, and his shallow heart brought on vast grief! The law of karmic causation never fails to work!

On Decreasing the Number of Stories in a Pagoda and Taking Down the Temple Banners, and the Penalty Received (3:36)

Fujiwara no asomi Nagate was chancellor in the reign of Emperor Shirakabe, who resided at the Nara Palace.[49] In the first year of the Enryaku era [782], his son Ieyori [d. 785] of the Junior Fourth Rank, Upper Grade, had a bad dream involving his father, and said to him, "Unknown soldiers, more than thirty of them, came to summon you, Father. This is an ill omen! Therefore, you should pray to ward off disaster!"

In spite of this warning, his father refused to follow his advice. Shortly after, he died. Then Ieyori fell victim to a prolonged illness. He therefore invited monks and lay brothers to recite formulas for his protection, but he was not healed. Among those attending him, there was a meditation master who made a vow, saying, "I live a life of discipline according to the teachings of the Buddha, so I may help others and pro-

---

48. A monk of Akishino-dera and Kōfuku-ji, Zenjū (724–797) devoted himself to the study of Yuishiki, or Consciousness-Only, doctrines.

49. The title of Dajōdaijin (prime minister) was conferred on Nagate posthumously by Emperor Kōnin. Nagate served Emperor Shōmu, Empress Kōken, Emperor Junnin, Empress Shōtoku, and Emperor Kōnin.

long life. Now I offer my own life in exchange for that of the patient. If the Buddha's teachings are true, please prolong the life of the patient!" Caring nothing for his own life, he grasped hot charcoal with his hands, burned incense, chanted spells, and circumambulated the Buddha. Then, suddenly, he began to run around and roll on the ground.

The patient then, possessed, began to speak, saying, "I am Nagate. I had the banners of Hokke-ji taken down, and later I was the one who ordered that the pagodas of Saidai-ji[50] have four corners instead of eight and five stories instead of seven. Because of these offenses, I was summoned to the office of King Yama, who made me embrace a pillar of fire and drove bent nails into my hands, interrogating and beating me. Then the palace became full of smoke. King Yama asked, 'What smoke is this?' An answer came, 'Nagate's son Ieyori is suffering from a disease. This is the smoke from the incense held in the hand of the monk who has been attending him.' Thereupon, the king released me and sent me back to the world. But my body has been destroyed, and I have nothing to live in. And therefore I must float in the air!" With this, the patient, who had not been eating, asked for something to eat, recovered from his disease, and left his sickbed.

As for banners, they are good cause for being born as a wheel-turning king.[51] And a pagoda is a treasury for holding the relics of the Buddha in the three ages of past, present, and future. Therefore, to take down the banners is to commit a sin, and to lower the height of the pagodas is to perpetrate an offense. How can we help but fear such actions? Thus they constitute an example of an immediate penalty of recent times.

---

50. There were two pagodas at Saidai-ji.
51. A wheel-turning king is one who rules the world. In India, banners were associated with kingship, and later were used as symbols of the Buddhist Dharma, or teachings.

On Doing Evil Because of Ignorance of the Law of Karmic Causation and Receiving a Penalty (3:37)

Saheki no sukune Itachi of the Junior Fourth Rank, Upper Grade, lived in the reign of the emperors who resided at the Nara Palace.[52] Once a man from the capital went to Chikuzen in Kyushu, was taken ill, and suddenly died. He proceeded to the palace of King Yama. Although he did not see anybody, he heard the voice of a man who was being beaten echoing far and wide. With each lash he cried, "It hurts! It hurts!"

The king questioned his clerks, saying, "When this person was in the world, what good deeds did he do?" The clerks replied, "All he did was make one copy of the Lotus Sutra." The king said, "Take his sins and match them with the scrolls of the sutra!" When they matched them, they found that the sins were many times greater, far outnumbering the scrolls of the sutra. And when they matched the sins with the 69,384 characters of the sutra, they were still greatly outnumbered; there was no comparison. The king thereupon clapped his hands and said, "I have seen many persons who committed sins and suffered greatly as a result. But I've never seen anyone who committed as many sins as this one!"

The man from the capital secretly questioned one of the bystanders, saying, "Who is it that is being beaten?" "Saheki no sukune Itachi" was the answer. When he returned from the land of the dead unexpectedly and was restored to life, he remembered the name. He sent a report on the case to the local government in Dazaifu, but they refused to believe it. He then took advantage of an opportunity to go by boat to the capital and submitted a report on how Lord Itachi had been detained in the palace of King Yama and the sufferings he underwent there. Itachi's wife and family, learning of this, were deeply grieved, saying, "During the extent of the seven-times-seven-day mourning period, for the benefit of his spirit we carried out good deeds and did what we could to obtain fortunate results.

---

52. The rulers were Emperor Shōmu, Empress Kōken (Shōtoku), and Emperor Kōnin.

How can it be that he has fallen into an evil state and is suffering so greatly?" They accordingly had another copy of the Lotus Sutra produced, dedicated it with all due reverence, and sent it to relieve the trials of his spirit. This, too, was an extraordinary event!

On the Appearance of Good and Evil Omens, Which Were Followed by Results Indicating Disaster or Good Luck (3:38)

It is said that when good or evil omens are about to appear, they are preceded by songs that spread through the land.[53] The people of the time in the lands throughout the country hear the songs, sing them, and thus communicate their message.

Retired Emperor Shōhō-ōjin Shōmu [Shōmu, r. 724–749], who had ruled the country for twenty-five years from the Nara Palace, summoned High Councilor Fujiwara-no-asomi Nakamaro into his presence and delivered a decree, saying, "It is my desire to see Princess Abe and Prince Funado rule over the land.[54] What do you think of my decree? Is it acceptable?" Nakamaro replied, "It is highly superior and acceptable. I receive your command."

The emperor then made him drink the divine wine and swear to him as follows: "If I fail to honor this decree, may Heaven and Earth hate me and inflict great disaster on me." At that time, Nakamaro swore, saying, "If in future times I violate this decree, may Heaven and Earth despise me, inflict great disaster on me, deprive me of body, and destroy my life!" After so swearing, he drank the wine and the ritual came to an end.

---

53. The custom began in China, where historians carefully recorded the words of popular songs that were believed to foretell important political events.
54. Princess Abe (718–770) was the eldest daughter of Emperor Shōmu and Empress Kōmyō, and a cousin of Nakamaro. In 749, when she was enthroned as Empress Kōken, Nakamaro was made High Councilor of the Senior Third Rank. Prince Funedo was appointed prince regent with the death of Retired Emperor Shōmu in 756. But the next year, Empress Kōken and Nakamaro replaced him with Prince Ohi. Funedo joined the rebellion against Empress Kōken and Nakamaro and was executed in 757.

Later, after the death of the emperor, he abided by the decree, making Prince Funado the prince regent.

When the empress dowager [Empress Kōmyō] and Empress Abe resided at the Nara Palace, all the people of the nation sang a song that said:

> Lost prince, dead at such an age,
> lost prince, like a lost jewel,
> a broken jewel, a torn scarf—
> When will your life be taken?
> Alas, poor flatfish!
> when will your life be taken?

Such were the words of the song.

Then, in the reign of Empress Abe and the empress dowager, on the eighteenth day of the Eighth Month in the ninth year of the Tenpyō shōbō era [757], the name of the era was changed to the first year of the Tenpyō hōji era. In the same year, Prince Regent Funado was seized as he emerged from the palace, imprisoned, and there put to death. With him Prince Kifumi, Prince Shioyaki, and their families were all killed.[55]

And in the Tenth Month of the Tenpyō hōji era [764], Emperor Ōji [Junnin, r. 758–764] was attacked by Empress Abe and dethroned, retiring to Awaji province. In addition, Nakamaro and all his family and associates were killed. The song had been an omen of the destruction of these princes. Again, in the reign of the empress dowager, there was a song that was sung by the population; it went:

> Don't look down on monks and their like
> for under their robes hang garters and hammers
> and when they stand up
> the monks become awesome lords!

---

55. Prince Kifumi was the son of Prince Nagaya, who had been executed earlier. Kyōkai is mistaken in listing Prince Shioyaki here. The brother of Prince Funedo, he escaped execution because he had not participated in the rebellion. In 764, however, Nakamaro replaced him as successor to the throne, and he and Nakamaro were executed.

Or another song that went like this:

> Lie down along
> the dark valley of my thighs
> till you become a man!

That was what they sang.

Then, in the reign of Empress Abe, in the year following the first year of the Tenpyō jingō era, the year *kinoto-mi* [765], Dharma Master Dōkyō of the Yuge family[56] shared a pillow with the empress and had relations with her. He listened to the governing of the nation and ruled the world. The preceding songs were a prediction of his relations with the empress, the shared pillow and intercourse, and his control over state affairs.

Also in the reign of the empress dowager, there was a song that went:

> Look straight at the roots of the tree—
> there the Most Venerable
> stands full up and fat!

That was how it went. And we know from this that this song was a prediction of the participation in state affairs of Dharma Master Dōkyō as Dharma King, and of Dharma Master Ingō of the Kamo family as spiritual councilor.[57]

Again, in the reign of the empress dowager who lived at the Nara Palace for twenty-five years and governed the nation, all the world sang this song that said:

> The morning sun shines
> west of Toyura-dera
> (press on it) at Sakurai[58]
> (press on it, press on it) at Sakurai

56. Dōkyō (705?–772), who came from Kawachi province, was put in charge of the court chapel and won the empress's favor. He died in exile in Shimotsuke.
57. Ingō (Ongō) was appointed senior assistant executive in 766.
58. Sakurai is said to be the name of a well. The words in parentheses are asides in the song.

A white jewel glimmers, sunken
a good jewel glimmers, sunken
(press on it, press on it)
Therefore the country will prosper
my family will prosper (press on it)

This was what they sang.

Later, during the reign of Empress Abe, in the fourth year of the Jingo keiun era, the year *kanoe-inu* [770], on the fourth day of the Eighth Month, Emperor Shirakabe came to the throne. And in the same year, in the winter, on the first day of the Tenth Month, a turtle from the province of Tsukushi was presented to the throne. Therefore, the era name was changed to the first year of Hōki [Sacred Turtle]. Thus we know that the song was a prediction of these events, the ascension to the throne of Emperor Shirakabe and his governing of the country.

Or in the reign of Empress Abe, who ruled the country at the Nara Palace, all over the country people sang:

Yamabe Slope, which faces the palace—
don't trample it
though it be earth!

These were the words they sang. And later, in the reign of Emperor Shirakabe, in the first year of the Ten'ō era, the year *kanoto-tori* [781], on the fifteenth day of the Fourth Month, Emperor Yamabe ascended the throne to rule the country. And the earlier song was a prediction of this.

In the reign of Emperor Yamabe, in the third year of the Enryaku era, the year *kinoe-ne* [784], on the night of the eighth day of the Eleventh Month and the morning of the next day, from around eight in the evening to about four in the morning, the star called the Emperor moved all about, flying around wildly.[59] On the eleventh day of the same month,

---

59. The Emperor, traditionally called Al Niyat, is the sigma star (actually, a star system) in the constellation Scorpius.

the day *tsuchinoe-saru*, the emperor, along with Prince Regent Sawara,[60] moved from the Nara Palace to the palace at Nagaoka. The movement of the star the Emperor was an indication that the imperial palace would be moved.

In the following year, the year *kinoto-ushi* [785], in the autumn, on the night of the fifteenth day of the Ninth Month, the moon appeared to be darkened, as though it had lost its light, and the sky was dark. Then, on the night of the twenty-third of the same month, around ten in the evening, Fujiwara no asomi Tanetsugu, Minister of Ceremony, Senior Third Rank, was shot and killed by an arrow in the residential quarters of the Nagaoka Palace by two members of the imperial guard: Ojika no sukune Kozumi and Hahaki no Imaro. The disappearance of the light of the moon was an omen of the death of Lord Tanetsugu.[61]

In the reign of the same emperor, in the sixth year of the Enryaku era, the year *hinoto-u* [787], in the autumn, the Ninth Month, the fourth day, around six in the evening, I, the monk Kyōkai, grieved, pouring my heart out, sighing and saying, "Alas, how weak, how shameful! I was born into the world, given life, yet have no means to sustain it! I am dragged along by the net of circumstance, caught in its meshes. Bound by its ties, I struggle in the battle of life and death. I race off in all directions, burning up my body. I remain in the secular world, feeding my wife and family, but I have no means to support them, no food for their mouths. I lack greens; I lack salt; I lack clothes; I have no firewood. Always I lack everything, my mind forever fretful. My heart knows no peace. In the daytime, hungry and cold; at night, again starving and cold. In my previous existences, I did not practice alms giving—how mean was my heart, how low, the things I did!"

---

60. Prince Regent Sawara was Emperor Kōnin's second son and Emperor Kanmu's brother. He was made prince regent in 781, but was deposed and exiled to Awaji province, dying on the way. Since his spirit terrified the imperial family and the Fujiwaras, he was given the posthumous title of emperor and ceremonially reburied.
61. A favorite of Emperor Kanmu, Fujiwara no Tanetsugu was put in charge of the construction of the Nagaoka Palace. Prince Sawara was deposed because of involvement in his assassination.

Then I went to bed, and around midnight I had a dream. A person begging for food came to my door, reciting a sutra passage and saying, "If you practice good deeds of the upper grade, you gain a body that is seventeen feet tall. If you practice good deeds of the lower grade, you gain a body that is ten feet tall." Hearing this, I turned my head and looked around. And I saw that the person begging for food was Novice Kyōnichi of the village of Awa in Kusumi, in the Nagusa district of Kii province. When I looked at him closely, I saw that he had a wooden tablet that was twenty feet long and a foot wide hanging down in front of him. On it were two marks, one at seventeen feet and one at ten feet. I asked him, "Are these marks for those who practice good deeds of the upper and the lower grades?" He replied, "Yes, they are."

Then, deeply moved in my heart, I pointed and said, "It seems that those who practiced good deeds of the upper or lower grades gained bodies of these two heights. But in the past, I did not even practice goods deeds of the lower grade! Therefore, I have a body that is no more than a little over five feet! How pitiful!" And I snapped my fingers in grief and repentance. The bystanders, hearing my words, said, "Alas, you are right!"

Then I took some of the white rice that I was about to cook and gave him several cups. He accepted them with a blessing and then took out a scroll and gave it to me, saying, "Copy this scroll, for it is an excellent work to guide people!" When I looked, I saw that it was a copy of the *Shokyō yōshū*, which, as he said, is an excellent work.[62] When I complained I had no paper to copy it on, he took out some used paper and gave it to me, saying, "Use this! I have to go elsewhere to beg for food, but I will be back." Then he went away, leaving the writing tablet and the scripture.

I then asked, saying, "This man does not usually beg for food. Why is he doing it now?" One of the bystanders replied, saying, "He has

62. *Shokyō yōshū* is a collection of quotations from a number of sutras.

many children, and they have nothing to eat. He is begging for food to nourish them."

Such was the dream I had, but I am not sure what it means. I believe it to be a revelation from the Holy One, the Buddha. The novice is one of the forms of Kannon. Why do I say this? Because one who had not yet been ordained is called a novice, and Kannon is one, too, for although he has reached enlightenment, he remains in the stage of self-discipline in order to save all sentient beings.[63] He is begging for food, which is one of the thirty-three incarnations of Kannon described in the twenty-fifth chapter of the Lotus Sutra, that called "The Universal Gateway of the Bodhisattva Perceiver of the World's Sounds." The seventeen feet of the upper grade is the result of all good deeds of virtue in the Pure Land. Ten feet represent perfection, for it is complete, whereas seven feet represent imperfection, for it is not yet complete. The ten feet of the lower grade is the result of the craving for the human and heavenly beings or gods. The words "deeply moved in my heart, I . . . snapped my fingers in grief and repentance" mean that one has been endowed with good causes, and by adding wisdom and practice, one may make up for sins of the distant past and in the long run attain benefits. "Deeply moved in my heart" refers to the shaving of the head and donning of a surplice, and "snapped my fingers" refers to banishing sins and gaining benefits. "I have a body that is no more than a little over five feet" can be analyzed as follows: "five feet" refers to the five lower realms of being.[64] "A little over" is uncertain in nature and refers to the tendency of the heart to turn toward a much higher state. Why do I say this? Because "a little over" refers neither to ten feet nor to seven feet. Therefore, it does not refer to a specific number, but to a tentative orientation with regard to the five realms. Making an offering of white rice to a mendicant indicates

63. In this stage, bodhisattvas accumulate causes to become Buddhas.
64. The five lower realms of beings are Hell dwellers, hungry ghosts, animals, human beings, and heavenly beings or gods. There are also a certain number of beings who had no fixed affiliation, but who may join any one of the five natures, depending on the circumstances.

that in order to gain a large cart drawn by a white ox,[65] he in the past had vowed to make a Buddha image, copy Mahayana scriptures, devote himself to good works, and cultivate an understanding of causes. When the mendicant accepted the offering with a blessing, it indicated that Kannon accepted it. When the mendicant gave me a scroll, it meant that I was given a new seed, a scripture that allowed me to understand the empty nature of humankind and to practice accordingly. Taking out and giving used paper means that, although the original deeds of goodness have long been hidden by worldly desires and have not been practiced for a long time, they are brought to light again through observance of the good Law and made relevant once more. He then says, "I have to go elsewhere to beg for food, but I will be back." The words "I have to go elsewhere to beg for food" indicate the great and boundless compassion of Kannon, which will fill the world and save all sentient beings. And the words "but I will be back" mean that if I, Kyōkai, fulfill my vow, I will gain good fortune and wisdom. When Kyōkai says, "This man does not usually beg for food," it indicates that, before he made his vow, he had no thought of the matter. "Why is he doing it now?" indicates that, now that he has made his vow, he is for the first time beginning to seek good fortune. "He has many children" refers to the countless beings whom he is going to convert. "They have nothing to eat" refers to those members of the five lower realms who have no fixed nature and lack any means of gaining salvation. "He is begging for food to nourish them" indicates that he will endow them with seeds that lead them to the realms of human and heavenly creatures.

Again I, Kyōkai, had another dream. In the seventh year of the Enrayku era, the year *tsuchinoe-tatsu* [788], in the spring, the Third Month,

---

65. This is a reference to one of the most famous parables in the Lotus Sutra, found in chap. 3, "Simile and Parable." A man and his many children are living in an old, dilapidated house. When fire breaks out, the father urges the children to flee, but they are too engrossed in their games to heed him. He promises to give them various carts if they will leave the house, and they obey. Once outside, however, he gives them all great carts drawn by white oxen, symbolic of his Mahayana Buddhist doctrine of salvation.

on the seventeenth day, the day *kinoto-ushi*, in the evening, I dreamed that I saw myself at the time of my death, when firewood was bundled together and my corpse was cremated. Then my spirit stood by and watched my body burn, but it did not burn as I wished. Therefore, I took a stick and poked my corpse, which was already on fire, to skewer it and make it burn. And to teach the others who were burning their corpses, I said, "Burn them well, the way I do!" And then when I looked at my burned corpse, I saw that its feet, its knees, its joints, elbows, and head had burned up and fallen off. Then my spirit began to cry aloud, putting its mouth to the ear of a bystander and calling out, trying to tell him my final words. But my voice sounded hollow, and the bystanders, unable to hear it, did not answer. I realized then that the spirit of a dead man has no voice. Therefore, he cannot hear me when I cry!

This dream has yet to be interpreted, although I would suppose that it means that I will gain long life or perhaps a high government office.[66] Sometime in the future, I hope, I may come to understand the meaning of the dream.

Then, in the fourteenth year of the Enryaku era, the year *kinoto-i* [795], in the winter, on the thirtieth day of the Twelfth Month, I was given the rank of Transmission of Light, Junior Rank.[67] And in the reign of the same emperor residing at the Nara Palace,[68] in the sixteenth year of the Enryaku era, the year *hinoto-ushi* [797], in the summer, around the Fourth and Fifth Months, a fox came to my room every night, crying. In addition, it dug a hole in the wall of the hall that I had built and entered, dirtying the seat of the Buddha with filth and, in the daytime, facing the door and crying. Then, after 220 or more days had passed, on the seventeenth day of the Twelfth Month, my son died.

66. This remark is based on the belief that such dreams customarily display the opposite of what actually awaits the dreamer; that is, dreaming of bad luck portends good luck.
67. Dentō jui. These clerical ranks were instituted in 760, in the reign of Emperor Junnin.
68. The text should read "Heian Palace."

Again, in the eighteenth year, the year *tsuchinoto-u* [799], around the Eleventh and Twelfth Months, a fox cried at my house, and at times a cicada was heard. In the following year, the nineteenth, the year *kanoe-tatsu* [800], on the twelfth day of the First Month, my horse died. And on the twenty-fifth day of the same month, another horse died. It is evident from all this that an omen of disaster appears first, and afterward the actual disaster occurs. But I have never studied the art of yin–yang divination taught by the Yellow Emperor, nor am I learned in the profound wisdom of Tendai Chisha.[69] Therefore, I am struck by disaster without knowing the cause. And not having any means to avoid it, I am worn out with worry. We must maintain discipline, must we not? We cannot but be in awe!

On a Monk Who Excelled in Both Wisdom and Practice and Who Was Reborn as a Prince (3:39)

Meditation Master Shaku Zenjū's secular name was Ato no muraji. He was named after his mother's family, Ato no uji. When he was a little boy, he lived with his mother in the village of Shikishima in the Yamanobe district of Yamato province.

After he was ordained, he worked very diligently, studying the doctrine and excelling in both wisdom and practice. The ruler and his ministers regarded him highly, and he was respected by clergy and laity alike. He worked to spread a knowledge of the Law and guide others, making these his concern. Accordingly, the emperor, in acknowledgment of his virtuous conduct, honored him with the post of Sōjō [Ad-

---

69. The Yellow Emperor is the mythical founder of the school of Daoism in ancient China. Its system of divination depended on the manipulation of the yin–yang dichotomy. Tendai Chisha, or Tiantai Zhizhe, is Zhiyi (538–597), the founder of the Tiantai school of Buddhism in China.

ministrator of Monks].[70] It may be noted that this monk had a large birthmark on the right side of his chin.

In the reign of Emperor Yamabe, who ruled the empire at the Nara Palace, around the seventeenth year of the Enryaku era [798], when the life of Meditation Master Zenjū was coming to an end, according to the custom among the laity and clergy, a diviner was summoned who, using the rite of boiling rice, was asked to question the members of the spirit world regarding his future existence. The diviner, possessed, replied, "I will surely take lodging in the womb of Tajihi no omina, the wife of the ruler of Japan,[71] to be reborn as a prince. He will have the same birthmark on his face as mine, which will confirm his identity."

After Zenjū's life had come to an end, around the eighteenth year of the Enryaku era, Tajihi no omina gave birth to a prince. Because he had the same black birthmark on the right side of his chin that Zenjū had had, he was given the name Prince Daitoku, or Prince of Great Virtue. But after living for three years, he died. When the diviner was summoned, the prince's spirit, speaking through the diviner, said, "I am the monk Zenjū, who for a while have been reborn as a prince. Hold a service and burn incense for me!"

From this, it is evident that the Most Reverend Zenjū lived two lives, first as Zenjū and then as a prince. When the scripture speaks of "a person being reborn in family after family," this is what it means.[72] This, too, was a miraculous event!

In Iyo province, in the district of Kamino, there is a mountain called Ishizuchi-yama. The name derives from that of the god of Ishizuchi, who lives on the mountain.[73] It is so high that ordinary persons cannot reach the summit. Only those who are pure in conduct are able to reach it and live there.

70. The office of Sōjō was established in 624 to supervise the clergy.
71. Tajihi no omina was a daughter of Tajihi no Nagano of the Junior Second Rank. In 797, the Junior Third Rank was conferred on her, and she was made a wife of Emperor Kanmu.
72. Abidaruma kusha-ron. See *Taishō* 29:124a.
73. Ishizuchi is the highest mountain in Shikoku, in Ehime prefecture.

In the reign of Retired Emperor Shōhō-ōjin-shōmu, who ruled the country for twenty-five years at the Nara Palace, and in the reign of Empress Abe, who ruled for nine years at the same palace, there lived on that mountain a monk who was pure in deed. His name was Bodhisattva Jakusen. The people of the time, both clergy and laypersons, praised him with the name bodhisattva because of the purity of his conduct.

In the ninth year of the empress's reign, the second year of the Hōji era, the year *tsuchinoe-inu* [758], Meditation Master Jakusen realized that he was about to die. He therefore put his written records in order and transmitted them to his disciples, saying, "Twenty-eight years after my death, I will be reborn as a prince with the name of Kamino. You may know that the prince is I, Jakusen!"

Twenty-eight years passed, and in the reign of Emperor Yamabe, who ruled the country at the Heian Palace, in the fifth year of the Enryaku era, the year *hinoe-tora* [786], a prince named Kamino was born to the emperor. This is the present Emperor Kamino [Saga, r. 809–823], who has been ruling the country for fourteen years at the Heian Palace.

Therefore, we know that he is surely a sage. And how do we know that he is a sage? The world says, "According to the laws of the imperial institution, someone who is guilty of murdering a person will surely be punished by the law for his crime. This emperor, however, makes us realize the meaning of his era name, Kōnin [Spreading Benevolence]. It means that he spared the life of one who deserved to be put to death for murder, replacing death with exile. Therefore, we know that he is a sage-ruler!"

There are those who speak ill of him, saying, "He is no sage-ruler! Why do we say this? Because in this emperor's reign, the country has seen the plague of drought! And there have been many other heavenly disasters and earthly plagues, and famines as well. Moreover, he keeps hunting birds and dogs with which to catch birds, wild boars, and deer. No one with a heart of compassion would do such!"

But these charges are not just. Everything within the land is the property of the ruler—there is nothing that is privately owned! All is for the use of the ruler, as he wishes. Although we are his people, have we the right to criticize him? Even in the time of the sage-rulers Yao and Shun, there were still droughts to plague the nation.[74] Therefore, it does not do to criticize him!

≈

Relying on what I have heard, I have selected oral reports and put down a record of good and evil actions, compiling this account of miraculous events. What benefits may accrue from it I confer on those of the populace who go astray, and I pray that I and they may all be reborn in the Western Land of bliss!

DAINIHONKOKU GENPŌ-ZEN'AKU RYŌIKI, VOLUME 3

WRITTEN BY MONK KYŌKAI OF THE TRANSMISSION OF LIGHT, JUNIOR RANK, AT YAKUSHI-JI ON THE WEST SIDE OF NARA

74. Yao and Shun were sage-rulers of ancient China, honored as paragons of virtue.

The Lotus Sutra. Translated by Burton Watson. New York: Columbia University Press, 1993.

Nakamura, Kyoko Motomochi. *Miraculous Stories from the Japanese Buddhist Tradition: The Nihon ryōiki of the Monk Kyōkai.* Cambridge, Mass.: Harvard University Press, 1973.

[Nakamura presents a thorough scholarly review of the problems related to the introduction of Buddhism into Japanese society, along with a complete and heavily annotated translation of the *Nihon ryōiki*. I am greatly indebted to this book for much of the material in my own translation of the same text.]

Nihon shoki (Chronicles of Japan).

Nihongi: Chronicles of Japan from the Earliest Times to A.D. 697. Translated by W. G. Aston. Transactions and Proceedings of the Japan Society of London, suppl. 1. 2 vols. London: K. Paul, Trench, Trübner, 1896; repr., Rutland, Vt.: Tuttle, 1972).

Taishō shinshū daizōkyō. Compiled by Takakusu Junjirō and Watanabe Kaigyoku. 100 vols. Tokyo: Taishō Issaikyō Kankōkai, 1922–1932.

Major Plays of Chikamatsu, tr. Donald
Keene 1961
Four Major Plays of Chikamatsu, tr. Donald
Keene. Paperback ed. only. 1961; rev.
ed. 1997
Records of the Grand Historian of China,
translated from the Shih chi of Ssu-ma
Ch'ien, tr. Burton Watson, 2 vols. 1961
Instructions for Practical Living and Other
Neo-Confucian Writings by Wang
Yang-ming, tr. Wing-tsit Chan 1963
Hsün Tzu: Basic Writings, tr. Burton Watson,
paperback ed. only. 1963; rev. ed. 1996
Chuang Tzu: Basic Writings, tr. Burton
Watson, paperback ed. only. 1964; rev.
ed. 1996
The Mahābhārata, tr. Chakravarthi V.
Narasimhan. Also in paperback ed.
1965; rev. ed. 1997
The Manyōshū, Nippon Gakujutsu
Shinkōkai edition 1965
Su Tung-p'o: Selections from a Sung Dynasty
Poet, tr. Burton Watson. Also in
paperback ed. 1965
Bhartrihari: Poems, tr. Barbara Stoler Miller.
Also in paperback ed. 1967
Basic Writings of Mo Tzu, Hsün Tzu, and
Han Fei Tzu, tr. Burton Watson. Also in
separate paperbacks eds. 1967
The Awakening of Faith, Attributed to
Aśvaghosha, tr. Yoshito S. Hakeda. Also
in paperback ed. 1967
Reflections on Things at Hand: The Neo-
Confucian Anthology, comp. Chu Hsi
and Lü Tsu-ch'ien, tr. Wing-tsit Chan
1967
The Platform Sutra of the Sixth Patriarch, tr.
Philip B. Yampolsky. Also in paperback
ed. 1967
Essays in Idleness: The Tsurezuregusa of
Kenkō, tr. Donald Keene. Also in
paperback ed. 1967
The Pillow Book of Sei Shōnagon, tr. Ivan
Morris, 2 vols. 1967
Two Plays of Ancient India: The Little Clay
Cart and the Minister's Seal, tr. J. A. B.
van Buitenen 1968
The Complete Works of Chuang Tzu, tr.
Burton Watson 1968

The Romance of the Western Chamber (Hsi
Hsiang chi), tr. S. I. Hsiung. Also in
paperback ed. 1968
The Manyōshū, Nippon Gakujutsu
Shinkōkai edition. Paperback ed. only.
1969
Records of the Historian: Chapters from the
Shih chi of Ssu-ma Ch'ien, tr. Burton
Watson. Paperback ed. only. 1969
Cold Mountain: 100 Poems by the T'ang Poet
Han-shan, tr. Burton Watson. Also in
paperback ed. 1970
Twenty Plays of the Nō Theatre, ed. Donald
Keene. Also in paperback ed. 1970
Chūshingura: The Treasury of Loyal
Retainers, tr. Donald Keene. Also in
paperback ed. 1971; rev. ed. 1997
The Zen Master Hakuin: Selected Writings, tr.
Philip B. Yampolsky 1971
Chinese Rhyme-Prose: Poems in the Fu Form
from the Han and Six Dynasties Periods,
tr. Burton Watson. Also in paperback
ed. 1971
Kūkai: Major Works, tr. Yoshito S. Hakeda.
Also in paperback ed. 1972
The Old Man Who Does as He Pleases:
Selections from the Poetry and Prose of Lu
Yu, tr. Burton Watson 1973
The Lion's Roar of Queen Śrīmālā, tr. Alex
and Hideko Wayman 1974
Courtier and Commoner in Ancient China:
Selections from the History of the Former
Han by Pan Ku, tr. Burton Watson. Also
in paperback ed. 1974
Japanese Literature in Chinese, vol. 1: *Poetry*
and Prose in Chinese by Japanese Writers
of the Early Period, tr. Burton Watson
1975
Japanese Literature in Chinese, vol. 2: *Poetry*
and Prose in Chinese by Japanese Writers
of the Later Period, tr. Burton Watson
1976
Love Song of the Dark Lord: Jayadeva's
Gītagovinda, tr. Barbara Stoler Miller.
Also in paperback ed. Cloth ed.
includes critical text of the Sanskrit.
1977; rev. ed. 1997
Ryōkan: Zen Monk-Poet of Japan, tr. Burton
Watson 1977

Lao Tzu's Tao Te Ching: A Translation of the Startling New Documents Found at Guodian, by Robert G. Henricks 2000
The Shorter Columbia Anthology of Traditional Chinese Literature, ed. Victor H. Mair 2000
Mistress and Maid (Jiaohongji), by Meng Chengshun, tr. Cyril Birch 2001
Chikamatsu: Five Late Plays, tr. and ed. C. Andrew Gerstle 2001
The Essential Lotus: Selections from the Lotus Sutra, tr. Burton Watson 2002
Early Modern Japanese Literature: An Anthology, 1600–1900, ed. Haruo Shirane 2002; abridged 2008
The Columbia Anthology of Traditional Korean Poetry, ed. Peter H. Lee 2002
The Sound of the Kiss, or The Story That Must Never Be Told: Pingali Suranna's Kalapurnodayamu, tr. Vecheru Narayana Rao and David Shulman 2003
The Selected Poems of Du Fu, tr. Burton Watson 2003
Far Beyond the Field: Haiku by Japanese Women, tr. Makoto Ueda 2003
Just Living: Poems and Prose by the Japanese Monk Tonna, ed. and tr. Steven D. Carter 2003
Han Feizi: Basic Writings, tr. Burton Watson 2003
Mozi: Basic Writings, tr. Burton Watson 2003
Xunzi: Basic Writings, tr. Burton Watson 2003
Zhuangzi: Basic Writings, tr. Burton Watson 2003
The Awakening of Faith, Attributed to Aśvaghosha, tr. Yoshito S. Hakeda, introduction by Ryuichi Abe 2005
The Tales of the Heike, tr. Burton Watson, ed. Haruo Shirane 2006
Tales of Moonlight and Rain, by Ueda Akinari, tr. with introduction by Anthony H. Chambers 2007
Traditional Japanese Literature: An Anthology, Beginnings to 1600, ed. Haruo Shirane 2007
The Philosophy of Qi, by Kaibara Ekken, tr. Mary Evelyn Tucker 2007
The Analects of Confucius, tr. Burton Watson 2007

The Art of War: Sun Zi's Military Methods, tr. Victor Mair 2007
One Hundred Poets, One Poem Each: A Translation of the Ogura Hyakunin Isshu, tr. Peter McMillan 2008
Zeami: Performance Notes, tr. Tom Hare 2008
Zongmi on Chan, tr. Jeffrey Lyle Broughton 2009
Scripture of the Lotus Blossom of the Fine Dharma, rev. ed., tr. Leon Hurvitz, preface and introduction by Stephen R. Teiser 2009
Mencius, tr. Irene Bloom, ed. with an introduction by Philip J. Ivanhoe 2009
Clouds Thick, Whereabouts Unknown: Poems by Zen Monks of China, Charles Egan 2010
The Mozi: A Complete Translation, tr. Ian Johnston 2010
The Huainanzi: A Guide to the Theory and Practice of Government in Early Han China, by Liu An, tr. John S. Major, Sarah A. Queen, Andrew Seth Meyer, and Harold D. Roth, with Michael Puett and Judson Murray 2010
The Demon at Agi Bridge and Other Japanese Tales, tr. Burton Watson, ed. with introduction by Haruo Shirane 2011
Haiku Before Haiku: From the Renga Masters to Bashō, tr. with introduction by Steven D. Carter 2011
The Columbia Anthology of Chinese Folk and Popular Literature, ed. Victor H. Mair and Mark Bender 2011
Tamil Love Poetry: The Five Hundred Short Poems of the Aiṅkuṟunūṟu, tr. and ed. Martha Ann Selby 2011
The Teachings of Master Wuzhu: Zen and Religion of No-Religion, by Wendi L. Adamek 2011
The Essential Huainanzi, by Liu An, tr. John S. Major, Sarah A. Queen, Andrew Seth Meyer, and Harold D. Roth 2012
The Dao of the Military: Liu An's Art of War, tr. Andrew Seth Meyer 2012
Unearthing the Changes: Recently Discovered Manuscripts of the Yi Jing (I Ching) and Related Texts, Edward L. Shaughnessy 2013